The Bikie Effect

Jennifer Brockie

The Bikie Effect

© Jennifer Brockie

National Library of Australia Cataloguing-in-Publication entry

Creator: Brockie, Jennifer, author.

Title: The Bikie Effect/Jennifer Brockie.

ISBN: 9780994382405 (paperback)

Subjects: Bicycles--Australia--Fiction.

Motorcycles--Australia--Fiction.

Motorcycle gangs--Fiction.

Crimes and criminals--Australia--Fiction.

Love stories--Drama.

Dewey Number: A823.4

Published with the assistance of: loveofbooks.com.au

www.jenniferbrockie.com

Contents

Do not speak evil against one another, brothers. The one who speaks against a brother or judges his brother, speaks evil against the law and judges the law. But if you judge the law, you are not a doer of the law but a judge. There is only one lawgiver and judge, he who is able to save and to destroy. But who are you to judge your neighbor?

James 4:11-12.

My heartfelt thank you goes out to all my wonderful

proof-readers for all their kind words,

helpful suggestions and their precious time.

Tania, Allison and Peter.

And to you, Sarah,

I cannot begin to thank you enough.

You are gold.

A huge thankyou to Cookie, Chris and Rachel

for all your help.

A very special thank you to one of the

most talented artists I know,

Mark Hollywood.

Thank you so much for the amazing work you did

on all the photography,

especially the book cover.

Mark Hollywood Photography.

"It doesn't matter who hurt you, or broke you down.

What matters is who made you smile again."

Author unknown.

Interview with Jenna

A few years ago, as the discussions on the Vicious Lawless Disestablishment Act were being tossed around, I heard rumours of an author who had a very interesting story to tell about bikies. From all accounts, the story was one which the author had shied away from sharing, and as the laws and new regulations began to take effect, the discussion of the story would grow even more guarded. For me, the investigative me, that would only make my desire to talk to this lady even stronger. I knew if I could just meet her, she would talk to me. So I began to all but stalk her. I watched her Facebook and Twitter pages. I even attempted to ask around in the biker circle. Now, that is one tight-lipped community. The more questions I asked, the more ostracised I became. But, from my knowledge of the lifestyle, I completely understood. I knew these people to be fiercely protective of their own and very little information was ever passed on. So I kept on searching. I gathered as much information on her as I could get my hands on. Then, as if by a stroke of luck, and almost a year of trying, I was fortunate enough to meet someone who was a close and personal friend of Jenna, the author.

On the first phone call I shared with Jenna, I knew instantly I was not talking to some run of the mill backyard author. I knew this woman was highly educated and had a deep knowledge of her subjects.

I must confess though, I did expect to be speaking with a rough, bikie type woman, someone with limited politeness and even less tolerance. But it quickly became apparent that I was mistaken. From the initial spark of the conversation, I found Jenna to possess a contagious personality. The more I spoke with her, the more I wanted to know about her and her story. Jenna entertained me and was quite gracious while engaging in the conversation, up until I touched upon the subject of her book. The change in her voice and enthusiasm was blunt and clear. She had no inclination to discuss her book with me, or anyone else for that matter. I pushed through her resistance and pleaded for her to meet with me.

Me: "Jenna, from everything I've been told about your story, this is something that could make a difference with these crazy new laws which are about to come into effect. It could change the way the normal everyday person views these bikies you so fiercely protect."

Jenna: "That would be an impossibility. People's perceptions are swayed and jaded by the things they see in the media. You can't really blame them though; it's how it's always been. If you see it on the news, it has to be true. Or so the public thinks."

Me: "So, are you telling me that what we see in the media is not real?"

Jenna: "No, not at all. That's not what I'm saying. Some of the things you see on the news are very real, and should be taken quite seriously, that's for sure. But, when it comes to the bikies being discussed, instant discrimination occurs. The public, already convinced that the bikie must be guilty from what they have already been exposed to, quickly jumps to the conclusion that what the broadcaster has just said, must, in fact, be true. But, if the viewer bothered to ask the right questions, maybe they too would understand that these bikies are simply, normal everyday men. Obviously, some of them may be criminally minded, but many are not. You think about that for a moment then ask yourself this; what makes it any different if it is a bikie or a member from the mainstream public who commits a criminal act? Are 'Bikies' not normal human beings? Are they not men made from flesh and blood just like any other man?"

Me: "Yes, of course, they are."

Jenna: "So why isn't it only the individual who is persecuted for his crime? Why is the entire club put on display and punished, or victimised because of an act perpetrated by one of its members? Do you see the public or the powers-that-be crucifying an entire religion if one of its parishioners commits a criminal offence? Isn't it called discrimination if we are biased against people based on race, colour, lifestyle choice or gender?"

Me: "Yes, it is actually. I didn't really think about it like that until you just said it."

I was left feeling a little naïve after assessing her reasoning of the topic and so my appetite to understand her grew. Our in-depth phone conversations continued on for the next two months and all would be well so long as I didn't broach the subject of her beloved novel being published. Then one day, simply on impulse, I just slammed her with my questions. I blurted it all out at once before she had a chance to stop me.

Me: "Jenna, you must have some sense of knowing me by now? Some depth of trust? Please, allow me some insight on what your story is about? Tell me what it means to you and shed some light on why you won't finish writing it?" The phone line went silent. No background noise, no familiar echo which was ever present each time we spoke. I said her name a few times quietly, before pulling the phone from my ear to check if the call was still connected. The timer run along like clockwork. I called her name once more.

Jenna: "Yes, I'm still here. Look, I'm sorry if all your efforts have been an attempt to gain my trust so I would share my story with you. But you need to understand that it's nothing personal, it's just that it is a part of my life that I don't really want to share with anybody. I'm sorry."

Me: "But, why Jenna? Why don't you want to share it if it has the capability of changing people's point of view on bikies?

Jenna: "Well one of the reasons I am hesitant to publish it is because of how judgemental our society has become. What do you think would happen if I went public with my story? If I openly associate myself with bikies I run a huge risk of ruining my career as a writer forever. As I have seen time and time again, instead of taking me on as a respectable author, I would be classed as "one of them". I have seen people lose jobs, friends and family over their association with bikies. It's wrong, but it's simply how it is. But even so, that's not the main reason I don't want to do it. The main reason I don't want to share my story with the world is because it is a personal story. This story is about my life, my personal life. A life of abuse and heartache and about the person who helped me overcome it. You don't seem to understand, I would do almost anything to change the way society views bikies, but nothing I can say will change their point of view. They've already formed their own single-minded opinions based on what they are consistently told by the media. The book isn't even really based on the laws, it's based more on a man who just happens to be a bikie and the fact that he is also, very much a human being. No, I'm sorry, I just can't."

Me: "So isn't that a reason to publish the book? Shouldn't you want to show the public that they are wrong? Won't your book prove to Mr or Mrs. Citizen that bikies are human, with real human emotional struggles and suffer from the same affliction of feelings just like everybody else? And, won't it dispel the myth that they are all the same?"

Jenna: "I suppose when you say it like that, I guess it does. Let me think about it. I'll call you in a few days."

And, with that she was gone.

To be perfectly honest, I didn't think I would hear from Jenna ever again. I thought about her and the things she had said constantly, barely able to focus on my other work. I kept wondering why this book was so difficult for her to write. What had been so painful in her journey that she would become almost mute over the topic? I thought about all that time and effort going down the drain. The book had taken Jenna close to ten years to write and almost double that time to live it. Despite the several offers she had received to publish the book, she always found an excuse not to carry through with the deal. I really wanted the opportunity to meet with Jenna and convince her to share her story.

One cold, wet morning, a few weeks after our last call, my phone rang and, to my surprise, it was Jenna. Something had changed and Jenna now wanted to talk. Sometime through the stormy night before, an epiphany hit her hard. It had suddenly dawned on her why she could not let her precious creation go and she finally understood why she could not bring herself to share her story. The realisation hit her harder than the lightning striking the ground outside. This was her story, a story from her heart. This was no ordinary novel, or piece of fiction she had written, this was their story; Jenna's and Rollie's story. She finally realised it was fear that was holding her back. Fear from her past, threatening to rear its ugly head and fear of what the truth could do to her future.

I spoke to Jenna at length that morning, learning about the other major difficulty she faced with finishing her book. Each and every time she drew the story to an end, another chapter would burst into life. The book had gained a life of its own. A life of which Jenna had no control over. As an author, that is an extremely difficult situation to find yourself in. Yet, I somehow managed to convince her that we, together, could control and contain the beast. I told her that somehow we would dominate that problem and she could soon be free of the emotion and fear that attached itself to this book. I assured Jenna that once we got the novel out there that the pain from her past would dissipate and her future both as a writer and an individual would look brighter. After an hour-long phone conversation, she finally agreed to meet with me.

The following Tuesday morning was the first day of interviews. I have to admit, I was quite excited. I couldn't believe that Jenna had chosen me. So many others had tried to get a chance to hear her story, but she had chosen me. To say I was thrilled would be a gross understatement. I arrived at Jenna's office at 10 am sharp, eager to embark on this once in a lifetime opportunity. I walked in and looked around, my eyes were immediately drawn to Jenna's double sided silky oak desk which was superbly organised, not like most of us writers. There were tidy methodical piles of paperwork, folders and memory sticks to the right and an antique silver writing tray to the left. In the centre, she had placed a vase of fresh red roses scattered with baby's breath. Hung carefully on the walls were photos of her family and closest friends. Jenna pointed out who was who. Towards the back corner of the wall was a framed picture of two men. Jenna explained to me that the burlier of the two was in fact Rollie himself. I stood there staring into the eyes of a man who would have terrified the life out of me had I met him in real life in a dark back alley. As a matter of fact, I think I would have been frightened of him if I met him in broad daylight, on a busy street. Jenna explained she had moved the picture from its original place so she no longer had to look at it all the time. I stood completely mesmerised.

This was not at all what I was expecting. Everything that surrounded me oozed with class. The aura and elegance surrounding Jenna and her things were pleasantly refreshing. I pinched myself, wondering if I was dreaming. I had waited so long for this and now standing directly in front of me was Jenna, the whole tiny five foot of her, dressed in a pair of figure-hugging blue jeans and low cut, soft mohair pink sweater. She looked so small and timid. The diamond-encrusted religious cross she wore around her neck shone brightly. There was nothing threatening or intimidating about her at all, but yet, a ball of anxiety knotted itself in my stomach as Jenna went off to make a pot of coffee, and I was left with her surroundings.

As the interview began, Jenna insisted that many of the things she would tell me would be strictly confidential and totally off the record. Once I agreed to her terms, we continued the interview. I kept getting tongue-tied and confused. I simply could not shake this uneasy feeling. I've always been a great judge of character and I liked Jenna, I liked her very much, but something didn't sit quite right. I fidgeted in my seat wondering what it was that was bothering me so much about this tiny woman. Once we began to talk, off the record, of course, I started to understand why I felt that way. This gentle woman, who sat directly in front of me has seen enough pain for all the men the world over. Some of the things Jenna has seen, some of the things she has lived and been through would buckle the bravest warrior and devastate the life of most women. Yet Jenna stands staunch; strong in her convictions and loyal to a fault. The admiration I have for this woman will stay with me for the rest of my life. I can honestly say to you, I could never endure even half of what she has been through. The dignity and sanity she has maintained is astounding. Jenna truly is an astonishing woman, who refuses to allow her past to determine her future. If I have it my way, we will be hearing a lot more about her life via several other books, but for right now, I hope we can get this book about Rollie down in print and into circulation. Either way, Jenna is not someone I will forget about in the near future or any time after I would imagine.

I steered the conversation back to Rollie and Jenna slumped back in her chair.

Me: "Tell me Jenna, why Rollie? What is it about this man that has you so guarded? Why have you gone to such great lengths to protect this man? Especially at the sake of a lot of money? And, if you were never going to publish the book, why did you tell people you were writing it?"

Jenna: "Well firstly, when I first decided to write the book I told a few select people I was doing it, and one of those people was Rollie. Before too long half of everyone we know knew about it, so that answers that question. Secondly, I am so protective of Rollie and his reputation because people and their rumours can be very vicious. Both he and I have suffered immensely due to the garbage people spread freely amongst others. And thirdly, the book was never really written for any kind of financial gain. The story was written in the way of a release. A way to express my feelings and thoughts and to dismiss some of my haunting past."

Me: "What are your feelings, Jenna? How do you feel about Rollie, right here, right now, in this very minute?"

Jenna sat quietly in deep thought for about five long minutes. Then eventually, you could see her mind slip into overdrive.

Jenna: "Okay, let's give this a go. You will be lucky if what I say makes any sense because Rollie is the only person I cannot sum up adequately no matter how hard I try. Well, here goes: Keeping in mind, that no matter how long you've known someone, or how much you trust them, the ghosts of your past will always remind you to stay on your guard. No matter how strong your friendship is, you will always remember that he is a bikie and as such, his first commitment will always be to his club. So it will always be with hesitation you move forward. Outwardly, he will look exactly like you expect him to look; he will dress and look like a bikie. But once you get close and begin to understand his soul, your mind will become like a tangled web of confusion. He will evoke feelings inside of you, you never even knew existed. He's a little like this: Have you ever been so close to a raging fire that you could feel its heat dancing through your hair, teasing your skin and seducing your mind? Have you ever had the urge to reach out your hands and to run your fingers through those enticing flames, even though you know that same fire will strip the flesh from your bones and leave you with nothing but skeletal remains?"

Me: "No, I can't say I have." I answered, looking at her bewildered.

Jenna: "Well, I have. That is what Rollie is like. Dangerous, yet alluring. He is like that raging fire. You know if he wanted to, he could burn you to the ground faster than you could ever envision. You know his mere presence could harm you if he so desired. But you know he has no intention of doing so. Instead of dancing with the devil, or touching the fire, you stand by, lapping up the heat from the flames, as they corrupt your thoughts from everything you have ever known as it sends them spiralling into a tailspin. Your past tells you to run, but the present tells you to stay. But if you look into his eyes and deep into his soul you eventually see what truly resides there. And, what I see there is not as daunting as one would imagine."

Me: "And you say you love and care for this man? He sounds dangerous and intimidating if you ask me. What is wrong with you, Jenna? I would have imagined you to be smarter than to tamper with someone like this."

Jenna: "Although I am the university educated one, Rollie is smarter than me; much smarter than me. He is wise and carefully manipulative. He controls his temptations like a trained lion tamer. But, if the truth were told, he has no control over it either. The relationship between Rollie and I is a life bond. A deep, sometimes dark bond, which at times plagues and torments us both. Sometimes I feel cursed by it, but to fight against it is futile, so I've learned to accept it. No matter how far apart we are, no matter how many rumours are spread, or lies are told, or how much we argue, we always end up back in each other's lives. No country, no law, no man, or woman, have ever been able to defeat or break the bond between us. So regardless of how dangerous people think he is or how unexplainable it may be, I just accept it as a fact and as a crucial part of my life. In all honesty, I may just be the only person in this entire world who truly knows and understands him, and even though we both at times deny it, he needs me. Everyone, even bikies, deserves at least one person in their life that they can truly trust and rely on. "

Tiny little goose bumps erupted over my entire body. My blood went cold and a sudden trickle of tears streamed down my face. I sat listening, although totally confused, to Jenna, wondering why she would be so protective of a man that the media had accused of murder, drug trafficking, and several other offenses. Yet somehow in the insanity of the moment, I knew her story needed to be told and I was determined to be the one to help her tell it.

The story of Jenna, the quiet author, and Rollie, the dangerous, powerful bikie, has more twists and turns than a Celtic symbol. This incredible story of their lives eventually, over time, grew stronger than the writer and the bikie put together. Theirs is a story about a forbidden love between the two most unlikely strangers, at its greatest strength and the assault their love took on both of them mentally, physically and spiritually. This is a story that will outlive them both, so, therefore, it must be written. Their past, their present and their future will continue to be entwined forever, leaving its mark on the generations of people they will eventually leave behind.

For the next few months, Jenna and I met every week and together, we worked tirelessly on her book. The more she wrote, and the more I read, the more I understood her devotion to Rollie and her commitment to show the public that not everything you hear should be believed. I can honestly say I have changed my view on classifying bikies, or any other minority group, as a whole entity rather than on an individual basis. I now believe that every single person on our planet deserves the right to a fair, unbiased trial. They deserve to be judged fairly by either the courts of law or by other human beings. I hope by encouraging Jenna to share her story that we can convince at least a few of you to form the same opinion.

Jennifer Brockie

A Word From Jenna

My name is Jenna and this is my story. Many years have passed since I first met Rollie, the bikie, yet the influence he had on me still lingers to this day. This part of my life began a long time ago. To be precise, it started almost twenty years ago. The story that I am about to tell you is a strange story, one with many highs and lows throughout the entire journey. No-one could be more surprised by my story than me. Believe me when I tell you, I am the last person on the face of this planet who would have ever thought they would end up in the situation I found myself in.

By the time I had met Rollie, I like many others, had already formed an opinion of what bikies and their lifestyles represent. I would neither go out of my way to speak to them nor would I make eye contact with them from across the street, as a matter of fact, I would go out of my way to avoid them. I wanted nothing to do with "their kind". From all I had known and experienced, they were all bad with no exception. Little did I know that I was soon to find out I was very, very wrong. And, the explosive interruption Rollie made in my seemingly happy little life would send me spiraling into an uncontrollable volcanic vortex of emotion that would change the way I felt forever.

All I ask in return for me sharing my story with you is that you use your open- mindedness to understand and comprehend what I am telling you. With each word you read, stop and remember that Rollie is a person. He is a man; made out of flesh and blood just like your father, your brother, your son or your lover. He may dress differently and he may be a part of something you do not understand, but he is still the same as all other men with human thoughts and feelings.

Come on this journey with us to learn the consequences and the real life struggles of a man society has classified as a monster. A man who apparently haunts your dreams and turns them into your worst nightmares. Rollie, so the media and your mother says, is the kind of man you should run from. Funnily enough, he is the same man I eventually ran to.

Chapter One

Uninvited Stranger

Fifty-three houses she inspected. Fifty-three of them! Doug began to wonder if the search would never end.

"I'll know it when I see it, Doug. None of these houses are even vaguely familiar. They just don't feel right. Once I walk into it, I'll know it straight away."

Rain fell at a sideways slant pounding hard against the front windscreen. The wipers and plump drops danced a perfect Charleston, so perfect, in fact, Joan Crawford would have been proud. Flashes of lightning struck the ground in front of the car as dark clouds floated down towards the earth.

"Are you sure you want to keep going, Jenna? This rain's bucketing down. It looks like it's settled in for the night. Why don't you call them and see if we can re-schedule?" Doug asked, wiping the fog from the inside of the windscreen with the back of his hand.

"No, we have to go on, Doug. What if this is the one?"

Doug eased off the accelerator and carefully maneuvered through the steadily flooding streets. Jenna gazed out the window and watched as the line of trees grew thicker. Odd sections of fencing trimmed the weather board houses, all of which were painted in a multitude of shades mainly favoured in the nineteen-seventies. Cream. Lots and lots of creams. Mostly, they were all trimmed in brown. A few white homes stood out, with their grey coloured window frames and doors, breaking up the monotony by dotting the street every so often. A canary yellow house came into view and surprised her. Jenna inspected those different coloured houses more closely than the cream ones. She noticed manicured lawns, a rope swing hanging from a Jacaranda tree, a dog kennel in the corner and a few sets of gumboots lined up outside of some of the front doors. Doug turned left into Orchid road and slowed the car down to a crawl. He wiped his side window and looked for the numbers on the letter boxes. As he pulled to a stop Jenna gasped and opened the door.

"This is it, Doug. I know it is. I just know it."

"Stop kidding around, Jenna. Get back in the car and we'll leave. Don't worry about it, honey, we'll keep looking."

"I'm not kidding, Doug. This is it. Come on, get out of the car and let's go in."

"Seriously, Jenna, stop being stupid! It's pouring down with rain. I'm not in the mood for you to humour these people today. Now get back in the car."

Jenna turned to face Doug. Her long blond hair stuck to the sides of her face and rain trickled from the end of her nose and chin. Her dripping wet clothing became transparent and stuck to her body. "I'm not humouring anyone, Doug. I don't know about you, but I'm going in. This is the place. This is my place."

"Have you gone mad, girl? Maybe the rain is screwing with your eyes. This is not what you're looking for. For fuck sake, Jenna, the fucking house is bright orange. Now get back in the car, I'm going."

Jenna swung the door shut and made her way over to the shabby metal gate. A plump woman, in her early to mid-forties, dressed in a black skirt suit and blue polka dotted blouse opened the front door of the house and stepped out onto the wooden deck verandah.

"Come on up before you catch your death of cold, Jenna. Look at you, you look like a drowned rat."

Jenna climbed the stairs, counting them as she went. Fifteen steps, not thirteen, that's the first good sign. She looked over her shoulder towards the car.

Doug remained in his seat. The woman handed Jenna a towel. Jenna patted her face and wrung out her hair. She wrapped the towel around her shoulders and walked in through the open front door. Standing just inside, Jenna scanned the room. The tiny lounge room with its tattered grey carpet appeared cluttered, yet friendly, with unfamiliar photographs lining the walls. A circle of friends' figurine sat in the centre of a small wooden coffee table. A large chipboard wall unit divided the space between the dining room and lounge room, making each of the rooms look even smaller than they actually were. Jenna followed the woman into the kitchen. One small breakfast bench divided the kitchen from the dining room. A unit of six kitchen cupboards lined the floors. The room felt crowded and awkward yet, the waft of coffee brewing on the bench danced in her nose making a smile spill out across her lips. A pot of soup simmered on the stove and the old refrigerator purred along like a content kitten.

"Follow me through the back here, Jenna. Even with the rain, I think you'll be pleased with what I have to show you," the woman said.

Jenna followed along silently, stopping only momentarily to inspect the huge carpet snakes in the six-foot fish tank across the back verandah. Something colourful caught the corner of her eye. The song of the Rainbow lorikeet toyed with her ears and she became totally mesmerized by their beauty. Her gaze caught the rolling green carpet that covered the quarter acre block. The land was flat, lush and more than suitable. The mango and mulberry trees swayed savagely in the storm. Jenna descended the stairs, held her arm out wide and spun around like a prima ballerina in the pouring rain.

"I don't need to see anymore, I'll take it," Jenna yelled, above the roar of the storm. "I'm home. I'm finally home."

After a lifetime of belonging nowhere, she now had somewhere to be. No-one could pack up her belongings in the middle of the night and move her and no-one could tell her what to do. For the next two years, the home Doug bought for Jenna became everything she had dreamed of, and way more than she had ever expected.

One cold, wet wintery afternoon in 1998, just as the sun had begun to slip from the sky, Jenna jumped as thunderous footsteps fell upon the rickety front stairs of the house.

She spun around from the vegetables she was peeling in the kitchen sink, as a tall dark figure stormed past the large lounge room window and moved into the frame of the front security screen door. Jenna stood motionless, peering out from the divider arch in between the two rooms. Standing in the doorway was a tall and handsome man, who stood at least six foot five inches tall. Jenna guessed he would have weighed around one hundred and ten kilos. His oval shaped face, which was trimmed with a gold tinged, well maintained, brown goatee was not smiling. His golden, ruffled hair fell down to his extremely broad shoulders and his pale blue eyes gazed out from beneath a heavily furrowed brow. As she allowed her gaze to fall to his chest, Jenna's jaw tightened and her heart began to race. Her body grew tense and her feet would not move. She could barely breathe. No matter how hard she tried, she could not raise her eyes from the Fearsome Devils patch attached to his leather clad chest. He raised his heavily tattooed arms up onto the security grill and took a firm hold of it.

"Hey, does Doug live here?" he asked, loudly.

Jenna just looked at him blankly. He asked the same question again, only louder. His deep, slightly accented voice vibrated through her. She began to twist her long blonde hair around her finger as her chin dropped to her chest. She raised her gaze up to his face. She opened her mouth to speak, but not a single word would escape her lips. Her voice became tangled in her throat like a tiny trapped sparrow in a net.

Doug, fresh out of the shower, sauntered up the hallway with only a towel wrapped around his hips. His bald head glistened and his full-face beard dripped onto the carpet. He smiled at Jenna before noticing the man standing in the doorway. Doug waved his hand at her, motioning for her to leave the room. Jenna stole another look at the man before turning to move away. Her heart skipped a beat as she noticed the size difference between the two men. To her, Doug had always resembled an invincible super-hero. He had successfully maintained a high level of fitness, due to his professional football training and athletic disposition, despite his average height and his love of the booze. Now, approaching the man at the door, his well taut, muscular, heavily tattooed frame, paled in comparison. The other guy looked like the giant, and Doug somewhat resembled a dwarf.

"Are you, Doug?" The man asked.

"Who's asking?" Doug answered.

"The name's, Rollie. I got told to come here and see you," Rollie replied, glancing down at Doug.

"What the hell for?"

"I bought a place down the road here a few weeks ago. I got robbed last night. I was told that you know all the young fuckers around the area and you could know who did it."

"How the fuck would I know?" Doug replied.

"Don't you have a couple of teenage kids? I got told they know all the other kids from around here." Rollie continued.

"You seem to know an awful lot about me and my family. But, yeah, I do have two teenage sons and a foster son. Whoever gave you that info is right. My boys do know just about everyone from around here. But I can sure as hell tell ya, that they wouldn't be hanging out with anyone stupid enough to rob a bikies house." Doug answered.

"I only just moved in so none of my stuff has been set up yet. I don't reckon they would've known I'm a bikie, as you put it." Rollie said, leaning into the grill. "Are you going to invite me in, or do you want me to stay standing here like a wanker in your doorway? I just want to talk to your kids if that's okay?"

Doug hesitated, Rollie gave him a half smile. Doug nodded his head and smiled back before unlocking the security door. Rollie stepped inside, extended his arm and introduced himself properly.

"Thanks, man. I appreciate you talking to me. Everyone calls me Rollie and I'm a member of the Fearsome Devils," he said, wrapping his huge hand around Doug's.

"Well, it seems you already know me, but I'm Doug," Doug said, grinning sheepishly.

"Yeah, one of my brothers, club brothers knows of you. He said you might be able to help me track down who broke into my house. I've got to get the stuff the little fuckers took back, man. Not only did they take some club stuff, but they also stole some rings and necklaces that were left to me by my late mother."

Jenna leaned against the kitchen wall and listened as Rollie and Doug discussed the break in. Bikie or not, Rollie hadn't deserved to be robbed. Butterflies swarmed in her stomach. The same twisted battle that had raged inside her for years began to simmer to the surface. She felt sorry for Rollie, yet at the same time, she prayed with all her might that he would just go away. Jenna slid down against the kitchen wall, pulled her knees to her chest and listened. She jumped as though someone had kicked her hard in the chest, when Doug startled her about twenty minutes later.

"What are you doing sitting down there, Jenna?" he asked, taking hold of her arm and helping her to her feet. "That Rollie seems like a nice guy. He'll be back tonight to speak with the boys," he said, guiding her towards the kitchen table.

"He what?" Jenna cried, turning wildly to face Doug. "You invited that bikie back to my house? To speak to my kids? What the hell do you think you're doing, Doug? I don't want people like that around my kids, period."

"Come on, Jenna, be reasonable. The guy's house has been robbed and he's lost a lot of stuff that can't be replaced. How'd you feel if it was you?"

"Well, it's not me," Jenna answered, loudly. "It's probably just Karma coming back to bite him on the ass. What goes around comes around, so they say. How many people's houses has he robbed? I don't want to get involved Doug. I don't want my kids involved and I certainly don't want you involved. We moved from Sydney so we could stay away from this shit. I'm sorry his house got robbed, I'm sorry he lost all his stuff, but he's not the first and he won't be the last person to get ripped off."

"I'm surprised at you, Jenna. You, little Miss fucking goodie two shoes, won't help someone in trouble? What makes Rollie any worse than some of these feral fucking kids you've been helping? They'd rob their own mothers for fuck sake!" Doug yelled as he heaved himself off the table.

"Those feral kids, as you put it, are victims of circumstance Doug and you know that! They have no one. They have to fend for themselves. Their parents are drug addicts," she said, without a pause. "Your new friend has probably been some of their parent's dealer. He is a God damn bikie, Doug, just in case you hadn't noticed. Get it through your head. They're drug dealers, murderers and thieves. I grew up around them, I'm not an idiot. I know what they're all about. I didn't get away from that lifestyle all those years ago for you to pull me back in now. Your new mate has many choices in his life and it looks to me like he has made them. He's a scum bag bikie, Doug. Look at the size of him.

Who's going to force him to do anything? He made his choices and now I'm making mine. I don't want him near my kids and that's it!"

"Well, that's too bad for you, Jenna. I've invited him back to speak to the boys and that's exactly what he's going to do."

Doug snatched his car keys from the breakfast bar and stormed out the front door. He screeched the tyres of the car as he tore off out the driveway. Jenna locked the screen door behind him and aimlessly wandered back to the kitchen.

She gazed out the window into the back garden. A smile snuck out across her face as she watched her two young daughters play innocently in the rain puddles. She stared at their faces as they giggled and splashed. She could not let this become an issue in their lives, the same way it had affected hers. She would not allow this guy Rollie to influence, or bother them in any way. Jenna refocused her attention back to the vegetables she had been preparing earlier in the sink. She'd been planning to make a special thank you dinner for Doug that night, in a way of appreciation for all he had been doing to hold down the fort as she worked away tirelessly on her book. She knew he was out of his league trying to juggle the children, the housework and his own work, but he was trying. Despite it all, and no matter how busy Jenna became, she had always loved to cook. She enjoyed making Doug's favourite winter meals, even after all these years of being together. She often giggled to herself when she remembered the time he announced that the sole reason he'd married her was for her cooking; he loved her food. His favourite meal had always been her roast beef, dripping with gravy, a vegetable medley, tasty roast potatoes and crunchy herb bread. The grin left her face as she heard the rattling of the front stairs.

"Hurry up and let us in, Mum," Harrison, Jenna's sixteen-year-old son called through the screen. "Me and John got places to go and people to see."

"Sorry guys, you can't go anywhere just yet, I need to speak to you first," she shouted from the kitchen.

"Why not? I was going around to see my mum today, Jen." John, her foster son yelled back.

"I know you were mate, but something really important has come up and I need to talk to you guys about it," she answered.

Jenna's resentment for Rollie grew deeper. It had not been an easy task reuniting John with his family after three long months of separation. John's brother had fallen victim to the increasing amphetamine problem. The drug, along with its complications had torn John's family apart. It had taken weeks for Jenna to persuade John to speak with his mother and now, all because of a bikie, she had to tell him he couldn't go and visit with her for too long.

"What's wrong, Mum?" twelve-year-old Hayden asked.

"Hang on mate, wait until Harrison and John come out here and I'll tell you all together. You probably won't know anything anyway, Hayden, but it's best if you listen in just in case."

Hayden nodded his head, grabbed a juice box from the fridge and swung his legs over the side of the black suede couch. Harrison and John came back to the lounge room and plunked themselves down on the floor.

"Okay, what seems to be the problem, lady?" Harrison asked, cheekily.

"Ha ha! You're funny mate," Jenna giggled. "But, this is serious, so stop mucking around and listen. We had a visit from a member of the Fearsome Devils bike club today. His name is Rollie."

Hayden coughed and spluttered the contents of his juice box all over himself. Harrison and John both jumped to their feet.

"What the hell? Rollie? Fearsome Devils? Rollie who? Why? What? What happened?" They all asked, cutting off each other's questions.

"Just settle down for a second and I'll tell you," Jenna said, motioning for the boys to sit back down. "Apparently he bought a house just down the road from us a few weeks ago and according to him, his house has been robbed. Someone stole all his dead mothers' jewellery, some bikie club stuff, along with a few other important items."

"Yeah right! Whatever! As if!" Harrison interrupted, lifting the left side of his lip up and rolling his eyes.

"That's crap," John chimed in, "as if anyone's stupid enough to rip off one of them blokes. Those Fearsome Devils are bad bastards, they'd kill you in a heartbeat.'

"Yeah, I reckon, the last time someone tried to rip them off, they got tied up and dragged for five kilometres behind a four-wheel drive and ended up in intensive care." Harrison added.

"Oh yeah, they did too," John said. "That was over that pot deal hey?"

"Yeah I think so," Harrison said, nodding his head.

"How do you guys know all this stuff? How do any of you know anything about the Fearsome Devils?" Jenna asked, raising her eyebrows.

"We hear all that crap, Mum," Harrison said, "It's part of being in a crew."

"That's true, Jen.' John agreed.

"What does he want with us, Mum?" Hayden asked quietly.

"We didn't do it."

"I know you didn't mate, but this bikie was told by another club member that you boys may have heard something about who could have done this. Or that you might even know who did do it." Jenna said, sitting down beside her youngest son. "And, if you do know anything about that robbery guys, you need to be honest and tell us," she added, resting her hand on Hayden's head.

"Well, we don't know anything about it, Mum. Haven't heard a word," Harrison said, "And even if we did, we aren't about to nark anyone in for that kind of crap."

"Someone would end up dead for rorting any bikie, let alone them bastards," John added.

"Well guys, you best be sure you don't know anything, or if you do, you will need to speak to this bloke," Jenna said, calmly. "He'll be back tonight to speak to the three of you."

"He's coming back here?" Harrison asked. "Why?"

"Because your father said he could speak to you," she answered, shrugging her shoulders.

"Oh shit," John said, climbing to his feet. "I'm glad I won't be here. I'll be at my mum's house," he added.

"Oh no, you won't, John. You go around to your mum's place now, but you be back home before dark mate. If any of you guys aren't here, you will look guilty and I really don't want you guys to piss him off. He's huge and quite frankly, I want you to tell him what he wants to know, so he can leave and not come back."

"Oh okay then, Jen, but it's a waste of his time. We don't know nothing." John said as he walked out the front door. "See you soon then."

Harrison walked to the couch and ruffled Hayden's messy hair.

"Don't you worry lil bro, you're okay. He won't want to talk to you anyway, you're too young. I'll be back before dark, Mum."

The cool winter afternoon quickly turned to dusk. Jenna called out to six-year-old Holly, and two and a half-year old Hannah, and asked them to come inside and take a bath. The two girls had remained completely oblivious to the afternoon commotion, and Jenna was determined to keep it that way. The girls had never before laid eyes on a man the size of Rollie. She knew his height alone would be enough to frighten them, let alone his leather vest full of bikie garb. She filled the bath and added watermelon fragrant bubble bath. The two girls laughed and squealed as they threw bubbles and water all over the bathroom. Jenna smiled at their innocence and wished their lives could remain this way forever; untouched and unblemished by everyday life and its problems.

Harrison arrived home at five thirty and John strolled in a little after six. Jenna rallied the troops and served the evening meal. The uncomfortable silence of the three boys and Doug was more than Jenna could bare. The usual noisy dinner table remained quiet with the exception of the two girls' cheerful babble. Hayden, usually first to finish his meal, pushed his beef around his plate with his fork and made mountains with his carrots. Hannah stole the peas from Hayden's plate and waited for a reaction. When she realised she wasn't going to get one, she took the rest of the peas and put them on her own plate. She smiled at Hayden and he smiled back.

"That's it, Doug. Look how much this meeting with your new friend is worrying them," Jenna said, rising from the table.

"I don't want you to let Rollie in here. Hannah is even stealing Hayden's food and he doesn't even care. When have you ever seen that before?" she asked, taking her dinner plate to the sink.

"I'm alright, Mum," Hayden said, looking to the older boys for reassurance. "I'm just not hungry."

"It's okay to be scared, Hayden," she said. "No one wants to be interrogated by a bikie mate; you would be a very silly young man if you weren't scared."

"What's a bikie, Mummy?" Holly asked, looking blankly at Jenna.

"Never mind Holly, Mummy is being silly," Doug answered, shooting daggers with his eyes towards his wife.

"No Doug, don't tell her that. Tell her the truth. What is a bikie, Doug?" she asked sarcastically. "A bikie Holly, is a bad person. A bikie is someone who rides a motorbike and hangs out with other bad people. That's what a bikie is."

"But Daddy rides a motorbike and he's not bad," Holly said, running her fingers through her blonde ringlets. "Are you bad, Daddy?" she asked, turning to Doug.

"No Holly, I'm not bad and neither is my friend who is coming here tonight. Like I said, Mummy is just being silly." Doug answered her softly. "But, when my friend comes over tonight Holly, I do need you to go and play with Hannah in your room and keep her in there for me, please. My friend, his name is Rollie, and he is a very big man, Holly and he might scare Hannah."

"I can do that, Daddy," Holly said, fluttering her big blue eyes. "I'll just play with her, or we can watch Anastasia? Hannah loves that movie."

"Good girl, Holly. Thank you for that." Doug said, gathering his and Holly's plates from the table.

Harrison, Hayden and John, cleared their plates and headed for their bedroom. Holly waited for Hannah to finish eating and then took her by the hand to their room. Doug went with them and placed the Anastasia video cassette into the video player. Jenna sat momentarily at the table with her chin resting in her hands thinking. She eventually got up and cleared the rest of the table. Doug emerged from the girls' bedroom not saying a word. They washed and dried the dinner dishes together in silence, neither one would even glance briefly at the other. Jenna, determined not to speak to Doug, took the vacuum out of the broom closet and begun to clean the floors. Doug went to the lounge room and turned on the television.

At around a quarter to eight Jenna heard a car pull up to the curb at the front of the house. Then, she heard two car doors slam shut instead of one. She went to the front window and peered out of the wooden blinds. Rollie appeared from behind the front fence, with a small brunette woman following closely behind him.

"Doug, your friend is here and he's taken it upon himself to bring someone with him. How nice of him," she said, sarcastically, as she headed down the hallway to warn the three boys.

Rollie and his companion approached the front door and Doug invited them in. Jenna emerged from the hallway with the three boys in tow.

"Doug, this is Candice, my girlfriend. A lot of the stuff that was taken from my house belonged to her." Rollie said, placing his large hand in the small of Candice's back.

"It's very nice to meet you," Candice said quietly.

Rollie then turned to face Jenna square on.

"And, I believe this is Jenna, Candice. This is Doug's wife."

"Nice to meet you, Jenna," Candice said.

Jenna offered Candice a forced smiled and stood to the side. Doug introduced the three boys one at a time. All three extended their hands like gentlemen and offered a good firm handshake. Rollie praised their perfect manners and Candice smiled at them, greeting each boy warmly. Rollie explained to the boys about what had happened to his house and asked them if they knew anything. None of them seemed to know a thing, but they all promised to keep their ears to the ground and let Rollie know if they heard anything.

Jenna was taken aback by Candice's striking features as she lingered behind the party of people moving towards the dining table. Candice appeared very young. Her long, thick, brown hair dangled down her back and over the side of her face. Her perfect almond shaped, brown eyes peered out from behind her hair. Her crimson lips shone as she spoke and her straight smile made many appearances throughout the conversation. Jenna wondered what a pretty young woman like her was doing with a bikie like Rollie.

"Jenna, how about making us some coffee?" Doug asked, interrupting her deep thoughts.

"Oh yeah, how rude of me. Sorry. Rollie, Candice, would you like a coffee?" she asked, making her way to the kitchen bench to switch on the kettle.

"Yeah, I'll have one thanks," Rollie answered.

"Yes please, I'll have one too, thank you," Candice said quietly. "We both have two sugars and milk, please."

Jenna made the four cups of coffee and cut four slices of banana cake before taking her seat beside Doug. Candice ate the cake and sipped on the hot coffee. Rollie and Doug continued their conversation about the break in and eventually replaced the coffees with Coronas. Before too long the verbal exchange became relaxed and extensive. Jenna sat back and soaked in the conversation as she toyed with the cake on her plate. Rollie explained that he and Candice had made the road trip to Brisbane from Melbourne a few weeks earlier. He shared his thoughts on the area and what he also thought about the state he'd left behind. He spoke briefly about his family and his predictions on his new future. Candice joined in the conversation at opportune moments, revealing her own thoughts on each matter. Doug revealed many parts of his past life; in fact, he shared parts of his life he would normally keep secret. Somehow he appeared to trust this uninvited stranger and that itself unnerved her. Perhaps it was the alcohol talking, she thought to herself. With every new detail Doug unveiled, Jenna would glance at him before continuing her small talk with Candice. She began to feel sorry for Candice, being estranged from her family and friends. Candice's childlike sweetness brought out Jenna's motherly instincts and she began to warm to her.

The night progressed into the early hours of the morning, and before too long, Doug and Rollie were arranging a meeting for the very next day. Jenna looked on in horror. All she could do was wait; so wait she did. Finally, after what seemed an eternity, Rollie and Candice left.

"Doug, what the hell are you doing?"

Doug raised his eyebrows and smiled "What?" he asked, shrugging his shoulders.

"What do you mean what? What part of, I don't want anything to do with bikies don't you understand?" Jenna asked. "I can't do this again Doug. You know I grew up around these bikie animals. It took forever for me to finally grow up and get away from them and now you are dragging me back into it! What the hell are you thinking? What planet are you from?"

"I'm too tired for this shit, Jenna, I'm going to bed. I have no intention of discussing this with you any further." Doug stated, as he locked the back door and made his way to the bedroom.

Jenna stormed around as she cleared the kitchen table. She roughly washed and dried the coffee cups and dessert plates before putting them away. When she finished, she sat down at the table and cried. She cried the tears that had threatened to pour from her soul for so many long years. Her memories, her nightmares had all come back to haunt her. Rollie, the bikie, had been right there, right in her house, right in her face. Everything that she had hated, everything that she had despised, and everything his lifestyle represented had just been sitting directly across from her. There he was, just like a nightmare, a stupid bikie, forcing himself on her family and indeed on her. Such a flurry of emotion spilt over the edge and the deepest rage grew inside her. What Doug had failed to remember, and what Rollie was yet to understand, was she had been partly raised within the bikie community. It was not a place she had planned to re-visit, not now, not ever.

Jenna's stepfather and many of her uncles, had either ties to or were members of, a notorious motorcycle club. She had learnt from a very young age the depth of brotherhood, the bonds that tie, and the pain that can be brought to anyone who dared to cross that invisible line of comradery. The memories Jenna held onto from her past were nothing short of being taunted, scarred and tormented. Her memories of violence and helplessness cascaded down around her, but the tears that flowed so freely did so for her most twisted pain of all. She had missed some of those brothers more than she cared to admit, yet she forced herself to live through that agony of knowing she could never return to a place such as that again. A little girl, who had lived mainly a life of abuse, who had now grown into a fully functioning woman, would not concede to such a temptation. Jenna had no intention of living that pain ever again, nor would she allow her children to be subjected to such misery either. Doug would have to make a choice; it could only be one way, he would ultimately have to choose her or Rollie.

Jennifer Brockie

Chapter Two

Resistance Is Futile

Jenna awoke before the break of day the following morning hoping that everything from the night before was nothing more than a nightmare. As she pulled the covers up around her neck and stared at Doug sleeping peacefully beside her, she knew everything that happened was true. Her thoughts quickly became a jumbled mess, so she quietly snuck out of bed being ever so careful not to disturb Doug as she left. As the children emerged from their bedrooms, Jenna routinely put the cereal into their bowls, poured the glasses of milk and helped Hannah get dressed. When the children were ready for school, Jenna bundled them all into the van and dropped them off at the school gate, waving to them as she drove away. She drove up the street a short way and pulled up to the curb.

"What's wrong, Mummy?" Hannah asked, almost yelling from her car seat in the back of the van.

"Nothing, baby. Nothing is wrong. Would you like to go and spend the day with Aunty Shari?"

"Yay! Yep. Can I? Will Bonnie be there?" she squealed, "Yay. I'm going to aunties," she cheered.

After stalling at Shari's for as long as possible, Jenna made her way back to the house. When she arrived, Doug called out to her from the kitchen.

"Do you want a coffee, Jenna?" he asked, as she entered the front door.

"No thanks, I don't want anything from you," she answered.

"Oh come on now, you're not still shitty with me are you? Doug asked, rounding the corner. "Where's Hannah?"

"She's at my sister's place."

"What's she doing over there?"

"Because Doug, we are going to have this bikie crap out once and for all, and we both know what your temper is like. I don't want Hannah to have to listen to that."

"Oh for fuck sake, Jenna, you're not still going on with this shit are you?"

"Of course I'm still going on with it. I don't want him in my house!"

"That's stiff shit for you then isn't it? I don't tell you who you can and can't have here, so don't try and fucking tell me," he shouted.

"Doug, I don't bring people like that into the house, or around our children. Why would you? Why would you even want to?"

"Because I can. I've always liked the Fearsome Devils and you know that. Rollie seems like a decent bloke and I'm happy to help him."

"Oh, so that's what this is all about? You still haven't outgrown wanting to be a big bad bikie? For God sake, Doug, don't you think it's time to grow the hell up? They're nothing but trouble."

"Yeah, that's your opinion. Fuck you and whatever you think about it, Jenna. It's time you let the past go. Times have changed. Bikies and their rules have changed. What makes you think Rollie is anything like the fuckwits your stepfather used to hang out with?"

"Poor naïve little Doug," Jenna answered, "You're a foolish, foolish little man. They are all the same. Nothing ever changes with them, not now, not ever. You make me laugh to think that I'm the idiot in this situation."

Doug stormed towards her, trapping her trembling body between his arms up against the lounge room wall. He moved his face in so close to hers, that she could feel the anger in his hot, alcohol-laced breath. He raised his fist, waving it in front of her before slamming it hard into the wall only inches away from her head. "Stop patronizing me you disrespectful little cunt. I will have who I want, when I want, in my house. If you don't like it, get your kids, get your stuff, and fuck off!"

Visions of Dennis, her first husband, picking her up and slamming her through the glass table, rose to the surface. She began to gasp for breath as though the memory had once again pierced her lung. She began to sob. Her cheekbone began to ache, her ribs began to throb and the memory of all the broken bones, which still ached in the cold weather, were enough to remind her to hold her tongue. Submission, she thought. Jenna remembered that crying, agreeing and submitting usually stopped Dennis in his tracks; at least until the next time. So that's exactly what she did with Doug.

After breaking free of his hold, Jenna went into her bedroom and laid down on her bed. She stared up at the illuminating stars and moons still stuck to the ceiling by the previous owners.

She remembered the day of her marriage to Dennis and all the agony it had caused her. Her mother, still caught up in her disgraced past of unwed mothers, was determined that Jenna would not suffer the same fate as she once had. But, no matter how hard Jenna protested that the times had changed now in the eighties, her mother refused to accept her resistance.

"Dennis is a respectable man, Jenna. He's been in the army. He comes from a good family. What more do you want?" she had asked.

"Mum, I don't want to get married. I'm too young. Besides, look how well it turned out for you."

"Just because your father was a violent man doesn't mean everyone else is going to be that way. Why can't you give it a chance? Not all men are the same."

"Dad wasn't just violent, Mum, he was a career criminal. He spent most of his young life in prison. For God sake, he was even inside when I was born. Why give it a chance? What is it you want from me? Do you want me to compete for the title of the world's youngest woman to ever divorce? As it is, you have to sign my marriage certificate. I'm only seventeen. I don't want to get married."

"Well, I'm sorry, Jenna. It can't always be about you. You have to think what will be best for the family."

"About me?" Jenna yelled, "It's never been about me, Mum. If it had been about me, I would never have ended up in that home for unwanted children now would I?"

Jenna's mother broke out in a red rage, pulled her arm back before striking Jenna hard across the cheek.

"I told you not to mention that ever again. How dare you judge me? I did the best I could by you kids," she said, taking Jenna's trembling hand in hers, "Look, you need to do this. You need to do this for me. You need to marry Dennis. If you do this, I can still help you, but if you don't, you know your step-father will kick you out of the house when he finds out you're pregnant. You'll be on your own with a little baby, with no financial help from him or anyone else. He needs to uphold the reputation of the family now that he is in so far with the elite."

"The elite?" Jenna asked, snatching her hand away to rub the side of her face. "They are not the elite, Mother. They're a bunch of crooked millionaires, with more money than sense. All you've managed to do is swap one bad bunch for an even worse one. You should've just stayed with the bikies. At least with them, you knew when they were after you or had a problem with you. Now look what you've got. A bunch of spineless fools who wouldn't dirty their hands on their own problems. They just cause the trouble and then pay someone else to clean up their mess. It's pathetic. I want nothing to do with them either."

"Jenna, Stop! You need to get dressed and get into that limo. Whether you like it or not, you are getting married today."

Jenna smiled as she remembered how she had ducked into the bathroom at the church and plotted her get away. Needless to say, her best-hatched plans never came to fruition. But then again, they never did.

Her next thought went back even further. She thought about the escape plan she and her brother had plotted to escape the children's home. In theory, in the minds of an eight year old boy and a five year old girl, rolling down that hill in a large tractor tyre should have meant freedom; but alas, a broken arm did mean freedom, even if it was only momentarily and all the freedom a hospital emergency unit could provide.

She sadly thought back to, Jack, her big brother and wished he could have still been here with her now. He had always been her hero and had always gotten her out of trouble. Since his death though, she had to work things out by herself. And, she thought she was doing a good job of doing so, right up until last night and the Rollie incident.

Just as she closed her eyes and began to accept that she had no control over Doug's decision, she heard the sound of the front gate creak open. She jumped up and peeked out of the blinds. It was Rollie. She threw herself back onto the bed and sulked. Muffled voices drifted in under the doorway and Jenna's curiosity began to grow. She opened her door, just slightly and strained to listen to the conversation between the two men taking place.

"I've got some info on my break in," Rollie said, "Do you know where Wattle street is?"

"Yeah I do. Why?" Doug answered.

"I got told that the low life's that live in that junkie den at number six, are the ones who broke into my place and they still have some of my stuff. Do you wanna come with me and check it out?"

"Yep, no problem, let me go grab my shoes and we'll go suss these fuckers out."

As it turned out the information Rollie had received was incorrect. After Rollie and Doug kindly kicked the front door to the house open and searched it, they proceeded to scold the occupants for showering their child on top of a mound of mildewed clothes. The people inside the house became terrified and offered in exchange for lenience, a world of information about who may have been involved in the break-in incident. Over the next few days, Doug and Rollie spent every spare minute together, going from house to house of all the local drug dealers, trying to unravel the mystery of the break in. They would often come back to the house gloating about the fear on people's faces as they approached them and questioned them about the robbery. As they revelled in the glory of terrifying people, Jenna's stomach churned even further. The more she protested about their behaviour, the more they justified their actions. Rollie had asked her if she believed the police would help someone like him to recover his possessions. In Jenna's heart, she knew the police wouldn't help him. Just like she also knew they probably highly doubted his accusations, just as she had. She knew this would be the only way he had any hope of finding his things, yet still, she feared for whoever may have been the perpetrator. The sheer size of Rollie's hands were enough to frighten anyone. To endure a deliverance from one of his punches would be like being crushed by a wrecking ball. No, she certainly wouldn't like to be on the wrong side of Rollie, actually, she wouldn't like to be on the wrong side of either of these two men.

As the friendship between the two men strengthened, Rollie became more of a permanent fixture. It didn't take too long before he was not only there to hang out with Doug during the day, but to also share meals with the family almost every single night. Over time, the children grew to adore Rollie, especially the boys. As he would talk about his travels and adventures, they would often hang off his every word, often repeating the stories between themselves for days after the event.

Even little Hannah, who usually didn't bother with visitors, had formed a deep affection for him. When Rollie would arrive at the house, Hannah would run to the front door and greet him, often swinging around his legs like a gymnast and asking him every question her two-year-old mind could come up with. Holly, being the more shy and reserved child, would stand in the hallway and wave and grin at him as though he were a celebrity. Jenna, on the other hand, avoided Rollie wherever she could. She only ever answered him in short yes or no answers and if possible, avoided running into him altogether. The only time it became a challenge for her was at dinner time. Every single night, Rollie would insist on sitting directly across from her or right beside her. Jenna eventually became accustomed to how uneasy it made her feel, until one night, he caught her gaze and almost made her choke on her pasta.

"You don't like me much do you, Jenna?"

She gulped down loudly and raised her eyebrows high before looking straight at Doug. Doug looked right back at her pleadingly.

"Umm, it's not that I don't like you, Rollie, I just don't really know you."

"Nice save," he laughed, "But, not good enough. Now, answer the question."

Feeling the unsettling urge to slip under the table and disappear, Jenna wrapped her legs tightly around the cast iron legs of her chair and squeezed her hands into tiny fists on her lap.

"Rollie, leave her alone," Candice said, "You can see you're making her uncomfortable. Now stop it!"

Rollie turned and glared at Candice. "I'm not making her uncomfortable, I'm asking her a question. You're not uncomfortable are you, Jenna?"

Jenna looked at Candice who shrugged her shoulders then rolled her eyes. "Don't worry about him. You'll get used to him," she laughed. "He just thinks he's being funny."

Jenna rose from the table and began to stack the dishes into the sink. As she turned around, to head back to the table, she walked straight into Rollie who was standing directly behind her with dishes in his hands.

"I don't know why you don't like me, or what your problem is with me, Jenna, but I will tell you this; from this moment on, I am going to make it my personal mission to make you like me."

Despite her objections when it came to Rollie, Jenna did find herself becoming fond of Candice. Candice, was the only daughter of a widowed miner, and found the commitment to her new life difficult. Unlike Rollie, Doug, and Jenna, who were in their late twenties, Candice, had only recently celebrated her twentieth birthday. She seemed much younger though, with her maturity level falling somewhere between a child and that of a young teenager. Being forced to leave behind her father and her friends in her small country hometown weighed heavily on her, often resulting in her throwing child-like tantrums and creating unnecessary dramas. Jenna recognised the behaviour from the children she had helped guide in her role as a Tough Love parent. Jenna felt confident she could help Candice mature into a decent and respectable young woman. The task, which was often met with huge challenges, became a welcome distraction for Jenna, even though she struggled to find a balance between her own family, her writing and the needs of Candice. In reality, Jenna thought all Candice needed was someone to help her adjust to her new life in a big city. She felt with the right guidance, Candice would be fine. Before too long, Jenna began to look forward to Candice's company, especially when she was on her best behaviour, while Rollie was away on club business. Jenna enjoyed his absences, as it gave her time to relax.

Each time he went away, she silently hoped he wouldn't return, but that never happened, as he always came home, and in spite of her desire for a contained universe without Rollie, Jenna felt her defences against him slowly melting away. She occasionally caught herself smiling at some of the things he'd said or done, but she was always careful to make sure he hadn't noticed her amusement. Ever since Rollie's confession of his intentions towards her, Jenna's recognition of his attention became paramount. Some days were harder than others as his boyish charm pierced through the layers of her toughened exterior.

If she were honest enough to admit the truth, undeterred by the fact she never wanted to surrender, she would have to say the true icebreaker in her friendship with Rollie, came the day he rode his ride-on lawnmower up a public street in broad daylight to visit. All the neighbours were out in their front yards going about their daily business; when low and behold, a huge, heavily tattooed man drives past them on a lawn-mower. Some nervous people ran inside their homes while others stood there in absolute shock. Rollie just rolled on by, nodding at them in acknowledgement as he passed by, even waving to the elderly lady sitting on her front porch at number twenty. Jenna had heard the commotion from in the fog filled bathroom, before rushing out to her bedroom window to see what was happening. When she saw it was Rollie putting up the street, she almost fell to the floor laughing. She thought to herself that he had surely lost his mind.

"Oh, Rollie, you didn't!" she exclaimed, between fits of laughter. "You can't ride that on a public street. I could hear you coming from in the shower. You were moving so slow I had time to dress and still watch you coming up the road. You live like two minutes from here, wouldn't it have been faster for you to walk? What were you thinking?"

"Top of the morning to you, Jenna," he said, grinning like the Cheshire cat. "It's too hot to walk, so I thought I'd test this baby out. What's wrong with that?"

"It's illegal Rollie. It's not registered. What if the police caught you?"

"Now there's a thought. I wonder if I could outrun them on this?" he added.

"I highly doubt that," she said, "Come upstairs and I'll get you a cold drink."

From that moment on, the ignorance ceased. Jenna decided to lower her guard towards Rollie. Anyone who could be that much of a child surely couldn't be too harmful, or so she thought.

One Friday morning in autumn, Rollie rang Doug and asked they were available to meet for lunch at the local tavern. Jenna's day was clear and Hannah was delighted.

"I bags sitting next to Rollie," she yelled at the top of her voice.

"Yes, Hannah, we know." Jenna answered, ruffling the top of Hannah's locks.

"I'm going to duck down the bank and put this cash in so I don't have to do it later," Doug said, heading out the door.

"Okay, see you soon," Jenna said, picking up the basket of laundry, before taking Hannah's hand and descending the back steps. Just as she loaded the whites into the machine, Jenna heard the screech of tyres on the driveway. She slammed the lid closed and bolted back up the stairs. "Fuck! Fuck!" Doug shouted, waving his arms around angrily.

"What? What's wrong, Doug?" she asked.

"I turned around the bend at the bottom of our street and there are cop cars everywhere. I mean fucking everywhere. There's three up this side and four down around the bottom corner."

"So? What does that have to do with us? What are they doing down there?"

"Jenna, it looks like they're going to raid Rollie's house."

"Oh my God, Doug. Why?"

"Well, I don't fucking know do I? Do you reckon I should call him and let him know or what?"

"I don't know. Is it legal? Can you get into trouble for tipping him off?"

"Oh fucked if I know. Fuck it, I'm doing it anyway."

Doug pulled out his phone and dialled Rollie's number. After several rings Rollie finally answered the call. "Top of the morning to you there. Would you like a chat with detective Jones would ya?" Rollie asked, sarcastically.

"So you already know? I was just ringing to warn you." Doug answered.

"Yep, I certainly do. I'll give you a call when I finish up here."

A little after lunch time Rollie called Doug and asked him to bring Jenna down to his house. He said he had something urgent to tell them. As they stepped through the door, Jenna's jaw dropped in horror. Rollie's house had been torn apart as though a tornado had just ripped through it. Pot plants were tipped over with potting mix spilled out all over the floor. Every drawer, in every room of the house, including Candice's personal drawer, had been upturned and strewn across the room. Paperwork and items of clothing littered the lounge room and the kitchen was totally destroyed.

Hannah gasped in horror as she stepped over the shattered glass coffee table.

"I'm scared, Mummy. I want to go home," she cried.

"It's alright, Hannah, I made all this mess looking for something," Rollie soothed, running his huge hand over the top of her shiny hair. "Silly me broke the coffee table when I picked it up. Do you want something to eat? Then you can go play with the puppies if you like?"

"Okay, Rollie," she answered, looking to Jenna for reassurance.

"Candice," he said, "Make the little one some food and play with her while I speak to Doug and Jenna."

Candice growled at Rollie, "If I have to."

"So what the fuck happened here?" Doug asked.

"Wait till the baby's out of the room," Rollie answered.

Once Candice made Hannah some pasta and took her out onto the back patio, Rollie shut and locked the glass sliding door. Jenna's legs began to shake uncontrollably.

"I want to leave, Doug. Go get my baby. I'm going home," she whispered quietly.

"You can't just leave," he whispered back, "Just wait until we hear what he has to say."

A wave of nausea washed over her and her mouth began to water.

"Are you alright, Jenna?" Rollie asked, moving towards her. "You look like you've seen a ghost. Look at her, Doug, she's gone white as a sheet."

"She'll be right," Doug said, "She just don't like cops much either."

Rollie swiped the bench top in the kitchen clean from all the clutter the police had left around. He switched on the jug, made three cups of coffee and invited Jenna to take a seat at the bench.

"I don't know how to break this to you, Jenna, and I seriously cannot apologise enough, but the cops have now got your phone numbers. Both your home number and your mobile number." Rollie said, "I'm sorry."

"How? Why? What do they want with my number?"

"It's not just your number they have, it's every number I had stored in my phone directory. They took the whole thing with them when they left."

"What were they doing here? What'd they want?" Doug asked.

"They were searching for evidence. That, my kind sir, was the homicide squad."

Jenna felt her body sway as her mind drifted off to another place. Her heart began to race and a bead of sweat broke out across her top lip.

"Doug, go and get my daughter, I want to get out of here now," she cried. "I knew this was a huge mistake. I want to go home."

"Please, don't go, Jenna. Please hear me out first?" Rollie pleaded. "It's normal cop tactics. They're trying to set me up. They're trying to make sure that everyone who lives in this street is terrified of me. Especially you."

"Me? Why me? They don't even know me," she said, gathering her handbag up in her arms. "I've never even had a parking ticket," she cried.

"They know that. That's why they're doing it. They track everywhere I go and everything I do. I'm a Fearsome Devil, Jenna. I'm a bikie. I'm everything they have nightmares about. They want you to be scared of me. But, let me tell you this, I didn't murder anyone, that much I can promise you."

Jenna held her breath and forced herself to look straight into Rollie's eyes. "You didn't?"

"No, I didn't. I promise you."

Something in his eyes told her he was not lying. She could see the pain the accusation had caused him. Jenna, who keeps herself at a safe distance from those who may be involved in violence or anger, hesitant to return to the pain of her past, is still fearful of intimacy. Her past is hidden, still too frightened to engage in the connections of yesteryear. Even now she cannot enter those episodes with safety. Unfortunately, the past is always brought into the present by small things; memories.

From that moment on, Jenna discovered she had a small admiration for Rollie. After all, he could have lied about the situation and fabricated an entirely different story about who those police officers were. He could have told her they were there to raid his house for drugs, or something slightly less horrifying. She studied him and watched as a picture formed over his face. He holds a formality which keeps him carefully guarded with others, yet his eyes told her of his innocence. That day would be their turning point; the point in which Rollie would slowly induct Jenna into his world. They have now stepped into an abyss that will change the way they will see each other forever.

Jennifer Brockie

Chapter Three

The Party

The introduction into Rollie's world and his people would begin slowly at first. He chose fleeting drop-ins to the clubhouse, small gatherings at his house with his brothers and their partners and other engagements he deemed not too threatening for Jenna. In time, she would gradually begin to relax, finding the company of the women to be quite pleasant. They were not at all what she expected. Nothing like the rough biker women from her childhood. These girls were wives and mothers. Some were even grandmothers. Most of them worked respectable jobs, such as dental assistants, florists and one was even a morgue attendant. The ladies who didn't actually have a job, instead invested their time maintaining their families and their homes. It didn't take too long before Jenna was really fond of some of them, especially Sarah.

Sarah, the sassiest of the bunch, was also the wife of one of the highest ranking members of the Fearsome Devils. Her laugh was contagious and she kept the boys amused by her many hidden talents. Sarah, being a farm girl, could out shoot the best of the boys with her eyes closed. The brothers had brought one of those shoot'em up machines for inside the clubhouse for amusement, only they hadn't planned on being shown up by a girl. Needless to say, the boys didn't hold many shooting competitions while she was around.

As Jenna's acceptance of his people grew, Rollie decided to step things up a notch or two.

"Guess what, Jenna?" he asked, one night over his mashed potato and steak.

"I don't know. What, Rollie?"

"You're coming to the biggest Fearsome Devil party of the year."

"I'm what?" she asked, almost choking on her food.

"You heard me. It's gonna be awesome. Anyone who's anyone will be there, including you."

"Yeah, na. I don't think so, Rollie. I'll sit this one out thanks."

"You can't sit it out. I already told everyone you were coming."

Jenna rose to her feet pushing the chair beneath her back under the table roughly. "Well, you shouldn't have should you? You shouldn't have said anything to anyone until you asked me first," she said, taking her plate over to the sink. "Now, you're just going to have to tell them I'm not going."

"Why not?" he persisted. "You'll be right. Nothing's gonna happen. You'll have a great time."

"I said no, Rollie. I don't want to go."

"Leave her alone, Rollie," Candice interrupted. "If she doesn't want to go, she doesn't have to. You can't make her go," she added, half smiling at Jenna.

"Shut up, Candice. I didn't ask you," he said. "I want her to go."

"Come on, babe? What's the problem? It'll be fun." Doug added.

"Doug, you keep out of this. I said I don't want to go. I'm not stopping you from going, so back off," she said, angrily.

"Jenna, listen to me," Rollie said, quietly. "You should come. It's the only way you're going to see for yourself what they're really like. Everyone will be together getting pissed and partying on. You'll love it."

"That's exactly my point, Rollie. Why do you think I don't even go to pubs? I can't stand obnoxious drunks hitting on everyone, starting fights and carrying on like idiots. I really don't want to go. You guys go and have fun," she added, as she continued to clear the table.

"I give you my word, the clubhouse is nothing like a pub. No-one is stupid enough to carry on like a fuckwit there. If they do, they get bounced and they know it. So everyone is on their best behaviour. I promise," he said pausing. "By coming to this party you can see for yourself. It's the only way I can show you that it's not at all about violence, rape and pillage. Please, come?"

Jenna looked at Candice who held her head down low. She looked at Doug as he pled with his eyes.

"Oh my God, Rollie. If it means you'll shut up. I'll go. But, I'm warning you now, if I get nervous, I'm leaving."

"Deal. But, you won't get nervous. I'll pick you up. You guys can come with me and then, I give you my word, I'll stay with you the whole night."

Jenna quietly cut the cheesecake, made the coffees and returned to the table. She looked towards Candice and smiled. Candice kept her face straight and stared.

"I don't want cake or coffee thanks," she said, looking at Rollie. "It's time we go."

The night of the big party finally arrived, when it suddenly dawned on Jenna that she had no idea what to wear to such a function. She decided to call Candice.

"Hi, Lovely, just thought I'd give you a call and find out what to wear tonight?"

"Oh, it's you, Jenna," she said, glumly, "I don't know about you, but I'm wearing my black leather pants and the new hundred dollar top Rollie brought me."

"Sounds nice, what do the other girls wear?" Jenna asked, detecting some hesitation in Candice's voice. "I don't want to look out of place or stupid."

'Oh, I don't know. Wear whatever you want. No-one will care anyway. Most of them just wear jeans. I've got to go. I've gotta finish getting ready."

Jenna hung up the phone and shook her head. She wondered what was wrong with Candice. Maybe she and Rollie were having an argument or something she thought.

After emptying her wardrobe and rifling through her drawers, she eventually decided on wearing a pair of white body-hugging jeans, a lace sleeved, black wrap around top and her platform heeled boots. She nervously applied a coat of earthy tone makeup then carefully painted her shapely lips with a luscious layer of cherry red lip gloss. With a sigh, she stood back and tentatively admired her own reflection in the mirror. It had been a long time since she'd had an occasion to fix her face in such a way. Once a much sort after, pretty teenage girl, pursued by all the most talented boys, she had exchanged her high street fashion for the true overalls of motherhood. There was no reason to dress in the latest trends now that she was a mother of four children and the foster mother of many. Instead, she dressed casually and comfortably as she made her way through her days filled with household chores and writing, simply preferring to slack around in denim jeans, a loose fitting top and even sometimes a beanie. As she thought about her past, her life before motherhood, she sprayed herself with her favourite perfume and curled her long blonde hair. She was startled back to the present by the ring of the phone.

"Hello, Jenna speaking," she said.

"Hey, Jen, its Rollie," he replied.

"Oh hey, Rollie. What's happening?"

"Not much. I'm just ringing to let you know l won't be at the clubhouse when you get there tonight. I'm really sorry." he said, quietly.

"Why?" she asked nervously. "You said you were picking us up."

"I know, and I'm sorry. It's nothing serious, I'll still be there. But I've got to pick up one of my brothers from the airport first. He won't get in until eight, so we won't get up there until around ten."

"Well, I'm not going then. I'm not going up the clubhouse without you. I'm scared to be there without you, Rollie."

"No, please still go. I'll be there, I promise. I'll just be a little late. When you get to the clubhouse, ring Candice's phone. I told her to meet you at the front door and keep you company until I get there. Please still go, Jenna, l want you to be there. It means a lot to me."

Jenna stared into the phone receiver long after Rollie hang up. She thought of every excuse she could think of to get out of going to the party. She even hoped Hannah would start whining because that way she really couldn't go. It would be too late by the time Rollie got there anyway. What could he say if they weren't there when he arrived? He couldn't exactly leave the party to come over and yell at her. Jenna made the decision not to go. Then Doug began to rant and rave asserting his aggression. Jenna wondered what she could do. After negotiating to have the keys to the car in her possession at all times, she relented and agreed to go. Besides, she had given Rollie her word. Not to keep it would make her everything she had accused the bikies of being. After stalling for as long as possible, by going over the instructions with the sitters and saying goodbye to her children, she finally pulled on her long black fur jacket and left the house.

On their arrival, Jenna was astounded. At least a hundred cars and just as many motorbikes lined both sides of the street as they approached the clubhouse. The clubhouse resembled a well-presented nightclub which had been lit up better than a New York Christmas tree. Security lined the door and gates as people swarmed towards the lights like moths to a flame. They arrived in droves, some by the car load, and others on their own. No matter how they arrived, they all appeared happy to have received an invite to be there. As they neared the gate, Jenna pulled her mobile phone from her handbag and dialled Candice's number. The phone rang out, so she dialled the number again. Every time she tried it went straight to voicemail.

"Why won't she answer the phone?" she asked.

"Don't worry about her. Let's just go in any way," Doug insisted.

"I don't want to. Can't we just wait here until Rollie gets here?"

"For fuck sake, Jenna. Stop being such a fucking sook. It's alright."

"Thanks, Doug. You know I'm freaking out. I've never been here without Rollie before and I'm scared."

"Thanks. What the fuck am I? It'll be alright. You don't need Rollie, I'll look after you."

Jenna raised her eyebrows in amusement. What did Doug think he could do against all of these men? These were bikies. Still, she lowered her head and followed quietly behind him. As they walked through the concrete car park she noticed all the Fearsome Devil brothers in their leather vests, displaying their colours and proudly mingling with the crowd. As they got closer to the entrance she stopped dead in her tracks. Off to the side of the building were other men, strange men wearing different patches than that of the Fearsome Devils. Her past rose to the surface to taunt her. She remembered from her childhood days that to wear your own colours to another clubs event was a massive sign of disrespect and was in fact, regarded as a total insult. The urge to run took hold of her. She had no desire to wait for the massacre begin. She turned to run, but Doug grabbed her hand and pulled her forward.

"Stop it, Jenna. You're being a fucking idiot. We're going in."

"Doug, do you not remember the Milperra massacre?" she whispered.

"There won't be no fucking massacre, those guys are invited guests. They're religious bikies. Now stop being stupid."

Relief washed over her as she reassured herself that she was safe once she could see the religious memorabilia hanging from their necks. She felt a little safer. These were men of God. Men of God would always do what was right, even at the Fearsome Devils clubhouse party she thought. She held her head high and moved forward in the line. Her body began to, once again, quiver as they neared the entrance of the clubhouse. She couldn't work out if it was the cold weather ripping through her fur coat, or if it was the fear of the unknown that made her teeth chatter and her knees to tremble. As they waited to enter, she gazed over her shoulder and soaked in the sheer size of the front door. It had always amused her.

This door would keep anyone out. Even worse, it could keep anyone in. The door was made of metal and was at least ten inches thick. It reminded her of a door to a bank vault. It would have been easier to drive through the wall of the building than it would be to get through that door.

Her thoughts returned to the moment as Doug paid for their tickets and they stepped inside. Jenna allowed her eyes to roam over the pictures of men in their colours all over the memorabilia wall. She had seen them a few times before, but tonight it felt different. Somehow that wall seemed to possess a power all of its own, a strong significant force that protected its secrecy, as it projected the band of brothers who stood before it. Pride lined those walls through the fallen brothers, the brothers lost, but certainly not forgotten. Symbols of the Fearsome Devils masculinity radiated around the entire bar. Their protective unity stood out as they assessed every new guest as they stepped through the door. Each member would raise their head, or glance over their shoulder to make sure the arrival was in fact friend, not foe. Jenna was pleased she was an invited guest. This certainly was not the kind of party she'd want to crash.

Groups of women sat huddled together in their close-knit circles and the men mainly stood, or sat at the bar. Smiles escaped from some familiar lips and Jenna shyly returned the affection. She moved closer to Doug as he approached the bar and ordered two drinks. The live band screamed out and vibrated the walls. People danced and laughed in every inch of the building. People from all walks of life littered the clubhouse, all enjoying themselves. Jenna's shock grew as she recognized people from the local shopping mall, the real estate agency and even some people she had seen at the children's school. She had never expected to find some of those people at the Fearsome Devil's clubhouse.

After Doug got the drinks they made their way through the crowd to the area that held high tables; tables which people stood at instead of sitting. Jenna felt so small. The table came up to her chest, even with her heels on. She placed her handbag under the table and she took a sip of her vodka. She began to relax as she soaked in her surroundings and   allowed her drink to take effect. A few minutes later, her peaceful mood once again became disrupted by a huge hand grabbing her by her tiny shoulder. Jenna jumped before hesitantly turning around.

"Hey, you!" Rollie said, smiling widely at her. "Hey, Doug, how's it all going?"

"Yeah good, mate," Doug answered.

"What about you, Jen?"

"Not too bad. Heaps better now you're here," she answered, reaching out to touch his arm.

"Good to hear," he grinned, "I really am sorry about that guys, but l got elected to go get Robbo from the airport. He came in from Melbourne for the party. We have heaps of Sydney brothers here too. Somethings just can't be avoided."

Doug nodded his head. "Yeah, no worries. It's a mad turn out anyway, bro. Looks like it's gonna be a kick ass night. Will you be right here with Rollie for a bit Jenna? I Just wanna go catch up with a couple of people?"

'Yeah, you go, Dougy. She'll be right. I'll stay with her." Rollie said, smiling. "Is that your handbag, Jen?" he asked, pointing under the table.

"Yes. Why?" she asked.

"Well, you can't leave it there."

Jenna looked puzzled at Rollie before grabbing a hold of her handbag and tucking it under her arm.

"Come with me," he said, taking her hand and leading her towards the bar, "It's a party night. You can't leave your handbag or anything else of value lying around."

Jenna raised her eyebrows and stared at Rollie. Was he finally admitting maybe some of these people were a tad dishonest? Was he actually saying they could not be trusted? Rollie raised his eyebrows back at her and grinned. "It's not my brothers you need to worry about, Jenna, it's everybody else. I can vouch for the members, but that's as far as the reassurance goes." He took her handbag and placed it safely behind the bar. "Come on, there are some people l want you to meet."

Over the hours that followed, Rollie introduced Jenna to many different men and women, from several different walks in life. Some were Fearsome Devil members who she had never met before and some were just normal, regular everyday people. She was astounded by some of these people's professions. Some were bankers, some were builders, and one of them was even a doctor. Just about any profession one could imagine, were here dancing and partying the night away at the Fearsome Devil's clubhouse, as though it were the most normal thing in the world. Just as she began to feel ashamed of her prior judgmental prejudice, Rollie warned her that not every person at the party were to be trusted.

"Don't ever be foolish enough to judge somebody for their title, Jen. Some people are well hidden away from the real world by what they do as a profession. Always judge a man, or a woman on how they treat you and others, not what their title is. There are a few people here that I will tell you to stay away from. I do expect you to listen to me. I wouldn't say anything if it wasn't necessary."

After Rollie concluded his introduction and warning tour, Jenna began to feel strangely comfortable. She couldn't believe how much she was actually enjoying herself at a bikie party. Surprisingly, she felt relaxed in this atmosphere, where no-one seemed to bother anyone else, as they all enjoyed each other's company. The entertainment, the food and the company were excellent. If she were honest, this was one of the best parties she had ever been to. After looking at Rollie's face, glowing with pride and happiness, Jenna admitted to him how wrong she had been about her fears about the party.

"Ah, so what was that, little lady? Are you saying you were the W word? Are you admitting that you were wrong?" he said, laughing. "Listen up, everyone" he pretended to yell, "Jenna here was wrong!"

"Shush! Stop it, Rollie," she squealed.

At some later stage throughout the night, probably close on two am, Candice stormed towards the table with her face glowing bright red.

"For fuck sake!" she yelled. "This idiot just came up to me asked me if I was the fucking flame thrower," she continued.

"Oh my God. Really?" Jenna asked, trying not to laugh. "Who asked you that?"

"I don't fucking know! Just some fucking idiot!" she yelled over the music. "Do I look like a fucking stripper to you? What drugs is that cunt on?" she roared.

Rollie rose from his seat and pulled Candice in close to him. Jenna followed his lead and stood up scanning the room looking for Doug. When she caught his attention, she waved for him to come over to her. When Doug weaved his way through the crowd, Jenna explained to him she thought there was about to be trouble. She told him Candice had just cracked it over getting called a stripper. Jenna had never seen Candice act that way before, let alone hear the disgusting language which spewed from her lips. As Jenna begged Doug to go and retrieve her handbag and her coat from behind the bar, Candice yelled obscenities at Rollie as she stormed off, almost knocking Jenna over as she went back to rejoin her friends. Rollie leant in over the table.

"What's wrong, Jen? Where are you going?" he asked.

"I think it's time we go, Rollie. Remember, I have a babysitter at home."

"What's upset you? Why all of a sudden do you need to go? I thought you were having a good time?" he asked.

"I was, I am. It's not that, Rollie, I just really need to go home," she said, reaching out to take her belongings from Doug as he approached the table.

"Is it what just happened with Candice that upset you? If that's what it is, don't worry about it. Nothing's gonna happen. You gotta expect these things when you mix alcohol with idiots."

"No, really Rollie, it's not that, I really do just have to go. I have to let my babysitter get to bed. Also, you have to remember, Hannah will be up at the crack of dawn. I don't have the pleasure of sleeping all day, the way some people do," she said, winking at Rollie. Rollie gave her a half smile and nodded.

"If you insist," he said, leaning in to give Doug a man hug. He then turned to Jenna and kissed her gently on the cheek. "I hope you had a good night, Jen?" he whispered in her ear.

During the car trip home, Doug bubbled with excitement over the party. He loved the clubhouse. He enjoyed and embraced the company of these men. Jenna smiled at him and turned her view outside the window. She instead remembered her retreat from bikies and anything to do with their kind. She recalled her reasons for the distance she had placed between herself and them.

Her first encounters as a child had been pleasant, even rewarding. Of a Friday evening, the members of the club her stepfather and uncles were involved in, would come to their small family house and gather. They would blast the music from Creedence Clearwater Revival and the Rolling Stones on the record player as they sung along in their drunken slur. They would drink alcohol, mainly scotch whiskey and beer. They smoked cheap cigars and cigarettes as they gambled. The evenings were always full of unruly chatter and laughter. The only rule for the bikies attending these card nights was that if any cash, whether it be a twenty cent piece or a twenty dollar note, fell to the floor, it had to remain there for the children to collect in the morning. It seemed a fair trade for the children's invisibility and silence, only as with children, nothing could ever be guaranteed.

One night, slightly after midnight, Jenna was awoken by the roars of the men's voices. In the same way as she had done many times before, she crept out of her room to see how much money had slipped to the floor. She quietly crawled over to the wood storage cabinet, carefully opened the rusty door and sat inside. If she left the door slightly ajar, she could see their faces and the floor beneath them. As she counted how many notes had fallen she overheard something that would almost pierce her eardrums and would affect her for the rest of her life.

"I've had it with that thieving fucking bitch. She aint nothing but a whore. It's the last time I tell ya. I'm gonna get that slut, rape her in the ass and hang her up on meat hooks, by her tits in the abattoirs."

The other men cheered him on, laughing as they did so. Could it have been a joke, she wondered. Her uncles always joked. But, something told her, that statement was real. Jenna's little body trembled fiercely beneath her nightgown. Those words had frightened her, as she had not understood much of the conversation at that time, but she knew she had breasts and she knew she wouldn't want to be hung up by them on meat hooks. She remembered seeing those hooks at the farm in Armidale. The sheer size of them and the splatters of blood that had dripped from the carcasses onto the floor had left a lasting impression on her innocent and vulnerable mind.

After that night, she never saw her "uncles" quite the same ever again. She no longer giggled as they wrestled each other to the ground. She no longer laughed at their cheesy jokes, and she no longer had any admiration for bikies. If they could hurt women, she wanted nothing to do with them. She would become forever scarred over what she had heard, but now as an adult, she wondered if what she witnessed ever truly happened. She couldn't imagine Rollie saying something like that, let alone doing it.

As Doug pulled the car into the driveway, Jenna became aware she had not heard one word he'd said during the entire trip home.

"So what do ya reckon?" he asked, "Jen. Jen. Jenna?"

"Sorry. What was that? I must've dozed off."

"I said, are ya gonna give him a chance now?"

Over the next few years, Jenna did give Rollie a chance, as a matter of fact; she gave him several of them. At one stage, he had decided he wanted to get into the business of camouflage clothing, combat gear and surveillance equipment.

"I've been thinking," he said, one day over a coffee. "I'm going to start bringing in camo gear from overseas and start selling it. Do you want to help me?"

"How can I help, Rollie?" she asked. "I've got the kids, uni and my books to write."

"Yeah, but this could be a sideline thing for you. You can help me source stuff and bring it in and then we can re-sell it."

"I wouldn't know how to Rollie, and like I said, I've got my hands pretty full now with this lot."

"Yeah, but that's what I mean. You're like a prisoner here, Jenna. All you do is cook, clean and run around after these people. You got to get out more. Come on, we'll make some money out of it. Don't say you couldn't do with the extra cash. Come on, it'll be fun. Candice has her job as a telemarketer at the pest control company now, so it'll just be the three of us."

After a little bit of hesitation, she decided to give it a go, after all, she really did need the money. Once he taught her the ropes, she delved into her role and began to have more fun than she had envisioned. She enjoyed checking out wholesalers, making deals with other stores and even sourcing seamstresses to make their own designs. Rollie surprised her with his intelligence and ability to get things done. He would work out what he wanted, make up a price he wanted to pay for it and then, whether it was right or wrong, he got the deal done. Jenna decided it was now time to reveal some of her own wicked sense of humour. On one of their trips to their new seamstress's house, she found a white frilly fronted shirt.

"Oh, Rollie, you would look beautiful in this," she said, holding it by its hanger to show him.

"What the fuck, Jenna?" he asked, "Who do you think I am? I won't be wearing shit like that."

"Oh come on now. It'll look beautiful on you," she said, struggling to keep a straight face. "You'll look like a pirate."

Rollie chased her across the room and gently wrapped his huge forearm around her neck. "I'll give you a pirate!" he said, laughing.

Time flew by as the business began to grow and prosper, until one day, instead of going to work, Rollie suggested Jenna and Doug meet him at their favourite restaurant for lunch. Jenna buzzed about happily getting Hannah and herself ready. He must want to discuss the container coming in she thought. They had worked so hard over the past few months to pull all this together. And now that Rollie had put her in charge, she enjoyed it even more. Her excitement level was phenomenal. She hadn't felt this accomplished in years. Rollie had been right; she really did need to do something outside of the home to maintain her happiness. When they arrived at the restaurant, Jenna noticed that Candice seemed unusually joyful and pleasant that day.

Candice smiled at Hannah as she ate her food and giggled at every word Rollie said. Just as they finished eating their main meal, Jenna asked Rollie had he heard anything about the container and its arrival.

"Yeah, I have actually. It will be here next Tuesday."

"That sounds good. You must be excited to see all the stuff you ordered?" she asked, placing the last mouthful of tomato in her mouth.

Candice shuffled over closer to Rollie on the booth seat and slid her arm through his.

"Go on. Tell her, Rollie," she said, smirking at Jenna. "Tell her."

Jenna raised her eyebrows and looked at her bewildered.

"Yeah, it'll arrive about three o'clock next Tuesday afternoon.' Rollie said, careful not to look directly at Jenna. "But, Candice will be running the show from now on. She has left her job at the pest control company and wants to have a crack at this," he continued quietly.

Jenna's eyes shot to Rollie's. She hoped she had heard that statement incorrectly. He bowed his head low and said nothing. Jenna stared blankly at him for a few moments before helping Hannah to finish with her food and tidying her up quickly.

"Come on, Doug, I need to go. I have stuff I have to do."

Jenna wrung her hands in her lap and bit down on her bottom lip. They excused themselves politely and left the restaurant. The minute Jenna got into the car and it pulled away, her heart began to break. Tears flowed down her cheeks as she wept like a betrayed child.

"What the hell just happened there?" she asked, once she could speak again.

"Fucks me!" Doug answered, looking as bewildered as she felt. "It's got to be that spoiled cunt, Candice. I told ya she didn't like you."

"But why? What did I do to her? All I've ever done is try to help her. She would've had no-one if it weren't for me. No-one else even likes her. They only tolerate her for Rollie's sake."

"Like I said, it fucks me. Fuck'em. You don't need them, Jen. Don't worry about them. Rollie was getting too close to you anyway. It's better if it goes back to just me and him. It might stop her being so jealous of you. Look at it this way, Jen, at least you'll have more time with the kids again now you won't to be at his beck and call."

Rollie's guilt was enforced by his absence over the next couple of weeks. If he wanted to see Doug, he'd call him and ask him to come down the road to his house. Jenna didn't mind at all. She had made up her mind she had been correct in the first place. She knew she should never have trusted a bikie, so the less she had to do with him, the better.

Candice, however, glowed in her victory. She convinced Rollie to buy her a thirty thousand dollar car so she could look the part of a successful business woman. She also encouraged him to enter into a lease in a complex he could not afford. Her theory was, play the part and success will come. Well, that success never did come. With no customers and Candice's appalling attitude, the business failed in only two short months, which left Rollie back at the same place he had started from, only now, he didn't have Jenna to help him. Jenna's tolerance for ignorance and ruthlessness was simply unbendable. Her philosophy was, and still is, treat others the way you want to be treated and Rollie should have been no exception.

However, sometime over the following weeks, Rollie once again began to visit the house. At first, Jenna would hide in her bedroom to avoid him having to speak to him. She had no desire to set eyes on him, let alone speak to him. She felt like a fool for trusting him in the first place. Before too long Doug insisted it would be in their best interest for her mend the friendship. He pleaded with her to forgive Rollie. He felt he too would lose him if she didn't fix the problem between them.

So to keep the peace, she eventually spoke to Rollie, as though he were a stranger with no feeling or pleasantness attached. After some time, she began to feel a little sorry for him. She saw the sadness in eyes when he looked at her. Never-the-less, the path to his forgiveness had not been easy for him with her bullet-proof resistance. He had to all but beg her to give him another chance and with that, she realised, her recognition for this contradictive man who had penetrated her life had softened her.

Jennifer Brockie

Chapter Four

A Wedding

After recovering from the financial devastation of his last company, Rollie needed to find a job or a business opportunity which could prepare him for his future. He thought over the many different ways in which he could make money. Despite his more than adequate educational background, gaining employment was always a challenge due to the fact that he was an active member from an outlaw motorcycle club.

Employers are generally hesitant to trust men who wear patches upon their back. In some ways, who could really blame them? The media tends to portray these men as a group, rather than as individuals; so if one member, breaks the law and commits an offence, then their whole club could quite easily be found guilty of the crime in the eyes of the public.

In the end, accepting his limited options, Rollie decided to try his hand at opening his own import-export company, bringing in delightfully different pieces of furniture from all around the world. He would then on-sell the pieces at a profit to other already existing companies. The business took off in a way no one could have expected. Before he knew it, he had to employ a large number of staff to tackle the many roles required to successfully manage such a fast growing company. One of those people would be Doug.

Doug went to work for Rollie managing the downstairs quarter of the company. His role was to receive the items as they arrived from the docks, repack them in business packaging, before finally sending them onto their final destination. Doug seemed to flourish in his new work environment.

Jenna often wondered how this loner, Doug, had become so close to Rollie. Until she had met him, he had been a wanderer and a drifter for most of his life. His drunken mother had thrown him out of the house by the time he was thirteen years old, forcing him to break into and sleep in abandoned cars. He lived mainly a life of crime, right up until the time he fell in love with Jenna. By the time, she met him at the age of twenty-two, Doug, owned nothing more than a bag of clothes and a motorbike. His reputation as a ferocious street fighter, in the western suburbs of Sydney, followed him wherever he went.

Each time he would take her out on a date, something dramatic would happen. Usually something he could handle within the first few minutes, but on other occasions, it would be much worse. On one occasion, a man at the bar, grabbed Jenna on the backside and made heavy sexual advances towards her. Doug told him in no uncertain terms to back off. The drunken man chose not to listen, resulting in him leaving the RSL in an ambulance with his left ear being bitten clear off.

From that moment on, she realised she had swapped one violent man for another. She understood, there would be no getting rid of Doug, even if she chose to. She now belonged to him and that's how things would stay for the next ten years. That's when, Rollie came along and his influence changed Doug in a positive way.

He respected Rollie and valued what he said and thought. Rollie attempted to calm his savage nature by pointing out that unnecessary violence led to unwanted attention. He reminded Doug it was something neither of them needed. So

Doug learned to make sure Rollie never suspected his violent tenancies, at least not towards Jenna. These two men had now become as close as blood brothers and Doug would do nothing to risk their friendship. Jenna often asked them did they ever get sick of each other now that they did everything together besides sleeping in the same bed.

While the men were working, Jenna seized the opportunity to see if she could repair the rift between herself and Candice. Candice, on the other hand, simply had no such interest. She was polite and courteous when put on the spot, but friendliness now eluded her. She had become far too involved in the nightclub scene and partying had become her escape. Unbeknownst to Rollie, Candice had begun her decline into a drug-addicted life.

Jenna noticed a huge difference in her one night as she introduced her to her new friend, Ivan and his brother. Candice reportedly met the two twenty-eight-year-old men in a popular nightclub in Brisbane city. Rollie appeared happy for her at first, almost relieved that she had someone to keep her occupied while he continued to work on building his empire. Jenna sensed something was wrong, but said nothing. Candice hung off Ivan's arm as though he were her partner encouraging him to escort her on every menial errand she had to complete. Ivan seemed only too happy to assist her.

In June of that year, Rollie had some club business he had to attend to in Sydney and Candice insisted that she go along for the drive. Rollie didn't mind hoping she would provide some much needed company. Candice then proceeded to invite Ivan and his brother to go along with them. Jenna knew instantly something bad would happen, she knew the trip would end in a disaster, but she dared not say a word. Rollie dropped the keys to his house off to her and asked if she could look after his plants and feed the dogs while he was gone. Jenna agreed, only too happy to help him. After the third night of their trip, at around nine thirty, she received a disturbing call from Candice.

"You have to help me, Jenna," she sobbed.

"Why Candice? What's wrong?" she asked.

"Rollie left me in Sydney. He's gone."

"What do you mean he's gone? Where is he?"

"He's on his way back up there."

"Well, what happened? Why did he leave you there?

"I don't know. He just got all shitty. I think someone spiked my drink and he got mad at me. I don't know what to do. If I don't get back there before he does, he will throw me out and it'll be all over for me."

"Oh my God, Candice, what can I do to help?"

"I know you won't want to, but if I catch a plane back, will you give me the keys to his house?"

"Oh Candice, I don't really want to get involved. He'll be pissed at me if I give them to you. Can't you call him and ask him if you can have them?"

"No! He won't let me take them. He told me to fuck off for good. I knew you wouldn't help me. I knew you wanted him for yourself."

Needless to say, after an accusation like that, Jenna agreed to give her the keys. She tossed and turned all night after Candice collected them. She didn't want Rollie to be mad at her, but she hoped this act would prove to Candice that she really didn't want Rollie in the way she'd been accused of.

When Jenna told Rollie what she'd done, he did get mad. Really mad. And once he told her the truth of the whole story, she wished she had never given those keys to Candice. Candice had taken drugs at a party they were attending and had embarrassed the life out of him by roaming around in nothing more than her G-string underwear and a leather vest. Rollie knew she had taken the drugs of her own free will and that her drink had not been spiked as she suggested.

The only people at the party were club members and the two brothers Candice had brought with her as guests. He knew his brothers would never give his girlfriend drugs and was insulted by the accusation. Once Jenna managed to calm him down by explaining it was just a foolish mistake on Candice's behalf, and that she only screwed up because she was young and silly, Rollie slowly began to soften. If Candice ever really knew the truth about how many times Jenna had managed to patch things up and keep her and Rollie together, she would be utterly dumbfounded and not to mention, positively embarrassed by her child-like and pathetic accusations.

But, as was promised by Rollie, things quickly returned to normal and everybody went about their business with not too much to mention for the next couple of weeks. Then one day just out of the blue, Rollie pulled in the driveway and rushed up the front stairs.

"Hey, you," she said, opening the front door. "What are you doing here and where's Doug?"

"He's still at work where he should be. I just wanted to stop by and see you by yourself for a second. I have something I want to show you."

"Oh, okay. What is it?"

Rollie dug deep in his pocket, pulled out a ring and handed it to Jenna.

"Do you like it?"

"Umm, what is it? What's the stone?"

"It's a full karat diamond. Do you like it?"

"Umm, are you sure it's a diamond, Rollie? It's orange."

"Yes, it's a real diamond. It's a really rare colour. Do you like it?"

"Umm, not really, it's not the kind of thing I'd wear. Why? What are you going to do with it?"

"Don't know yet," he said, placing the ring back deeply inside his pocket. "I thought you'd like it?"

"Yeah, na, I love crystal clear diamonds. I have a few black diamonds too, but orange isn't a colour I'd wear. It's probably worth a bit though. Take it to an appraiser and have it valued"

"Yeah, probably. I don't know yet, I'll see. Anyway, I got to go."

Jenna shook her head and laughed. That was not unusual behaviour from Rollie. He often dropped in and showed her things he'd brought, or found, or was given. Most of the time she approved of them, but she just really didn't like that ring. She never really thought about it again until around a week later when Candice called her.

"Guess what? Guess what?" she delightfully sang into the phone.

"What? What?" Jenna squealed back.

"I found a ring in Rollie's pants pocket. I think he's going to propose."

"Really? What kind of ring is it Candice?" she asked excitedly.

"It's a really big diamond, but it's the most pretty orange colour. I absolutely love it. Should I tell him I found it or should I just wait?"

"Umm, I don't really know. Maybe you should just wait. He might get angry about you going through his things."

"Oh no he won't, I always go through his stuff. He's used to it. He probably knew I would find it. Maybe that's why he left it there? I'm so happy, Jenna. I was starting to wonder if he'd ever ask me to marry him."

"That is so exciting, honey. I'm really happy for you."

To this day, Jenna still has no idea if Candice told Rollie she had found the ring, or if he actually proposed to her. But by the next time she saw Candice, she was engaged. Brisbane's biggest party girl was about to be a bride. Jenna hoped and prayed that this would change her immature ways and help her settle down.

The wedding became the focal point in both Jenna and Candice's lives. With no mother to guide her, Candice needed all the help she could get. Jenna loved the magic and happiness that weddings brought to people's lives. Firstly they chose an Anglican church, on a cliff beside the ocean. Then they chose the restaurant fifty metres up the road from the church. They went over menus, music, invitations and colour schemes. Candice asked if Harrison, Jenna's son, could write her a poem for the invitations as he had a pure talent for such things. Harrison was only too happy to oblige and Candice was delighted. So with the invites in the mail the girls needed to concentrate on the flowers, centrepieces and decorations.

Then, with just weeks to go until the big day and only the finer details to settle, Jenna curiously noticed that Candice's interest in her upcoming nuptials began to diminish. The only thing she hadn't lost interest in was her dress, so the fitting schedule stayed on track. Jenna then hurriedly arranged for Candice to decide on a cake before all her enthusiasm was completely gone.

"Come on, Candice, I know all these preparations are draining, but we're nearly done. The only thing you've got left to choose is your bridal waltz. What do you think it should be? It's got to be something that captures you and Rollie as a couple."

"To be honest, I could give a flying fuck. Just choose whatever you reckon."

"Are you serious? It's one of the most intimate parts of your wedding. You must like something?" Jenna asked, totally shocked by her reaction.

'Nope. I'm done. I just can't wait to get it all over and done with now. I'll be happy once he's married to me and then things can change. Change to my way."

Jenna raised her eyebrows in disbelief, "How about, Hero, by Enrique? I love that song. I wish I had a wedding coming up, cause that's what I'd choose," she answered, not really knowing what to say.

"Yep. That'll do!" she answered.

Jenna didn't take much of the conversation on board believing instead that Candice had simply become frazzled by the amount of work that is required for such a huge wedding.

A few days later, just after she had dropped the children at school, Doug called her and asked her to stop in at the warehouse and drop him off some cash. Far from being a stranger at the workplace, Jenna obliged with no argument. When she arrived, she found Doug down stairs in his quarters powering into his work. He stopped, had a quick chat and thanked her. Jenna had just got back to the car when Rollie put his head out the upstairs window.

"Hey you, what's happening?"

"Hey, not much. Just dropping some money off to Doug. Silly bugger forgot his wallet. How've you been?" "Yeah, good. Stop making me yell. Come upstairs and I'll show you the new stuff we're about to bring in."

Doug nodded for her to do so, so Jenna agreed. She joined Rollie upstairs on his computer as he went through the lists of furniture available.

"Some of this furniture looks pretty good, Rollie. You should be able to make a fair bit off some of this."

"Yeah, some of it should go alright," he answered, glumly.

"What's wrong, Rollie? You don't seem your normal bubbly self?"

"Ah, nothing. It doesn't matter."

"Are you sure? Looks to me like something's bothering you."

He didn't answer. He just kept scrolling through the list of furniture on the screen in front of him.

"Are you getting excited about the wedding at least? Its only two weeks away, you know?"

Rollie looked up at her and turned in his chair to face her. Suddenly he was only mere inches from her face. "I don't really know, Jen. If you want to know the truth, that's what's bothering me."

"What do you mean?"

"I mean, I want you to tell me, should I marry her, Jenna?"

Jenna stared back at him, not knowing what to say. "Well, you have to now, I've already ordered the cake," she said, trying to force a smile onto her face.

Just at that moment, the office door swung open. Mike, the leading hand stepped in.

"Oh ooops sorry, I didn't mean to intrude," he said. "I'll just be a sec."

'Don't be silly, Mike, you weren't intruding. Rollie was just showing me the new arrivals. They look pretty good to me." Jenna said, "I'm just about to leave anyway.

The big day was finally here. Jenna slipped into her long black diamanté studded gown and pulled the soft organza shawl around her shoulders. She adjusted the tiara on her head and examined herself in the full-length mirror. It had been so long since she had attended such a formal event and still felt quite insecure about how she looked. She had mentioned to Candice on several occasions that she thought the formality of this wedding would be way too much for Rollie's liking. Formal ball gowns, tuxedo's and tie were a far cry from his normal club t-shirt, jeans and boots. She wondered if Candice had at all considered what he might like. But when Jenna addressed it with Rollie, he just said let her do what she wants. I don't really care, he'd answer. She sensed his unhappiness and his non-commitment to any of the decisions, but Jenna couldn't do anything. It certainly was not her place to do so.

At three fifteen in the afternoon, Doug and Jenna arrived at the church on the edge of the cliff. The ambience of the sandstone church, which was built in the 1800's held a somewhat, eclectic charm and an enticing atmosphere. Rollie was waiting at the wooden gates of the sanctuary to greet the guests as they arrived. When Jenna and Doug reached the top of the stairs, Rollie stepped off the curb and dropped his jaw open.

"Well!" he said, "Don't you scrub up alright, Dougy?"

"You don't look too bad yourself," Doug answered, "Feel like a monkey in your suit?"

"Yeah," he answered, chuckling, "Feel like a fuckwit."

"You don't look like one," Jenna added. "You look really good. Your mum would be so proud."

"And look at you, little lady, you look amazing. You look absolutely beautiful," he said, taking her hand to lead her in.

Jenna could feel the heat rush to her cheeks. "Aww, thanks, Rollie," she answered, lowering her gaze. "Are you getting excited now?"

"Na, not really. Just want to get it over and done with."

"It'll all be over before you know it," she said, smiling. "So, where do we go from here?"

"When you go inside the church, sit to the left. That's my side. You guys are here for me so sit with my people."

The church bells rang out and everybody began to flock towards the double wooden doors at the entrance. Rollie walked ahead to join his best man and his groomsmen at the front of the church. As Doug and Jenna entered, the ushers assisted them in finding a seat in the second row from the front on Rollie's side of the church. Jenna sat beside Doug and one of the members from the club. Before too long, she was wedged on a pew between several Fearsome Devils members, all of them big burly men. Jenna was the only female in that pew. She felt out of place, yet somehow totally relaxed. When Stocksy arrived and sat directly behind her, she felt even better. He and his wife Helen were two of her favourite people from within the club. But since Helen was a part of the bridal party, Stocksy was let loose to behave on his own. Not always the greatest idea; especially not at something so formal.

As the wedding commenced, Jenna found herself having to turn around and chastise him on several occasions. She felt sure Stocksy suffered from ADHD and on this particular day it appeared he'd forgotten his medication. He wriggled, kicked his legs and squirmed around like an earthworm. Jenna couldn't help but laugh at him. Once the minister began the service, everybody began to tone their behaviour down and tried to listen to the service.

"Do you, Candice, take this man Rollie, to be your lawful wedded husband, to have and to hold from this day forward, for better or worse, for richer, for poorer, in sickness and in health, to love and to cherish; from this day forward until death do you part?" asked the little Irish minister in his thick accent.

"I do," she answered, smiling widely.

"Do you Rollie, take this woman, Candice to be your lawful wedded wife, to have and to hold from this day forward, for better or worse, for richer, for poorer, in sickness and in health, to love and to cherish; from this day forward until death do you part?"

Rollie looked around the church and said nothing. Stocksy poked Jenna in the back. "Did you see that? He didn't even answer."

"Shush, Stocksy, maybe he couldn't understand what he asked him. His accent is pretty heavy."

"Ha! Yeah, whatever. I bet he's changed his mind," he said, loudly.

Whether Rollie had understood what the minister had asked or not would remain a mystery to all of us. But as far as we could tell, Rollie wasn't married.

Meeting back up outside the church everyone offered their congratulations as the photographer set about taking the wedding pictures. Candice's only concern was getting professional photos of her German Shepard pups dressed up in wedding attire. Jenna listened as several people commented on how bizarre her behaviour was considering it was her who had just been married. Jenna thought the pups looked cute but certainly would never have gone that far. Even the photographer commented on her obsession with the dogs rather than her own wedding photos with her new husband.

"Did you see that, Jen?" Stocksy asked, rushing up behind her. "I think our old boy is still a single man. He didn't even say I do. How fucking funny was that?"

Jenna tried not to laugh. "Stop it, buddy, it's not funny. He probably didn't hear what he got asked, or he was probably freaking out. You know he hates attention."

"Na. I say more power to him. I'd have never married her, she's a bigger mutt than her fucking dogs. I say good on him," he said, laughing. "Can't wait to get back to this reception but. Make sure you find me and I'll shout you a Cock Sucking Cowboy!"

"A what?"

"You know? A Cock Sucking Cowboy? The cocktail?"

"Oh oops, yep sorry. I didn't know what you were talking about for a second there," she laughed.

Once they reached the reception at the restaurant Jenna became confused by the seating arrangements. She and Candice had planned it out to the finest detail weeks prior to the wedding. When Jenna went to find her and Doug's seats she noticed they had been moved to a table of the people Candice had felt obligated to invite; not the people she wanted to attend Rather than making a fuss, Jenna took her seat and pretended she hadn't noticed. She chatted with the other people at the table and smiled throughout the meal. Helen, Stocksy and Sarah came to her table and sat down with her.

"Well, what did you do to get put all the way over here?" Helen asked.

"I don't know. Maybe it was a mix up by the staff?" Jenna answered.

"Ah stop being so fucking nice, Jen," Stocksy said. "The girl's a cunt. She would've done this on purpose."

"No, I'm sure it's just a mistake," Jenna added.

"Na, Stocksy's right, it's just her being her normal asshole self," Sarah said. "Don't worry about her. As soon as all this formal shit's done, we'll all come over and sit with you"

Jenna looked towards Candice as she picked at the chicken scaloppini on her plate and wondered why she would do such a thing. She had done everything she could do to make this wedding run smoothly for her and this is how she repaid her. She excused herself from the table and went into the bathroom to catch her breath. She looked into the wall length mirror and fought back her tears.

When Jenna returned to her table, Rollie was sitting in her seat.

"Hey, you, you having a good time?" he asked.

"Yes, it's been a beautiful day. How about you? Are you happy, Rollie?"

"Happy about what?"

"Are you happy you're married?"

He just stared blankly at her.

"Are you happy it's all over then?" she asked.

"Yep. That I'm happy about. I felt like a fucking penguin," he said, relaxing back in his chair with his vest now placed over his white business shirt.

For the rest of the evening, right up until Jenna left to go home, Rollie sat at her table, drank with her and chatted. Jenna suggested on several occasions that maybe he should go and join his new bride. Rollie seemed hesitant, only ever rising out from his seat to yell at Candice who danced upon the dance floor like a stripper. She pulled out a cat of nine tails and danced with it like she was the queen of bondage. Jenna could see the flame of embarrassment rise in his cheeks as his elderly father stood at the edge of the dance floor and watched this woman his son had just married dance like a temptress toward any man in the room who would give her attention.

The following day Rollie and Candice left Brisbane and headed to Hawaii for their honeymoon. Doug and Mike were left in charge to run Rollie's business in his absence. One afternoon as Doug arrived home from work, Jenna couldn't help but notice his distressed expression.

"What's wrong, Doug? You looked pretty annoyed," she said.

"Ah, nothing. Don't worry about it. You can't do anything anyway."

"I might not be able to do anything, but it might help if you get whatever's bothering you off your chest."

"It's one of them times when I just don't know what to do."

"What do you mean?"

"Well, some pretty serious shit is going down at work at the moment and I'm not real sure what to do about it."

"How serious? Should you ring Rollie?"

"Na, I'm not going to be responsible for ruining his honeymoon."

'Well, how serious is it? Why don't you go see Taz? Isn't he the go to member if something goes wrong?"

"Yeah, he's supposed to be. But it's more about being a dog, Jenna. I don't want to go dobbing on people. I've told Mike I'm not happy with what he's doing so we'll just wait and see if he pulls his head in."

"Wow. Sounds pretty serious. What's going on? You know telling me isn't dogging. I won't say anything." "Yeah, I know. I'll tell you, but don't say nothing to anyone till I see what happens now I've spoken to him."

"I promise."

"Well you know how Rollie put Mike in charge of ordering while he's gone," he asked, waiting for her to nod. "Well, I can't prove it yet, but I know it's happening. I saw it with my own eyes."

"What?"

"He's ordering stuff in and then selling it for cash and sticking that cash in his pocket."

"Are you serious? So, he's stealing from Rollie?"

'Yep. I'm pretty sure he is. And to top that off, he's bringing people into the office and snorting cocaine pretty much all day long too."

"Oh my God, Doug. You can't keep a secret like that. I see it like this: you have one of two choices. You can either ring Rollie direct in Hawaii or you can tell Taz so that someone other than you knows about this. You don't want to end up with egg on your face and getting the blame when Rollie does find out."

Jenna could never have known the impact of those words she had said to Doug until the day it finally happened. Even though Doug had gone directly to Taz and told him what was going on, when Rollie did return from his honeymoon, it would be Doug who was fired from his job and turned away in disgrace. Not from the members of the Fearsome Devils, but from Rollie himself. If the story that lingers is actually the truth, Candice was instrumental in the decision Rollie made that day. From all accounts, it was her who convinced Rollie that one of the two men had to be fired. In her own words, she felt Doug was less beneficial to Rollie's empire as Mike was the furniture specialist after all. She convinced Rollie that he needed him more. Someone later repeated her statement that by Rollie firing Doug, it would be like killing two birds with one stone; taking out Doug, would also remove Jenna out of Rollie's life once and for all. And she was right, once Rollie fired Doug, Jenna refused to speak to Rollie again.

"Now do you see what I mean, Doug? They're all the fucking same. He used you!"

"It's not like that Jenna. He had to choose one of us and Mike is more important to the company than I am."

"Oh, so you're going to defend him and forgive him for this one too? For fuck sake, Doug. How stupid are you? He basically called you a liar, made an idiot out of you by firing you, his so-called good mate, instead of that drug fucked idiot he has working for him. What does he have to do before you will get rid of him?"

"Shut the fuck up, Jenna! The difference between you and me is that I understand why he did what he did. He and I have got other plans that will more than make up for it. So I'm not worried about it. It could've been worse, he could have believed Mike's lies and then I would've been kicked out of the circle too."

"You make me sick! You can be his little lackey for the rest of your life if you want, Doug, but I will never speak to that piece of shit ever again. I hate his fucking guts."

Jenna stuck to those words for months on end. Doug would usually go and see Rollie either at his house or at the clubhouse, but Jenna never went. She refused to answer her phone to him and she wouldn't answer Doug's phone for him either if she could see Rollie's name flashing across the screen. Rollie made his presence at their house very scarce at first, knowing only too well the depth of Jenna's resistance and stubbornness.

Over time though he began to ask Doug to get her to talk to him again and Doug foolishly obliged. Jenna always answered the exact same way. She reinforced her hatred for the man and refused to budge an inch. She had no desire to re-engage in any form of friendship with a man who claimed to love them like family, yet had no issue taking food out of her children's mouths.

At times, Jenna would be out in her front yard, either washing her car, playing with Hannah, watering the plants or simply taking in some air on her front verandah when she would see Rollie's car coming down the street. When she would see it coming she would quickly duck for cover behind the lattice work across the verandah or behind the little fence. She never wanted to talk to him or lay eyes on him ever again. Then one night, as she slipped downstairs to soak some whites in the laundry, she heard his car pull up outside. Jenna decided to stay put and continue doing what she was doing knowing full well Doug would never be foolish enough to bring Rollie to where she was. She loaded the whites into the machine and added the soaker before turning the machine on.

Once she had finished, she grabbed the broom and began to sweep the floor waiting for the sound of his car to drive off.

Just then, Doug walked straight past her in the laundry into the downstairs living area. Following closely behind him was Rollie. Jenna shook with anger. She turned her back to the door.

"Jenna," Rollie said. "Turn around and talk to me."

Jenna spun around and went to walk away before she noticed Rollie had extended his arms across the width of the room. She couldn't go anywhere. Not without pushing past Rollie first. She glared at him not saying a word. She could feel her heart rate quicken and her throat narrow over.

"Jenna, can you please talk to me?"

"I have nothing to say to you, Rollie."

"But I have something to say to you. I'm sorry."

"Yeah, it seems to be becoming a pattern with you, Rollie. You're always sorry but yet you do the same thing over and over again."

"Can you just hear me out?"

"No. I don't want to hear anything you have to say. You said it all the last time with the camo gear. I don't care if Doug is your mate Rollie, but I'm done with you."

"Oh no, you're not. I'm not going anywhere until you hear me out."

Jenna's anger grew when she realised that no matter what she did, she truly could not get out of that laundry without walking straight into Rollie. Her anger grew even more when she realised Doug was not going to do one single thing to stop Rollie from holding her prisoner in her own laundry. "Just move, Rollie! I'm not playing with you. I am done!"

Rollie just stood there looking at her. "No, you're not done. I'm going to say what needs to be said and then you can go." Jenna narrowed her eyes wishing for him to be anyone else but who he was. She couldn't push past him. She was trapped. "Well spit it out. Just say it. But I'm telling you, whatever you have to say won't make one ounce of difference to me. I hate you, Rollie!"

"I'm sorry, Jenna. I am so so sorry. If I could take it all back I would. I should've never listened to Candice and I should have listened to Doug. I knew he had my back, but I needed Mike to try build up my empire."

"See, it's all about money with you," Jenna said, angrily. "Money can't buy you loyalty Rollie."

"I know and that's why I'm apologizing. It was my mistake. It was all my fault. I want you to forgive me and let me make it up to you."

Jenna looked into his eyes and once again felt the same pity she had felt for him the day of the homicide squad incident. "Rollie, you can't make something like this up to me. If I just

90

started being friends with you again everyone would think I am a complete idiot who lets you do what you like when you like to me and I'll just forgive you. I can never show my face back up the clubhouse, or around our so called friends ever again. You embarrassed the hell out of me by doing what you did. I thought you were supposed to be ruled by loyalty, not by money."

"You're right. I fucked up big time, but I can't make it up to you if you won't let me. Of course, you can come back up the clubhouse. Who would say anything to you? I'm the one who looks like a fuckwit. Taz said straight up that Doug did nothing wrong. So who do you think Taz is pissed at? You or me?"

"That's because, Taz is a good bloke, Rollie, she said, trying not to smile. "He's not like you."

Once again, Jenna forgave Rollie, even if it was a somewhat fake forgiveness. She hadn't wanted to forgive him, after all, this was the second time he'd built her up only to tear her down. The pure unadulterated trust she once had in him remained somewhat fractured. Yet her pity for Rollie grew as he began to suffer the consequences of marrying Candice. It seemed nothing he ever did or said was ever enough for her. The more power and control he entrusted to her, the less effective his life or his empire became. Due to her constant attention seeking and trouble-making schemes, Rollie eventually, once again, lost everything he had worked for. His import-export company suffered the exact same demise as his camo venture. He lost everything, with the exception of a desk full of unpaid bills.

Jennifer Brockie

Chapter Five

Work

As the curtain to summer drew to a close and the familiar heavy cloak of humidity finally began to lift, Jenna breathed a sigh of relief. The sticky fingers of restriction had slowly begun to release their grip, and for that she was ever so grateful. She hated the summer season and always would. She didn't see the summer-time as others did with sunshine, lollipops and rainbows, she saw it instead as a reminder. The nights wrought with sweat and fretfulness reminded her too much of her past. A past in which at any moment any member of her family could betray her with their next travesty, leaving her once again abandoned in a hot dry desert. Alone, weakened and stranded. But those episodes were gradually becoming a thing of her past.

Now as an adult, she could muster the strength to say no. She could somewhat control the situations which life brought forth by choosing her friends and family wisely. There was no longer a closeness between her extended family and herself. Whatever intimacy had once existed between them had long since vanished. She no longer desired their approval, nor did she wish to please them, to be accepted by them, or even to be loved by them. She now rolled the dice in her future and made the choices most emotionally beneficial to her and her beloved children. Her children were all that mattered to her now.

But yet, she would make mistakes with her decisions, sometimes huge mistakes and each time she did, layer upon layer of trust and respect for mankind would be pulled away like the flesh from a carcass. However, the next poor decision she would make would be one that would cause her more pain than she had ever known before.

As the season began to change, so did the course of bikie education that Rollie was introducing to Jenna. Now she was comfortable around his brothers, he decided the next path in the course was to teach her a little more surrounding the police and government stance on bikies. Way before the VLAD and anti-association laws came into effect, Rollie had predicted exactly what would subsequently happen.

"You know, the day will come when you could be arrested for being friends with me," he said, as he lazed about on the couch one Saturday evening.

"Don't be silly, Rollie. Why would they do that? I'm not a criminal. And, as far as I know, you're not either." Jenna answered, giggling as she spoke. "Why would they want to arrest me?"

"For knowing me," he said, sitting up straight. "You don't get it do you? The police and the government don't see us blokes like you do. They see us as a threat."

"Oh my God, Rollie! Don't you think that's going a little overboard?

"Overboard? I'm actually understating it for you, Jenna" he said, anger slowly rising in his voice. "There's no need for me to tell you the ins and outs of everything, but it is important that you understand the added attention you'll receive by knowing me. Knowing the boys, supporting who and what we are. It's like a game of us and them."

"Unless you're breaking the law, Rollie, I'm sure they couldn't care what you're doing. I'm pretty sure they have a lot more important things to worry about than a group of men who ride bikes and hang out together."

"Yeah, that's why they bug our houses hey?"

"What are you talking about? Rollie, stop it."

"So you think I'm just paranoid? You don't think what I told you about them seizing our assets and treating us like second rate citizens will ever happen?"

Jenna did think he was being paranoid and she never dreamed his predictions would ever come to fruition. She assumed Rollie was just having an insecure day. Jenna excused his bizarre behaviour and concentrated on the present.

Even though her trust in him had been badly damaged, she admired him, his drive, his passion, and his refusal to let negative effects hold him down. After losing his import-export company, his enthusiasm plummeted. Jenna witnessed his decline in passion towards so many different things. Where he'd once come calling full of excitement and happiness, the visits were now plagued in frowns and problems. She often wondered if he could make it through the loss. Over all the years she had known him, nothing could compare to the destruction of his beloved empire. His faith in doing the right thing was waning, sometimes believing that her way, Jenna's way of righteousness was completely wrong.

"You know, Jen, I might have to resort to a life of crime," he said, one day completely out of the blue.

"Rollie, don't talk like that. You of all people don't need to make your money from crime," she answered back harshly. "Don't even say such things."

"For fuck sake, Jenna. I really don't know what to do. I need to make some money."

"Well, use your head. You're one of the smartest men I know, Rollie. If you want to make money, put your thinking cap on and work out how to do it."

He looked at her and grumbled. Jenna's fears of Rollie resorting to a life of crime and truly becoming an object of interest to the police were completely unwarranted. Within six months of losing everything he had worked for, he was back up on his feet all over again. As the cash and sunshine returned to his life, so did his smile.

At a chance meeting late in September, Rollie was approached by a professor of natural medicine who asked him if he was interested in some work as a security guard, or a bodyguard. Rollie had declined at first as that field of work was not usually his forte. But the spindly, ninety-year-old professor begged him to consider it, insisting that his life was in danger. The professor believed an old rival from medical school was having him followed, trying to steal his ideas and inventions. Rollie humoured him at first, believing that the old guy may have been suffering from a touch of dementia. Even though Rollie was a bikie, he held high morals and principles pertaining to children and the elderly. He later told Jenna that he believed that if this little old man approached the wrong person, they could easily take advantage of him and take him for everything he was worth.

In the early days, Rollie was more of an assistant to the fragile professor, helping him to find a factory suitable and secure enough for him to go about his business. Jenna had laughed the day Rollie showed her the lock he had put on the mesh wire gate for security. The padlock was almost as big as her head. Jenna had told Rollie there was no point in such a big lock because if anyone truly wanted to enter the premises they would just simply cut through the wire fencing. Rollie agreed with her, admitting it was purely for show and to give the old man reassurance. Before too long, Rollie became more of a son to him than a worker and was all but his constant companion.

In the meantime, Jenna continued to work on her book, raise her children and look after her home. One afternoon, just as she finished baking blueberry muffins for the children's school lunches for the following day, Rollie bounced up the front steps and made his usual grand entrance.

"So what's new with you, Jen?" he asked.

"Nothing at all, my friend. How about you? Anything exciting happening in the life of Rollie?"

"Yeah, shit loads! Life is good, little lady. Life is good."

"I'm so pleased to hear you say that Rollie. I truly am. I was starting to get pretty worried about you before you got this new job."

"Never worry about me, Jenna. It might take me some time, but I'll always bounce back. Nothing ever holds me down for too long."

"Yes. So you always say."

"It's true," he said smiling. "I keep telling you. It is what it is! So how about a coffee?"

"Why not. Do you want a muffin while you're at it?" she asked.

"Of course. But make yourself one too, Jen. I want to talk to you."

"Oh no. that doesn't sound good," she said, turning the jug on and looking back at him.

"Na, it's all good. I want to ask you something."

Jenna made the coffees and took the two steaming cups to the table together with a fresh muffin for him to eat. As Rollie scoffed the muffin down and sipped on his coffee, she began to wonder what on earth he could want to ask her.

"So, what is it you want to ask me, Rollie?" she asked, looking directly at him.

"Well," he said, rubbing the crumbs from the muffin out of his goatee. "I was wondering......."

"Wondering what? Stop stalling Rollie, you're making me anxious."

"Don't be anxious, it's just a question. I was wondering, would you like to come and work with me and the professor?"

Jenna stared at him in disbelief. He couldn't be asking her this all over again. Her mind screamed. She wanted to lean over the table and slap him silly. How could he be stupid enough to ask her this all over again after the last two times?

"You could be my personal assistant with all my projects. You can come to all the business meetings and lunches and take notes. I need your organizational skills, Jenna. Things are getting a little out of control and I can't do it myself."

"Why don't you ask Candice to do it, Rollie?" she asked, glaring at him.

"Because I can't rely on her. She's useless. Especially now she's drinking like a fucking fish and I'm pretty certain she's taking drugs just about every other day. And besides, we need someone who's reliable and up to the job. It's important work you know, Jen? If this medication works it could help so many different people."

Jenna raised her eyebrows, shook her head and stood up. She grabbed the two empty coffee cups and took them over to the sink.

"And, you don't even know the best of it yet. I got asked if I want to do some business with the Singaporean government. It's got to do with their eco system."

"Sounds great," she said glumly. "I hope it turns out well for you."

"No, turns out well for us! Come on Jenna, I want you to do this with me. It's not a lot of work. It's just making sure I stay on track. Get me out of bed in the morning," he said, laughing. "It's keeping my butt in line and making sure I do what needs to be done.

"Rollie, you know I would do just about anything for you, right?"

He propped his face up on the table with his hands. "So, you'll do it?"

"No. I said just about. I can't come back to work with you, Rollie. Not now, and not ever. Not if you want our friendship to survive. I can't go through all that shit again. As it is, you are so God damn lucky to be sitting here with me right now. If you were anybody else, I would never have spoken to you ever again. I can't do it. I'm so sorry, Rollie, but no. I'm not doing it."

"It won't happen again, Jenna. I promise," he said, moving in closer to her at the sink. "I said I was sorry and I meant it. I give you my word, it won't happen again. Please at least say you'll think about it."

"Okay, I'll say I'll think about it, but I won't, because I'm not going to do it. Our friendship means way more to me than the money."

When Rollie left that afternoon, that question was the only thing she could think about. What on earth would possess him to ask her such a thing? Surely he wasn't stupid enough to honestly think she would re-enter a place in which he held all the cards all over again. A place where he had already betrayed both her and Doug. He'd hurt her so deeply the last time he fired her that she had truly believed she would never have uttered a single word to the man ever again. Even though she knew in her heart it was Candice who had instigated the action, she still believed that he, as her friend, should have stood his ground and told Candice no. After all, it wasn't like she hadn't taken more than her fair share of ridicule and disapproval from all who knew her over her loyalty to him.

As far as Jenna was concerned, the door to that space in their relationship was well and truly snapped shut and bolted tight. And it should have stayed that way. As far as she was concerned it would have been, but then, she could never have imagined the reaction she would receive from Doug.

When Doug arrived home that afternoon, Jenna felt confident that he would side with her as she explained to him what Rollie had asked her to do.

"Yeah. I knew he was going to ask you," he said.

"You what?"

"Yeah, he asked me to ask you. So I told him to ask you himself. I told him it was pretty unlikely and if he wanted to get his head ripped off, he could do it himself."

"Why, Doug? Why didn't you just tell him you didn't want me to do it? What the hell is wrong with you two? Hasn't he already put me through enough? Don't you think he hurt me bad enough last time? You want him to have another go at it? If you want to work with him again after what he did to you, then by all means, you do it. But don't expect me to ever work with him again."

"For fuck sake, Jenna. Stop being so fucking dramatic! He told you both times it was because of his fucked up wife. What do you want him to do? What would you do if I stuck with another woman other than you? The bloke had no fucking choice! Give him a break. Fuck knows he needs it. And besides, he said he'll pay you really well and I'm telling you, babe, we need the money."

Jenna glared at Doug in disbelief. Their marriage, now completely in tatters due to his control, alcohol binges and violence, hung only by a thread, and here he was, her so called husband, pushing her closer to another man; a man who through his wages and contacts could provide her with freedom. A freedom she so desperately yearned for. She thought about what both men had said overnight before waking in the morning and deciding to take the job. But her decision was not based on either of their wishes, it was now based on her own desires; her desire to live an uncontrolled, free life. Now that both, Harrison and Hayden lived in their own places outside of the home, she figured she could stash some money away each week without Doug knowing and then she could eventually find a place of her own. A place where she could live in peace with her two daughters.

Hesitation plagued her start with the new job as she waited at every corner for Rollie to once again drop his almighty deliverance of destruction. But as the pages on the calendar began to turn and it still hadn't happened, Jenna began to slowly relax. As the company grew so did her confidence. It wouldn't take long at all before Rollie had put her completely in control of the everyday management of his business, only ever needing to go to him for major issues. He made it perfectly clear to every single person, whether in Australia or any other country, they needed to deal with that she in fact, had as much authority over each matter as he did, calling her his right-hand girl on several occasions. Rollie often told her that she was much better equipped at dealing with the finer details than he was. He knew he could get the important factors in place, but then accidently overlook a major incident due to the speed at which his mind was now operating. He solely relied on Jenna to go over each and every contract and he quickly realised why it was so imperative that she did so.

At one stage over the course of this venture with the government, Jenna noticed the irrigation systems they were working on had not been cleared by the Safety Approval Seal. Without the seal, the multi-million dollar business deal would be worth nothing. So she diligently set about getting Rollie to ensure that it was covered before commencing any further into the project. It was this exact work that she thrived on doing. Finally, after so many years of just being Mum, she found herself important in many other roles, and she could all but taste her freedom. With everything, she was learning and the respect she now commanding, she knew she'd eventually be alright. She knew she could make a decent life for herself and continue raising her daughters without the control of Doug or anybody else.

Each day of her job brought about new adventures. Her mornings usually consisted of helping ten-year-old Hannah get ready for school before dropping her off, doing the housework and checking her email. Once that was complete, she would ring Rollie, making sure he had risen and was on track for the day. She could always tell if it was going to be a good or bad day by whether or not he chose to answer his phone. Some mornings he would greet her with his friendliest "Top of the morning to you, little lady. What's on the agenda for today?" They were the good days. Then on other days, she would call his number ten times with no answer at all- these were the bad days. When those days occurred, Jenna always felt like a stalker; someone obsessed with controlling the life of another.

Even though she was paid to do precisely that, she felt uncomfortable in that role because even after all these years and all the reassurance she received from him, she never forgot that he was a bikie and backed up by the memories of her past, she knew he could make her life very difficult if he ever turned on her. Fear aside though, when he finally would call her back, she would always have something to say about his inability to answer his phone. He would usually offer some pathetic feeble excuse. Excuses she rarely ever believed, but tolerated regardless. They had a different deal however, that suited them both when it came to down his club business, and that was, that it was not her business. That suited Jenna down to the ground, preferring instead to know as little as possible about any such matters, as she could still in the back of her mind, only accept Rollie as a man, not so much as a bikie. So when he did go away on club business, the morning ritual would change. He would ring her, not vice versa.

Aside from the above, Jenna adored most of the roles she had taken on within the company due to the wonderful array of people she met during their frequent meetings. As a general rule, Rollie would arrange for the meeting to occur around lunchtime and usually at fine restaurants in or around Brisbane. On one such occasion, prior to lunch, they had to first meet at the professor's house to supervise the signing of a contract between the professor and a new team of medical assistants. Jenna knew she needed to take notes and observe the board's behaviour while attempting to pick up any negative vibes they might send off. She rose early that morning, before going about her morning routine, then showering and getting dressed for the day. She decided on wearing a pair of tailored brown slacks, a red button up business shirt and a pair of designer sling back four inch heeled sandals.

On arrival at the professor's house, Rollie introduced Jenna for the first time to the professor's wife, Adele. Adele, a soft-spoken Scandinavian woman, was well-travelled, in her late sixties and was an avid doll collector. On entering their home, ceiling high glass cabinets full of dolls from all around the world filled the formal lounge area. Jenna stood in awe of them. The dolls were absolutely beautiful, mainly dressed in their traditional costumes. Adele had told her that she had handmade many of them herself and that she had a room attached to the back of the house in which she was currently making a few more. She had asked Jenna if she would like to see them. Of course she agreed. Adele told Rollie that she was stealing Jenna away for a moment but promised to bring her back. Rollie had laughed and told them to take their time. Jenna picked up the most exquisite baby doll, dressed in layers and layers of lace, more beautiful than she'd ever seen. She fussed over the creation and she gently stroked the golden rooted hair in the baby doll's head.

"She's beautiful isn't she?" Adele asked.

"She is simply adorable. You're a very clever lady, Adele. Did it take you long to learn how to do this?"

"Oh, I've been at it for years. I mainly make them now for my grandchildren back in the home country. They love them."

"Oh, they would. They're just gorgeous."

As they stood and spoke, Jenna heard a mass of chatter coming from the boardroom just on the other side of the wall.

"Thank you so much for showing me these Adele, but I best get back to work or Rollie will fire me," she said, smiling. No, he won't," she said, raising her hand for Jenna to wait. "Rollie, can I still keep Jenna or do you need her back?" she yelled at the top of her voice.

"No, she's right. She can stay with you for now," he yelled back.

"See, I told you he'd be fine," she said, gloating. "He'll never fire you. He needs you too much."

Jenna smiled and continued to pick up each doll on the craft table.

"Do you know, Candice, Jenna?" Adele asked.

'Yes, I do actually. I've known her for many years now," she answered, puzzled by the question.

"Do you like her?" she asked, looking directly at Jenna.

"Umm, that's a strange kind of question," Jenna said, stopping to look back at Adele. "She's Rollie's wife."

"Yes, we all know the devastation of that union. I don't like her. As a matter of fact, I think she is a mean spirited nasty bitch. And I wish Rollie would leave her. He's not happy with her you know?"

Jenna just stared. She stared at Adele, she stared at the ceiling and then to the floor. She didn't know what to say. If the truth were known, she herself had begun to completely hate Candice, but she certainly didn't think it her place to answer such a question. "I don't really get involved in people's relationships, Adele. Not if I can help it anyway. All I can say is whatever makes Rollie happy, makes me happy," she finally answered. "He's the one I care about."

"Yes, me too," she said, softly. "But he isn't happy and we all know it. But hey, he does smell great today doesn't he? I love the scent of his aftershave," she answered, sensing Jenna's hesitation to continue.

As the meeting in the boardroom came to a close, Rollie sung out to Jenna at the top of his voice and told her they were leaving. Jenna bid her farewells to Adele and followed Rollie out to the car. He opened her door to let her in, then climbed into the driver's side and started the engine. "What the hell, Rollie? What the hell was that all about? I thought I was coming today to meet these people and to take notes?"

"It's all good, Jenna. Don't stress, I'll fill you in on everything that you missed. I thought you'd like Adele?"

"I do like her. I like her a lot, but I thought I was there to work?"

'Well consider it a paid break then," he said, smiling.

The remainder of the afternoon was just as strange as the morning meeting had been. When they arrived at the seafood restaurant, Rollie told Jenna to go and ask for their reservation and to take a seat. He explained to her that he had to meet some other people regarding club business while they were there. Jenna did as he asked, then took her place at the table. Just as her patience began to grow thin, the professor arrived and began making idle chit chat. Every few seconds Jenna would glance over her shoulder towards the area in which Rollie held his meeting with several other men and noticed that he was looking back at her too. He would muster a coy smile then turn away. The professor began to ask her similar questions to what his wife Adele had asked earlier, but in true Jenna style, she sideswiped his enquiries as though she were dodging a bullet; only retorting with evasive answers. Once Rollie sat down at the table they all ordered their lunches. The professor insisted they order the best on the menu for a job well done on closing his deal. Jenna sat and thought about what she had done at that meeting; nothing! Still, Rollie insisted she order something she liked. She ordered a lobster mornay, a salad and a glass of white wine. She didn't really feel like eating, as the claws of nervousness began to converge on her calmness. What were all these questions about? Was she about to be fired? Were they testing her loyalty to Rollie? Whatever it was, she wanted it to stop. So once the lunch meeting was over and they were safely back in Rollie's vehicle, she bombarded him with questions.

"Rollie, seriously, tell me what the hell is going on? Am I about to be fired again?"

"Don't be stupid. What would make you think that?" he asked.

"All these bloody questions! Did you ask them all to ask me this stuff? I want to know what's going on."

Rollie just looked at her. "Nothing's going on. It's all good. I already told you that."

"Well, tell me something, does Candice know I'm with you today?" she asked, not really knowing why she had asked that question.

"Of course she knows. I wouldn't do that to you and I wouldn't do that to Dougy," he said, before leaning down, turning up the radio full blast and smiling at her. "I like this song."

Jenna just stared out the window totally bewildered by the morning's events.

Rollie had some legal paperwork he had to sign at a solicitor's office in the city, but on their way to do that, they needed to stop by a place of someone whom Rollie knew. This particular person had called Rollie and told him about a container which had been brought in from China and asked him if he was interested in having a look at what was inside it.

"Now when we get to where we are going, Jen, I want you to not act at all surprised. No matter what I show you, I want you to keep your emotions in check and don't show any real interest."

"Oh my God. Why? What is it, Rollie?"

"Nothing to be scared of," he said laughing, "Just wait and see. I think you'll love it."

When they reached their destination, Jenna got out of the car and followed closely behind him. They stepped into the triple car garage of a mansion on the North Side of the city. A small hippy-looking man rushed out from the connector door between the house and the garage.

"Hey, there, Rollie, my friend. Glad you could make it. Come on in and I'll show you what I've got."

They followed the hippy inside. Jenna's jaw immediately dropped in awe as she found herself surrounded by the most magnificent oil paintings she had seen in the longest time. Rollie nudged her and winked.

"Stop it," he said quietly, smiling at her.

"I can't help it. These are Van Gogh's," she whispered back.

"No, they're not. They're repos," said the hippy. "I've got Monet's too."

Jenna strolled through the two-story house looking in great detail at all the paintings that completely filled each room. Some of the paintings were six foot tall and wider in length. Rollie steered the hippy into the kitchen and spoke business, as Jenna continued her inspection of his art. Once they left the house Jenna could hardly contain her excitement.

"So are you going to get them? They're so beautiful, Rollie."

"Let's see if we can get them at the right price first," he said, "He's asking too much for them right now. But see, I told you, you'd like them."

On their last stop for the day, Rollie parked his car in a loading zone on the main street of the city.

"Don't you dare stop here in a loading bay and leave me in this car, Rollie" she cried, as he pulled on the handbrake and turned the engine off.

"It's all good, Jen. Look, I'm leaving my wallet here. If anyone comes, just tell them I'll be back in a second."

"If anyone comes, I'm going to tell them that I was hitchhiking and you kidnapped me," she answered, sarcastically.

Rollie laughed as he jumped out of the car and ran towards the solicitors building. Five minutes later a parking inspector started towards the car. Jenna began to panic. Just as the inspector reached the back of the vehicle, Rollie appeared from the building and ran across the street. When the inspector noticed him entering the car, he put his ticket book down and walked on.

The late afternoon traffic was beginning to congregate on the busy motorway. Rollie and Jenna didn't really seem to notice as they chatted about the paintings and what they could do to move them along. Rollie's phone began to ring. He looked at the caller ID before answering it.

"Hey, Candice, what's up?" he asked, rolling his eyes at Jenna.

"Don't you what's up me," she yelled, loudly enough for Jenna to hear from the opposite side of the car. "Did you eat my fucking chocolate bar?"

"What chocolate bar?" he asked, before pulling the phone away from his ear as Candice verbally crucified him.

Jenna didn't know where to look or what to say. Her embarrassment for him flamed her cheeks. Considering the depth of respect this man demanded from other people, her heart ached for him being spoken to like that from his wife. Rollie put the phone back to his ear and told her to stop yelling. The next thing Jenna heard was, "You kick that filthy slut out of your car right now and leave her in the fucking city. I'm fucking sick of you spending all your time with that ugly dog cunt!" Candice screamed. Rollie's jaw tightened and the blood drained for his face.

"You fucking listen here. I am not leaving her in the city and I'm getting off the phone," he yelled at her.

Candice continued to hurl abuse as Rollie disconnected the call. "I'm so sorry, Jenna."

"I thought you said she knew I was with you."

"She did, but she reckons someone ate her chocolate bar, so now she's cracking a shit. She probably just got too drunk last night and forgot she ate herself. Somehow, that's your fault and she wanted me to leave you here."

110

"Yeah, I heard."

"I'm sorry," he said, somberly.

Jenna turned in her seat to fully face him. "It's okay, Rollie. It wasn't your fault. You can't control what she says," she said, quietly, "You know I don't usually say anything, or try to involve myself in other people's problems Rollie, but I'm going to say something now after that little performance. I have seriously done everything I can to help that girl for years now. I've tried to be nice to her and yet she still hates me. I hate that you have to go through this shit because of me. Maybe it would be best if I didn't work with you anymore?" she nervously suggested.

The traffic came to a complete stop. He turned and looked directly back at her. "No fucking way, Jenna. I need you. Just ignore her, she's just being a bitch. I just don't know what to do with her anymore. I thought she'd get better once I married her, but she didn't, she just got worse."

"I'm sorry, Rollie. I feel so sorry for you, but I don't know what to tell you to do. The only thing I do know is that you better do something or you will end up as unhappy as me."

"What do you mean as unhappy as you?"

"You've known me long enough now to know I can't stand people who treat people poorly. What Candice just did to you, is exactly how Doug speaks to me all the time. Well, not anymore. As soon as I can get it all together, I'm getting out. I'm taking the girls and leaving."

Rollie looked at her inquisitively before he gave her a sympathetic smile. They travelled the remainder of the drive home in silence.

Around a week later, Rollie called Jenna and told her he had secured the paintings.

"Guess what?" he said. "I got your paintings. They're all yours."

"Really? You got them?"

"I sure did. So all you need to do now is book a truck for them to be collected and we'll put them in Gavin's warehouse."

"You're the best Rollie, you really are," Jenna squealed with delight. "I can't wait to get started on them."

The following day Jenna arranged the truck for the collection of the paintings. Rollie told Holly, she could help with them, perhaps even open a studio in which she could sell them for the company and she could do all her artwork on the premises. Holly could hardly contain her excitement. Holly's talent and passion for art controlled her every waking moment. If she was not drawing, she was painting. Then on the same afternoon, Rollie called Jenna back.

"Sorry, Jen, but we can't collect the paintings today. You'll have to ring and re-book the truck for next week. I've got to ride to Sydney with my brothers," he said.

"Oh, really?" she asked sadly. "So, we can't get them today?"

Once he heard the disappointment in her voice he changed his mind. Rollie told his brothers to go on without him and he would fly down the following morning and catch up with them. Jenna could not have loved him more than she did in that very moment. He really was staying true to his word and not going back on his promises. Instead of enjoying the company of his brothers, Rollie picked Doug up and together they collected the paintings and delivered them to the warehouse.

Life was looking good. Business was booming and the empire Rollie had worked so tirelessly on was finally coming together. Jenna's confidence and her escape fund grew. The trials of the herbal medication were about to commence and the safety seal for the irrigation system had been approved. Finally, after a lifetime of being owned, Jenna could see a free and happy future staring straight back at her.

Chapter Six

And, So It Begins

Rollie returned from his interstate trip full of life and stamina. He called Jenna from the airport and asked her if she was happy.

"Of course I'm happy, Rollie. You bought me the paintings. I love what I'm doing and life is looking good."

"I was thinking," he said, "You know, once we get this up and going with the paintings, you could take the company credit card and go over to China. That way you can tour their painting factories. I think you'd find that really interesting, the artists all sit in rows and paint away so you can see the art work as they are being created. It would be a real experience."

"You would be coming with me, wouldn't you? Remember, I've never flown before. I'd freak out if I had to go by myself."

"Jenna, I couldn't come with you."

"Why? We could do it at a time when you're not busy. It would be so much fun. I want you to come with me."

"I can't."

"Why?" she persisted.

"Jenna, if I came to China with you, you wouldn't be coming back."

"Why? What does that even mean?" she said, apprehension rising in her voice. Her mind raced with questions. "Why, Rollie, what did I do wrong? Why wouldn't I be coming back?"

"Nothing. You didn't do anything wrong, Jen. I just can't come with you. I can't be implicated in you running off with a little Asian man," he answered quietly.

"Oh my God, Rollie. You must be mad my friend. Why in hell would I do that?" she asked laughing.

She let the conversation slide and didn't really think about it again. She had more pressing issues to consider and bigger decisions to make rather than worrying about going to China, with or without Rollie.

Two days before Rollie brought up the China trip, Doug arrived home from work mildly intoxicated. As the night drew, on the more he drank and the more verbally abusive he became.

"I know we've talked about this before, babe, but I really want you to reconsider what I asked you to do about your job."

Jenna looked up from the email she was reading on the computer and took a sip of her white wine. "What about my job, Doug?" she asked, flatly.

"I want you to give it up. I want you to give Rollie up."

"What are you talking about, Doug? We've spoken about this too many times before. I'm not giving up my job. I want to get out of this area. How do you expect me to buy another house if I don't have a job?" she asked.

"Because I have a job. We can use the equity in this place and I can get a loan on my wage. Can't you see how much trouble you working with him is causing?"

"How is it causing trouble? I still take care of all my responsibilities. I still look after the kids, the house, run all the errands. I still do everything. Why is it causing you any grief?"

"Because I hate your fucking attitude now you work for him."

She knew things were about to turn ugly fast. She rose from her chair and tipped the remainder of her wine down the sink.

"I'm going to bed, Doug. I'll talk to you in the morning."

Doug grabbed hold of her arm as she went to pass by. He twisted it hard causing pain to shoot through her shoulder.

"Let go of me, you're hurting me," she cried.

"Nope, you're going to listen to what I've got to say. You will chuck in that fucking job and you will cut Rollie off. I don't want you having anything to do with him or his stupid fucking business anymore."

"I said let go of me. You're hurting me."

"Why don't you call your fucking boyfriend then? He only lives down the street. It'll only take him a second to run up here and save you," he yelled.

Jenna sharply turned around and glared at Doug. She wriggled free from his hold and quickly walked towards the hallway. Doug reached out, took hold of a handful of her hair and pulled her back. "Go on, ring him you cunt. Ring your big bikie boyfriend to come up here and save your ass."

"Stop being silly Doug. He's not my boyfriend. He's my boss. He's your mate, not mine."

"Yeah, he used to be once, but he's not now. He don't even speak to me now you two are so fucking chummy."

"So that's what all this is about? It's not about me, it's about Rollie not giving you any attention. Oh my God, Doug, that is the single most pathetic thing I've ever heard you say."

Doug twisted his hand, ripping strands of Jenna's hair out by the roots, pulled her arm up her back and steered her towards the bedroom. He threw her down on the bed and spat directly in her face. "I'll give you pathetic you filthy fucking whore," he yelled as he straddled her body.

By now both Holly and Hannah were standing outside the bedroom door screaming for their father to stop. The noise must have been alarming as the next thing Jenna knew, the police were knocking at the front door. Doug forced her to go and answer it in the state she was in. Both Holly and Hannah followed her. As they opened the door the police officers told them to go down the stairs. Doug then approached the door.

"What the fuck do you fucking pigs want?" he yelled.

"We received a call for a domestic violence disturbance and by the look of your wife it looks like you're lucky we did."

"How does it make me lucky? I own her, I can do what I like to her, she's my wife," he yelled back at them slurring his words heavily.

"Sir, can you just open the door so we can come inside and talk to you?"

"Have you got a warrant little piggy?" Doug asked. "If not, fuck off."

Needless to say, the incident left a bitter taste in Jenna's mouth. So when she returned home a few days later, she finally convinced Doug that she wanted to sell the house. He agreed to it, with the condition attached that she let him make it up to her and buy her a new house. By this stage, she would have told him anything he wanted to hear. She didn't know how she was going to do it, but she was leaving him, with or without the money from the sale of the house. Over the last few years she had heard every excuse in the book, and each and every time he broke a promise to her, or smashed up something else she owned or called her another obscenity, an extra little piece of her died inside. She had finally had enough.

Once Jenna told Rollie she was selling her house, he had asked her why all of a sudden she wanted to move. She did not utter one word about what had happened with Doug, instead preferring to tell him she just wanted to get out while the housing boom was on and make some money. He agreed, deciding now was the right time to move also. The area was going to the pits and on top of that, he told her that he thought a change of scenery might be good for Candice. Once Rollie listed his house, it was sold and the deal completely wrapped up all within three weeks.

At around eight thirty one Sunday night, Jenna had the urge to go to the warehouse to do some inventory on the paintings.

"Come on, ladies," she said to Holly and Hannah, "If you're coming with me, go and grab a jacket, it's really cold outside."

"I'm coming," Holly yelled, from her room. "Hang on a second."

"Me too," Hannah said. "I like that warehouse, it's creepy."

Jenna laughed at her and told her to hurry up. As she took the keys to her car out of her handbag her mobile phone rang.

"Hey, Rollie, what's happening?" she asked when she answered.

"Not much. What are you up to? Are you busy? I was wondering if you could possibly drop off one of the professor's trial medical packs for me?" he asked.

"What? Do you mean now? Tonight?" she asked.

"Yeah, if you could. I'd really appreciate it if you don't mind," he said in a quiet voice.

"I guess, if you really need it tonight, 1 can drop it off on my way to the warehouse," she replied, raising her eyebrows at the strange request.

"Are you going back to work tonight?" he asked.

"Yeah well, some of us really do have to work you know," she said, giggling.

Rollie laughed quietly. "Oh good on you, Jen. See you soon then hey?"

"You most certainly will," she answered.

By now, Doug was like Jenna's darkest shadow. He followed her wherever she went, insisting on driving her everywhere. He pulled the car to a stop outside Rollie's house. A twinge of sadness shot through Jenna's body. Even though she had all intentions of moving from the street herself, the thought of him moving out after ten years stirred her thoughts and emotions. She looked at the jasmine plant growing wildly over the fence and thought of how many times she'd floated its sprigs in a bowl at her own house. As she approached the front door Candice called out for her to enter. Jenna stepped inside and stopped dead still. Everything was gone. His huge wooden kitchen table with the carved chairs that looked as though they belonged in a castle, the couch, the hutch and even the hand painted portrait of Rollie were all gone. A shiver soared through her body. Candice bounced around like a jumping jack full of life and vigour. She yelled out orders to the cleaners working hard into the night cleaning the mess Candice would have left behind.

"This feels really weird, Candice. I mean this house being so empty. I can't imagine you guys not living here anymore," she said, glancing around.

"Not for me. I couldn't be happier. My life will finally be what it should've been all along. A brand new house and Rollie all to myself. I can't wait to get out of this hell hole," she replied.

Jenna stared blankly at her. She knew she was wasting her time and sentiment on someone like Candice.

"Where's Rollie, Candice?" she asked, backing out of the house.

"Well, he's not in here like he should be. He's around somewhere. Go look in the shed."

Jenna shook her head and walked out the door. As her eyes adjusted to the darkness she noticed Rollie leaning up against her much loved, old beat up Mercedes-Benz, speaking to Doug and her daughters through the open window.

"Hey, Jenna," he said, raising his head to look at her.

Jenna smiled at him, instantly noticing the emptiness in his eyes. He seemed listless, buckled or broken. She wondered why he looked so sad at a time he should have been his happiest. Maybe he was angry at her for harassing him over her pay. But she had a right to be angry. Up until recently, he had always paid her on time every time, but for the last few weeks, each time she would try and discuss it with him, he'd make an excuse, more often than not saying he needed for one of their deals to close first. She accepted that and tried not to make too much of an issue out of it. The longer she stood there looking at him, the more she wanted to reach out and hug him. She had no idea why, it was just an urge that took control of her body. Her desire to wrap her arms around him and take away his pain, whatever that pain was, became excruciating. But, she knew she couldn't hug him. She couldn't touch him. There was nothing at all she could do to help him.

"Hey, Rollie," she replied, quietly. "Here's the pack."

"You can have it back, Jen. I just need it for now," he said, reassuringly.

Jenna just smiled and silently wondered what he would need that medical pack for right here, right now. After all, he was meant to be moving. "No problem, Rollie, whenever you're ready."

Candice rushed up the gravel path bubbling with excitement. "You should see my new house, Jenna," she said. "It has four bedrooms, a spa and an in-ground swimming pool. It's finally the kind of house I deserve. I don't know if you'd like it, but I do. It's a house fit for a queen. I'm finally getting out of the ghetto. I can't wait till I never have to see this pathetic street ever again."

Jenna turned away as Doug congratulated her. She allowed her mind to slip back to ten years earlier and the first time she entered Rollie's house. At that time, the house was perfect for him. That house was fit for a king. But it had never been good enough for Candice. Jenna wondered if the new house would be good enough for her. It seemed nothing stayed good enough for Candice for very long. While off in her own world, reminiscing alone, she noticed the same pink four wheel drive which had been sitting in their driveway for a few days prior was still sitting there.

"Candice, whose is that car?" she asked, pointing to the vehicle.

"Oh that cute little thing? That's mine. Rollie bought it for me so I would have a girlie car to drive for work." Candice answered, smiling widely.

"Oh, really? Aren't you a lucky girl then? Jenna asked, sarcastically, as she turned to face Rollie.

"Yeah, I traded in the big white four wheel drive for it," he said, tilting his gaze away from her.

Jenna glared at Rollie, and shook her head. She rolled her eyes and stared into space. You surely can't be serious Rollie, she thought to herself. Jenna's confusion consumed her as she attempted to understand how Rollie could afford to buy Candice a brand new car, but couldn't afford to pay her the wage she'd worked for.

What was the deal with that she thought? Maybe Rollie really was, as he had told her a million times before; just purely selfish. Or maybe, he actually was just thoughtless and uncaring like other people had accused him of being? Jenna began to shake with anger. Rollie knew what she had planned to do with her future because he had become her best friend. She told him almost everything. He knew how much she relied on her pay so that she could save her money and start a new life for herself and her daughters. He also knew her pay was much less since they'd made the deal between themselves of getting most of their money when their deals with the companies settled. He also knew she had declined many other, much better-paying jobs, so she could help him and this is how he wanted to repay her? In that exact moment, her anger towards him escalated. She wondered how she could be so blind. How had she been so foolish as to trust him again? She really did know better.

Maybe it was because of all the things he had told her. Maybe it was the promises he made her about always being there for her and reassuring her how big his shoulders were and how they could take on anything she needed him to handle. Maybe it was that single statement about how she could always trust him. He promised her he would never again let her down, yet here he was, doing the exact same thing all over again. It was in that moment that she realised no matter how true to his word he was to others, he would never be like that with her. An ache soared through her head as though she'd been hit with a tomahawk right through the centre. She knew now, he would disappoint her time and time again. Jenna regained her composure as Candice once again drew her attention.

"Come and look at the inside of my car, Jenna. It really is kind of cute for a cheap little car," she said, walking towards the driveway.

Jenna reluctantly followed behind her. "It is a lovely car, Candice. You're a very lucky girl. Rollie really does take good care of you," she said, glaring at Rollie.

Candice got inside her car, stretched out her long, fake tanned legs and leaned back. "Yeah, he knows value when he sees it," she said, reaching into the console. "Hey, do you want these?" she asked, passing her two pieces of cardboard.

"What are they?" she asked, taking them into her hand.

"They're VIP premiere movie tickets for two. I don't want them. I'm not interested in seeing this movie. You might as well have them if you want. But, they're for the fourteenth of this month, so you have to go on that night."

Jenna looked down at the tickets, knowing she really didn't want to accept them. She truly hated accepting anything from

Candice. But, in keeping true to her well-mannered style, she took them.

She looked down at the date on the tickets and thought to herself, Happy fucking Birthday, Jenna. The movie premiered on her birthday. She had no intention of going to that movie, VIP tickets or not. She had deliberately not made any plans for her birthday. She hadn't allowed Doug to make any either. Jenna smiled and thanked Candice before moving away from the car. Rollie intercepted her in the driveway as she headed towards her own car.

"Oh, yeah," he said. "By the way, you know my brother, Fingers? Well, he had a really bad bike accident yesterday and he's in intensive care."

Jenna took a second for the information to filter through her mind. "Oh my God! Is he okay?" she asked.

"We don't really know right now. He's not doing too good. No-one can say whether or not he'll make it." Rollie answered, quietly.

"I'm so sorry, Rollie. I hope he'll be okay. Keep me updated on how he is won't you?" Jenna pleaded, as she walked around to the passenger side of her car and got inside. "Doug, get me out of here. I want to leave now!" she whispered almost silently.

Doug turned and looked at her as Rollie leaned inside his window. "Hey, I'm sorry I'm a bit weird tonight, I'm just buggered with all this moving house and stuff. It really does take it out of you," he said, as he stepped back from the car. "This car is running like shit!" he continued, as he stepped back from the curb. "Hurry up and buy her another one. She shouldn't be getting around in this piece of shit."

"Fuck this shit, Doug, let's go," she whispered quietly, through gritted teeth.

"Oh well, Rollie, we'll catch you later," Doug said as he shifted the car into gear.

"Okay then buddy, catch you later," Rollie answered. "Bye girls" he added to Hannah and Holly, before looking straight at Jenna and pausing briefly, "Well, I guess I'll see you later, Jenna," he said, looking at her intensely.

Jenna stared straight back at Rollie, her normally gentle eyes now full of rage. She knew he was only attempting to delay her departure for no real reason. She forced her lips to release a shallow answer. "Yeah bye, Rollie," she said, instantly turning to face out the side window at absolutely nothing.

Doug had barely pulled away from the gutter before Jenna launched her emotional rollercoaster into overdrive. Her pent up frustration and confusion had found a brand new high and for her, someone well equipped to control her own anger, had suddenly snapped.

"What the fucking fuck?" she cried, "What the fuck just happened there? Fuck him! He is so fucking nasty, I don't know why I have anything to do with him." she yelled. "Does he even consider the fact that my car wouldn't be such a piece of shit if that weirdo would fucking pay me? Does he think I want his fucking charity movie tickets instead of my pay? And, how is his fucking form? He buys that nasty bitch a brand new car, even though he says he's broke. He can't be too broke, now can he? I can't even say anything to him about it either because if I do, I'll just look like a jealous bitch!"

Doug interrupted her ranting "You're not a jealous bitch, babe, you've always been happy for him to get new stuff and improve himself. As a matter of fact, I think you get more excited for him than his own wife does. I don't blame you getting pissed off, the amounts of times he's fucked you around. I'm surprised you even bother to work for him or to be his friend. He just fucking hurts you and like I've told you a million times before, you need to fuck him off for good! You would if he were anyone else."

Jenna shook her head in disbelief. Was Doug really going to use this as a way to reinforce his stance on her job with Rollie? And, was Rollie seriously doing all of this all over again? She wondered how her life, the new life she was planning, had begun to crumble so quickly.

She remained quiet and in deep thought for the rest of the drive to the warehouse. She knew Doug, or anyone else, couldn't understand the bond she shared with Rollie. This bond had saved their friendship time and time again. Her thoughts became a tangled web. She thought about the way Rollie had looked at her when she'd first arrived at his house. She thought about her sudden urge to comfort him from something unknown to her. She thought about his insults and his ignorance. Her confliction was crucifying her. She felt so bitter and twisted towards him, but yet, she also felt deep sorrow. She remembered the huge disagreement they'd had in January regarding their friendship. She recalled his commitment and promise to try harder and to this end, he had. After all, he had just told her about Fingers being hurt in the bike accident, unlike when one of her closest friends, King was hurt in his accident and had nearly died. Jenna recognised and appreciated his effort to stay true to his word, but the anguish this man inflicted on her was inexcusable.

When they finally reached the warehouse, Jenna's level of agitation grew. The inner doors to the warehouse had been locked by the cleaners and she couldn't gain entry to the paintings. Hesitant to speak to Rollie at the time, she asked Doug to call him and find out how they could get in.

"Tell her to call Gavin and ask him what to do," Rollie told Doug, and Doug relayed the message.

"Well, why not? Why wouldn't I call, Gavin? After all, it is my job to look after everything to do with King Rollie," Jenna sarcastically replied. "God fucking forbid if that asshole had to make a fucking phone call."

Doug put his finger to his lips and mouthed for Jenna to shut up. "He heard that," he whispered, covering the mouthpiece to the phone.

"Quite frankly, I don't give a fuck what he heard," she answered, as she dialled Gavin's number. "Fuck me! That's it. I'm going home," she said, becoming more disappointed when Gavin didn't answer his phone.

She threw her phone in her bags and ushered the girls back out to the car. Just as she opened the door her phone began to ring.

"Hi, baby," Gavin said when she answered.

"Hey, Gavin. How are you?"

"Better than you, by the sounds of it," he said, laughing. "Are you at the warehouse? Did I lock you out sweetheart?"

"Yeah you did. Then when you didn't answer your phone, I thought I'd wasted my time coming out here tonight," she answered, a smile beginning to erupt across her face.

"I wouldn't do that to you, baby. I should've called you and told you that the cleaners do that sometimes," he soothed. "Go through that door to your right and go upstairs. Hey......... just watch out for those guys up there, won't you?"

"What guys?" she asked, stopping dead in her tracks.

Gavin laughed loudly. "I'm just teasing you, baby. There are no guys up there. When you go through that door at the top, go to that cupboard straight in front of you and grab the set of keys. They're the ones that will let you in."

"You're a true gem, Gav. Thank you for that," she said, beginning to relax.

"You're welcome, baby. Help yourself to that tea, coffee or even my alcohol if you like. Actually, you can have anything you want. Except, you can't take my paper clips," he added, trying to make her laugh.

"You're such a smooth character aren't you, Gav?" she giggled.

"Na, I'm not. You're giving me too much credit. I just think you're so sexy." he laughed.

"Okay, Gav. I think that's about all you can help me with for now. I better let you go," she said, laughing.

"Okay, sexy lady, I'll talk to you soon."

"You will Gav, you will."

Jenna opened the inner doors to the warehouse and once again, was surrounded by all the magnificent paintings. Her mood lifted as she soaked up the pleasure at being enveloped by such beauty. The gorgeous oil paintings lined every wall and filled each room to the brim. Everything you could imagine from Van Gogh reproductions down to the most simplistic beach scene.

Each and every painting oozed with character. The very heart and soul of the artists poured out into every single picture. Each one displaying a sea of colour and mountains of talent. As Jenna threw herself back into her work she asked Holly and

Hannah to gather the small Van Gogh paintings together so she could take them home, to trace their names and inventory them. By midnight, the two girls were cold and tired. Jenna decided to head home. After returning the inner door keys to Gavin's office, she set the alarm code and locked the outer doors.

The drive home seemed to take forever. Her thoughts quickly returned to Rollie. She wondered how he could've been so thoughtless, or cruel with the comments he'd made about her car. On one hand, he'd give to her, but on the other he'd take away. She knew he needed her and relied heavily on her, yet still, he was foolish enough to insult her. She began to wonder if maybe he had no realisation of his actions, or if maybe he didn't really care about her after all. She knew he had something he wanted to say to her, but she had no idea what it was and with his reluctance to spit it out, she grew more and more confused and frustrated. Jenna's impatience amplified as her craving to hear his thoughts took over and the distance between them formed an ugly life all of its own.

His suspicious absence became more apparent over the next few days. Where once she would hear from him at least a few times a day, she now rarely heard from him at all. On the rare occasion he did call her just for a chat, he would mainly ask her questions delivered in the way of riddles which she struggled to understand. This resulted in him quickly retreating as she frustrated him further. She knew he had to stay guarded because of the police activity on his phone, but surely he could ask his questions in a language she could understand. She could feel the cloth of their friendship hanging by a thread. The fact was, Jenna was not used to missing anyone, yet here she was missing Rollie every single day. Unbeknownst to her, he had somehow managed to saturate her thoughts and had become an integral part of her life.

The next Friday came around and still she hadn't seen or heard from him. She left him a voice message on his mobile asking him to call her as soon as he could. He finally called her around seven thirty that night.

"Hey, you," Jenna said when she answered the phone. "Did you forget about me again?" she asked.

"No, Jenna. I could never forget about you," he answered. "I've been busy on club business all day. I'm sorry I didn't get back to you earlier."

"That's okay. I just thought I might've seen you today. I really haven't seen or heard much from you lately with your move and all. And, I've missed you," she said, moving to a quiet place in her bedroom, so she could hear him talk.

He made small talk about his day, his new house and other trivial matters before finally telling Jenna he had something to ask her.

"You can ask me anything, Rollie, you know that," she answered, softly.

"What is it you want from me?" he asked, with deep feeling in his voice. Jenna removed the phone from her ear and looked at it for a moment, then put it back to her ear.

"I bend over backwards for you, Jenna. I'd do anything for you and you know that. But I don't know what it is you want from me anymore," he continued.

Jenna stumbled over her thoughts. She didn't know what to say. She was reluctant to make the same mistake she'd made with the China statement so she answered the question the best way she knew how.

"What I want from you is for you to stop forgetting about me. I realise how much you have on your mind with work, the club and even your social commitments, but can it really be that hard for you to ring me? Or text message me? Don't you understand how frustrating it is when I need to talk to you, but can't? She asked. "You know what? Don't worry about answering that question because I'll do it for you. You wouldn't know what it's like because I am different to you. I am always here for you, Rollie. Day or night or anywhere in between. Whenever you need me, I'm there. But when I rely on you to do the right thing by me, you always let me down. You gave me your word that you'd always be there for me, but where are you? I'm a forgiving and understanding person, but if anyone in this whole entire world drives me nuts, it's you," she said, knowing full well she hadn't understood what he had actually asked from her.

She bit down on her lower lip and waited for him to respond. It was then that she hoped, wished and even prayed that Rollie would finally say what the true problem was between them. Her yearning to know what was bothering him had hacked away at her for so long now, the gnawing had become as familiar as an annoying little sister. Rollie hesitated and said nothing to address her concerns. He told her instead, he would be over in the morning to pay her and that they could work it out from there. With that he hung up the phone. Once again, he'd left her alone with her confused thoughts and feelings.

Chapter Seven

Never Again My Friend

Jenna rushed to the front window and watched as the four wheel drive pulled into the driveway the following morning. Her eagerness to see Rollie and sort out their problems almost consumed her. As she looked outside, she wondered why he was driving Candice's new pink car. Then as the driver side door opened and Candice swung her long, fake tanned legs out, Jenna gasped and took a step back.

"What the hell is she doing here?" she whispered to herself.

Candice fluffed up her hair, rubbed her lips together and adjusted her skimpy mini skirt, before strutting over to the steps. She bounced up the stairs like she was going for gold in the Olympic Games. The smile smeared across her face told an all too familiar story.

"Oh, hey, Jenna, Rollie asked me to pop in and drop off your money," she said, as she stepped in through the front door.

Jenna reluctantly took the cash and thanked her. "Why are you here, Candice? Where is Rollie? Isn't he meant to be coming over to see me himself?"

"No, he's not actually," she gloated. "He asked me to come over and see you. He wants me to give you your money. Oh, and while I'm here, he wants me to pick up the keys for the warehouse and to get all the paintings while I'm at it."

"He what?"

"He wants the keys to the warehouse and the paintings, I said."

"Oh, really?" Jenna said, tilting her gaze to the floor.

"Yes, really," she added, nodding her head.

Jenna could feel Candice's eyes fixed firmly on her. She knew to react would be exactly what. Candice wanted; a reason to run back to Rollie and cause even more trouble.

"Okay, sure. Hang on for a sec and I'll go get them for you then."

Jenna raised her eyebrows and shrugged her shoulders at Doug, as she slowly made her way down the hallway and into her bedroom. She carelessly fumbled around in her handbag, trying to suppress the tears that were threatening to spring to her eyes. Once she located the keys she pulled them out and dangled them in front of her eyes, staring at them intensely without moving an inch. These were meant to be the keys to her freedom; the keys to make a difference in her life, and now Rollie was taking them back. Even though she had never told him exactly what the keys represented to her, she assumed that he already knew. After all, when he'd arrived back from his last interstate trip he knew something was wrong. He had hounded her, wanting to know what the problem was. She told him in no uncertain terms that regardless of what Doug said or done, due to his violence, she was leaving him. He kindly offered the use of his solicitors so she wouldn't lose her share in her house and promised to be there for her. But, just like every other male in her life, it now appeared Rollie too would let her down. She squeezed the keys tightly, kissed her closed fingers wrapped around them and whispered a quiet goodbye to them and her freedom to boot. She straightened her back, tidied her hair, forced a half smile to her lips and dawdled back into the lounge room.

"Oh, and, by the way," Candice added, as Jenna emerged from the hallway, "I'll be doing all Rollie's emails from now on in. All his business emails and his personal ones. My internet is not set up at the new house yet, but just send them to my email account and I'll get to them when I get to them. You know my email address."

Jenna almost laughed thinking to herself how interesting that was going to be. Candice had never been able to deal with Rollie's affairs before, what made her think she could do it now? And the even bigger joke was, why Rollie all of a sudden thought she could be a reliable or responsible human being?

Candice smiled, narrowed her eyes and said, "That should make it easier for you to deal with your own business instead of his from now on, shouldn't it Jenna?"

Jenna swallowed hard, as she attempted to dislodge the lump of pain caught up in her tightening throat. She turned her head quickly, trying to avoid Candice's querying eyes. She would not allow her to gloat, or to bask in a victory that was not rightfully hers. Jenna had been through this too many times before with her. She stood staunch and smiled.

"Yes, I guess I will, Candice," she answered, "The paintings are in the office and here are the keys to the warehouse," she said, as she walked towards the kitchen with a cloak of disbelief settling on her shoulders. One thought after another raced through her mind. After everything they had been through, after all they had talked about and dreamed of, how could Rollie possibly want to do this…again? She had warned him; told him if he ever did this to her again that would be the end of their friendship, forever. He had even signed her mock-up contract saying he understood that message. Surely this couldn't have been his doing? It must have been her; it must have been Candice who insisted on her being fired. Jenna's breath became fast and shallow, her mind began to race, and she struggled to inhale. She poured a tall glass of water and sipped it slowly as she waited for her heart rate to drop back to normal. Doug placed his hand in the middle of her back and rubbed it.

"It'll be alright, Jenna. We'll get this mess sorted," he said.

Jenna wriggled her shoulders away from Doug and stepped back.

"Please, don't," she said, "Please, just go and ring Rollie right now. This can't be right. Maybe she's taken it upon herself to collect all this stuff? This isn't what he told me last night. This can't be right. Surely he's not stupid enough to do this all over again? He promised he'd never do it again."

Doug groaned deeply, "For fuck sake, Jenna. I'll do it, but I'm only doing this for you." He snatched up his phone and descended the back stairs.

She went back to the lounge room and looked around. Half the paintings from the office had already been removed.

"Where is she, Holly?" she asked.

"Out the front putting my paintings into her car," Holly answered, angrily. "What is she doing here? And why is she taking the paintings?"

"I honestly don't know, Holly. I really don't," she answered, gently rubbing her teenage daughter's arm. "Do me a favour and help her with these paintings will you?"

"What? You want me to help her to take the paintings to her car after Rollie gave them to me?"

"He didn't actually give them to you Holly. He said you could help with them. They do belong to him, so there really is nothing we can do. Just help her so I can get her out of here so I can try and speak to Rollie. At least that way we'll know what's going on."

"Why don't you stop being so nice to her, Mum? You know this is all her fault. It's no different to the last time or the time before that. I hate her fake ass guts!"

"Stop it, Holly. I can't stop her from taking them. If I could, I would, but I can't so please stop doing this."

"So what will happen to the paintings now then?" she asked.

"I don't know. I won't know anything at all until I speak to Rollie."

"You shouldn't have bothered answering. I already know what will happen to them. He'll leave them in the warehouse to rot. What happened between you two anyway? What did you do to him?"

Jenna looked up and raised her eyebrows high into her forehead.

"What did I do to him? Holly, seriously, you didn't just ask me that did you?"

"Well, something must have happened, or else he wouldn't be doing this. And again, Mum, why are you being so nice to her?" she asked.

"What do you want me to do, Holly? I don't like her any more than you do, but, I refuse to look as pathetic as she does. I can tell her she can't come in here. I can go off my head at her, but what will that solve?"

"She'll just go running straight back to Rollie with a whole heap of lies like she always does and that will just make it worse. Out of respect for him, I'll keep my mouth shut and wait and see what's going on. I guess we'll find out soon enough. Dad is downstairs calling him now. Hopefully, he can find out what the hell is wrong."

Holly shot her mother a disgusted stare before taking a painting under each arm and storming out of the house. Candice tried to talk to her when she got to the car, but the only response she received from Holly was a dark silent stare. Holly's passion for the arts had only grown since Rollie had purchased the shipping container load of paintings and told her she could help with the sale and distribution of the pieces. The gesture had only made her fondness of Rollie grow deeper. Jenna's heart broke as she watched Holly's disappointed face loading those paintings into the car.

Doug disturbed her thoughts as he entered through the back door looking totally bewildered.

"Yep, Rollie sent Candice here. She's doing exactly what she's meant to be doing. He told her to get the keys to the warehouse and all the paintings you have here.

He wants her to deal with his emails, exactly like she said. Something's not right but, he sounds all fucked up and confused. Trying to get anything out of him was worse than pulling teeth. He said he just can't work with you anymore, Jenna. He said it's just too hard for him." Doug said.

"Huh? That's not what he told me last night. He told me he was coming over to talk so we could work out this miscommunication problem once and for all. What the hell does any of this even mean?" she asked, frowning.

"How can it be too hard for him to work with me? I do most of the work anyway. We've never had a dispute over work, ever.

Has he been drinking? Is he on drugs or what? Something is really, really wrong, Doug. Are you for real? Did he really say all that? And, what is too hard for him?"

"I don't know, Jenna, that's all he would say. I didn't even think he was going to answer the phone to me. He doesn't sound right, that much I can tell you." Doug answered, speaking softly.

Jenna steadied herself against the kitchen table as time dragged on like a heavy anchor behind a loaded ship. Candice made trip after trip from the office to the car loading up the precious paintings. The temptation for Jenna to erupt became overwhelming. She watched Candice haphazardly throw the paintings in the rear of the car with her two beloved dogs. The drooling pups jumped all over the paintings, dragging their doggy claws over the oil paints and down the expensive wooden frames. Jenna cringed at the sight. After an hour or so of Candice stalling for time, hoping to get a glimpse of Jenna's devastation, she finally jumped into her car and sped away. Jenna stepped out onto the front verandah and watched after the four wheel drive as it drove down the street and around the bend. Jenna wrapped her arm apologetically around Holly's shoulder and led her inside the house.

After settling Holly on the couch, she grabbed her mobile phone and dialled Rollie's number. The long ring of the phone became deafening. It rang and rang until it finally switched to voice mail. Jenna knew Rollie never listened to his voice mail so she decided not to leave a message. Instead, she dialled the number again, only to receive the same result. Jenna knew her attempts to reach him were futile as she painfully tried again to no avail. Her tears gushed down her cheeks faster than the flow of Warragamba Dam when the release gate is opened. Jenna dropped to her knees and wept until her chest was stricken with pain from her shallow breathing.

"Why are you doing this? Why won't you answer me?" she cried. She looked at Doug as tears dripped from her chin. "Why is he doing this to me? What the hell is wrong with him?"

"I don't know, babe, I really don't know," Doug answered.

She dialled the number again.

"What the fuck is wrong with you, Rollie?" she screamed as the phone once again fell silent. "I have never done the wrong thing by you. I've never done anything but help you and this is how you want to treat me?" she yelled into the dead line. "This is the last time you get to hurt me, Rollie! Fuck you and everything about you! You will live to regret this decision, Rollie that much I do promise you!"

Doug crouched down beside her and tried to lift her to her feet. She shook her shoulders fiercely and pulled away from him.

"It'll be alright, babe, we'll sort it out," he said.

"No, it won't be alright, Doug! It has never been alright. I told you right from the start this is the kind of thing that bikies do to people," she yelled, "Just leave me alone."

"This is all your fault. I told you I would never work with your so called mate ever again. I told after the last time, and the time before that with the camo gear that I would never help him again. But did you listen? No! Instead, you insisted that I did. Now look. He's a user. He uses people up and spits them out. This is the third time Doug! The third time I've helped him get into a position to make a shit load of money and this is how he repays me. "He repays me by dumping me flat on my ass again! If I could turn back time to just after that homicide squad was at his house and that anonymous guy called me to warn me about him, I would. I should have listened to them. The cops and the media are right about them. People mean nothing to him, we're all just puppets in his pathetic little show, and he is the grand puppeteer. Once the show is over, he dumps you off like discarded rubbish. I hate his guts! I hope he goes broke and then dies a slow and painful death. I hope he rots in hell!"

Doug hung his head and walked away silently. Jenna snatched up her mobile phone and scrolled down to her messages with Rollie. Her hands trembled as the rage inside her grew. Her hands now so shaky she could barely type out a text message to send to him, but when she did this is what it said:

"Why have you done this, Rollie? What have I supposedly done? What happened since last night? Rollie, PLEASE talk to me. Seriously, you can't cause all this heartache and trouble and then not answer your phone. You best be sure that this is what you want my friend, because I swear, this WILL be the last time. Ring me."

Throughout the day, Jenna's phone remained silent. Not one single word came back. Not via text message or a simple phone call. Buckled at the knees with grief, she wept like an abandoned child on the floor in her office, right where the paintings had previously been. An abandoned child? No, not an abandoned child, she had already been one of those and the pain she was feeling right now could not compare even to that. Jenna had never experienced anguish like this before. Not even the death of her beloved siblings could compare to this.

The pain she felt by Rollie's betrayal soared through her like a raging storm. She sat and wondered why this was hurting her so much. It must be the shock she thought. She knew she had done nothing to deserve this treatment. She knew she did her job well. She knew Rollie loved to work with her and to be around her as often as he could. He had proven that time and time again, through the way he looked at her. The way he smiled at her. She felt it through his massive bear hugs, his gentle cheek kisses and the way he smelled the top of her hair every time he held her. Jenna knew this had to be some kind of misunderstanding. She needed to find the truth.

"Doug, could you please try calling Rollie again and ask him why he did this to me?" she cried.

"I don't want to keep ringing him, Jenna. He's only going to get pissed off. Let's just worry about us now. Forget about him."

"He's not angry with you, he's angry with me. Please, please call him? I need to know what I did," she begged.

Eventually, Doug agreed to make the call for her. He escaped down the back steps again to speak in private. Jenna stared out the office window and watched as the rage Doug felt built up inside him. His face reflected the heavy black clouds which had begun to roll in. He walked laps of the backyard as he listened to and answered Rollie for around fifteen minutes. When he finally emerged, he sat beside Jenna and took hold of her hand.

"I think he's off his fucking chops. He went out of his way to try and piss me off. He's so angry with you, Jenna."

"Why? What did I do?"

"He didn't say you did anything wrong. He just said you're too moody and too hard to work with. He said you're doing his head in and he just can't do it anymore. He also said he can't speak to you right now."

"Huh? What does he mean I'm too moody? And, why can't he speak to me?" she asked, tears springing back to her already bloodshot eyes.

"I don't know what he meant by either statement, babe. I told him I've been with you for almost twenty years and you're far from moody, and, on the contrary, you're easy to get along with. I asked him why he couldn't talk to you and he fobbed me off. He really didn't want to answer that question. I also told him you've got every right to be pissed off when he tells you he's going to do something and then doesn't do it. I told him the only other time you get upset with him has been when he screwed around with your pay. I told him you have every right to get pissed over that. He totally agreed but didn't offer any kind of explanation."

"What else did he say, Doug? Did he say anything about the paintings or the contract, or anything else we have been working on?"

"He only said when the next container lands he will stick to his deal and pay you what he owes you. I'm sorry he has done this to you, Jenna, but he just sounds really confused."

"Confused? Don't talk to me about being confused. How do you think I feel?"

"Yeah, I know you'd be confused, but I think something else is going on here. I asked him if he would let me buy the paintings off him for you and Holly. He flat out said no, which was pretty weird. But saying that, I don't think the paintings have got anything to do with this."

"I think he's trying to cause trouble. He got all seedy at one stage and tried to tip me off to the fact that you were having an affair with some bloke named, Terri. I got pretty pissed off until I realised he was talking about your girlfriend, Terri. He got fucked off when I told him that she was a girl. After I didn't bite at that, he didn't have much else to say. I don't know what else to tell you, Jenna." Doug said soothingly.

"Me have an affair? What a joke! If you believe one thing that stupid bikie tells you, Doug, you'd be as stupid as he is!" she yelled. "He's a liar! If you think he'll pay me when that container lands you're deluded. He won't pay me one red cent! I don't get where he is coming from. Where the hell would he be now if I hadn't worked with him? Who helped him get the contract in place? Do you know what would have happened if he had of signed that contract without that safety seal? He would be exactly where he was almost a year ago; nowhere!" she continued to ask and answer her own questions. "I don't get it, Doug. Why has he done this to me? He knows how much I love my job and all the people we work with. If he even had one legitimate reason for firing me then I could understand. But I've done nothing wrong. The only thing I did wrong was to trust him. I don't get it. I find it so hard to trust and love people, but he ended up being one of them. He forced me to love him. Do you even remember back then? Does he remember back then? It took a lot for me to care for him, and look what he does. I never thought I would see him do something this stupid ever again. I truly thought he loved and cared about me. I thought I knew him better than this. I would've never expected him to betray me again. Ever! I thought he understood how it was meant to work."

"Jenna, you need to listen to me, and you need to listen very carefully. You did nothing wrong. Not to Rollie and not to his business. If you did anything at all wrong, it was doing too much for him. You were too good to him. You did everything for him. You even put him before your family at times. You let him get too close to you and this is the result of that. He doesn't want to understand what he's done to you. It's not about you as far as he's concerned, it's all about him. I guess people only understand what they want to understand, Jen. It's like having a safety guard around himself; if he doesn't acknowledge what he's done to you, he doesn't have to suffer the consequences of his shame. Whatever you do, don't you ever doubt yourself, Jenna, you're a good person and you certainly didn't deserve this." Doug said, pulling her into his arms. "I wish I never insisted on you helping him. You said he'd betray you again and you were right; he did. I'm so sorry babe. But, on the other hand, I'm glad the fucker's gone. Good riddance to the fucking thing."

Jenna wriggled free from Doug's grip. "It's too late to be sorry, Doug. It's too late for Rollie. It's too late for you, and it's way too late for me. I just can't do this anymore. I'm tired of doing everything for everyone else only to be stabbed in the back. I'm sick of it. Everyone can find themselves a new puppet. You can all find someone else to use and abuse. The next time Rollie decides he's human and he needs me, and he will, just as he has done every other time, I won't be here. I refuse to be here for him ever again. I'm moving out and I'm taking the girls with me. I can't be hurt anymore!"

Jenna paced wildly around the kitchen, before holding the sides of her throbbing head, as tears slipped down her face and silently dripped onto her already drenched top.

"You know what?" she asked, "Laura and I were only talking about this exact scenario last night. She asked what would happen if my friendship with Rollie ever came to an end. She asked me straight out how I would feel about it. Obviously she could see a catastrophe on its way, but me being me, I didn't. Laura had asked me, what is the worst thing that could happen out of this situation between you and Rollie? I asked her what she meant and she told me he was becoming too attached. He depends on you, Jenna. If you want to know the truth, I think he's in love with you, she said. I laughed at her and told her not to be so stupid. He's married I'd said. He loves his wife; he'd have to or he wouldn't put up with all her bullshit."

She switched on the jug and continued with her story.

"I told her that I loved Rollie with all my heart and would do almost anything for him, but that she had got it wrong. I told her that Rollie loved me like he loved ice-cream. She told me I was as blind as a bat and that Rollie adored me. She said you can tell by the way he looks at you. He is in love with you. Then she insisted I answer her question. And stupid me, I said to her, the worst thing I could imagine is that Rollie would decide all this working with me would become too hard due to the fact that I ride him so hard. I told her I was scared that if he walked away we would lose everything we were working for and it would be gone forever."

She poured the boiling water into the coffee mugs and kept right on talking. "You won't believe what she said to me Doug, you really wont. She told me, well that is never going to happen now is it? Rollie will never walk away from you; the bond between you two is too strong. At this stage of the game, your job is the only way he can hold onto you, she said. I laughed at her. I truly thought she was being funny."

She placed her coffee cup on the table and slunk down in the seat.

"Well, how wrong was she? He did walk away. Actually, he didn't just walk, he threw a flash bomb in at full force and waited for the explosion, then ran. You know, I thought something was wrong when he called me from the airport. When he told me he couldn't come to China with me because if he did I wouldn't be coming back, I thought he was angry at me. I reacted so poorly I couldn't believe it myself. Especially the thoughts rolling through my head. I thought he meant he would kill me and leave my body there. But when I told Laura about it last night, she laughed at me. She told me that she thought he meant that if he had a chance to take me away, that he wouldn't allow me to come back, that he'd keep me with him. She again insisted that he loved me and wanted me to be with him. I thought she was nuts."

"See, I told you that's what he meant, Jenna. I told you it wasn't about him hurting you. But as usual, you shut me down." Doug said, "You can't be that stupid. You've got to know by now the man wants you. He knows how rocky our relationship is and he's been waiting for you to make your move. The only advantage I have over him is that I know you'd never hit on someone. He's not used to that. He's used to women throwing themselves at him. So maybe that's what this is about; he's sick of waiting."

"For God's sake, Doug. We're not doing this again. Rollie's not like that. His wife might be a piece of shit, but he has morals, he has standards; he doesn't act like that. And besides all that, he knows I'm not the kind of girl who'd ever have an affair. We've talked about it plenty of times, he spends enough time with me to know that I don't hit on men. He would know if I was to move on, a man would have to pursue me, not vice versa. So that puts paid to your theory. As far as I'm concerned you're just as crazy as Laura. "

"You're a fucking idiot, woman!" he yelled as he plonked himself down in the chair across from her. "Are you seriously telling me that you don't know how Rollie feels about you?"

"Well, yeah, I do now! I think it's pretty obvious how he feels about me. He hates my guts! Look what he's just done to me. Don't try and tell me that's what a man who loves someone does." The tears once again began to flow. "So even if you were both right, you have nothing to worry about now because he's gone."

Doug's outburst forced Jenna to think about the other matter Laura had brought to her attention last night. She had told Jenna how much she loved her and how much she valued their friendship. She also told her how worried she was about her. Jenna couldn't comprehend what Laura was concerned over. Her life for the first time in forever was finally heading in a direction that she was happy with. She finally felt like she was taking control. Laura had told her to be careful as she felt something shifty was going on. I'm not too sure what it is I'm picking up on, but both of these men are pulling you apart like a little soft filled ragdoll. One is trying to tie you to the past and the other is trying to pull you into a future. Jenna had told Laura that she loved her too, but not to be so dramatic. If only she could have seen what everyone else had apparently seen, maybe she wouldn't be suffering how she was now. She began to wonder why she didn't see things the same way as others. But then she remembered, she was Jenna and Jenna saw things through Jenna eyes.

Doug perched himself up on the wooden kitchen table right in front of Jenna. He took her tear soaked face in his hands and turned it up to look at him.

"Look, I really don't know what to say to you to make you feel better, babe. I really don't. But, I'm sorry you're hurting so much. If I could turn back time or take away your pain I would. I'm sorry I ever introduced you to Rollie. I never expected any of this to happen."

Over the next couple of weeks, time passed by in a blur for Jenna, as the grip of unhappiness pulled ever so tightly around her throat. What had once been done as her daily routine, now became a challenge for her to manage. The most mundane and simple tasks had become difficult, and the difficult tasks became impossible. Her pining for Rollie affected everybody, as the tourniquet of sadness lured her deeper into a dark and empty pit. She still had no answers; answers she so desperately needed to gain closure to this nightmarish event in her life. It wasn't through a lack of trying to resolve the issue on her part, it was the lack of response from Rollie that kept her where she was; sinking in a pit of misery. She had tried endlessly to contact Rollie. She called his phone every day for the first two weeks, but with every rejection she got from his calls, the lower she sunk. Eventually, everyone around her insisted she let go of him and the hypnotizing effect he'd had on her life. Jenna was unsure if she could do that. She hadn't even realised he had meant so much to her until he was gone. Now he was gone, she failed to thrive without him. He had represented everything she wanted from her life. He had represented a powerful kind of freedom; her freedom.

Freedom had been a stranger to Jenna. Her whole life had been controlled and manipulated by others who were supposed to love and care about her. But with Rollie at her side she had been learning to take that freedom for herself. As he had pointed out, it was time for her to live her life.

It was time for her to do as she pleased when she pleased, with whom she pleased and however she pleased. She had just started to become accustomed to that new lifestyle, when he made his sudden exit. She knew without him in her corner, that her new status as a free woman would be impossible. She knew Doug would once again step up and try and claim his prize. It suddenly dawned on her, Rollie was her strength! He had been the one who nurtured her determination and fed her ambitions. Together they were unstoppable. Separated, Jenna drowned.

With the help from family and true friends such as Laura and Earl, the third week promised to be a little brighter. A fraction of trust began to slowly appear as they proved their loyalty over and over again. No matter how, or when, she needed them they would drop whatever they were doing and rush to her aid. Whether it was midnight or the middle of the day, they would come running. Laura even insisted on leaving a restaurant without finishing her meal one night when Jenna called her sobbing. Their selfless acts of kindness were heartfelt and appreciated. Jenna began to wonder if maybe she could go on. Maybe she could live a life without Rollie. After all, emotional pain was nothing new to her and she had survived before.

One afternoon as she watered the front garden while playing with Hannah, Jenna could hear her mobile phone ringing.

"Holly," she called, "could you answer my phone for me, please? It might be your dad."

Holly rushed out the front door with the phone still ringing.

"Can't you just answer it for me, please? I'm soaking wet."

"I'm not answering it, you get it,' she said, leaning over the front verandah to pass it down.

"Why? Who is it?"

"Mum, it's Rollie," she said, pointing to the caller ID on the phone.

Jenna tripped on the steps, whacking her shin as she stared at the screen and saw Rollie's name flash up on it. Her descent back down that emotional spiral staircase took control of her body. She bit down hard on her bottom lip drawing a spot of blood, as she plonked herself down on a wet wooden step. Her hands shook violently as she sat there and stared. Answer it, Mum," Holly ordered. "You've waited for too long not to answer it. Just answer it."

"I. I can't.' Jenna cried. "I can't answer it."

The phone stopped ringing. Jenna looked at it in her hand.

"You should've got it, Mum. You should've given that asshole a piece of your mind."

"I couldn't get it, Holly. I don't even know what to say to him anymore."

"Yes, you do. Ask him what his problem is and then give it to him."

Just then the phone rang again. Once again it was Rollie's number flashing before her eyes. Jenna just stared at it.

"Answer it!" Holly yelled.

Jenna fumbled with the phone then hit the talk button.

"Hello," she mumbled.

"Hey, Jenna, it's me, Rollie. I'm just returning your call," he said, calmly.

"What call? I haven't called you in weeks," she answered, quietly.

"I've got a missed call from you, but if you don't need to talk to me, I'll let you go and catch you later," he said.

"Rollie wait. I do want to talk to you. Of course I want to talk to you," she said, fighting back her tears. "But the question is, are you going to talk to me? Are you going tell me what happened? I need to know what I did wrong. Please, tell me, Rollie, tell me what happened between us? Why did you betray me again?" she pleaded.

"I didn't betray you, Jenna. You betrayed me! You hurt me. You fucked me up so bad and Dougy's supposed to be my mate." Rollie said, his tone turning to anger.

Jenna pulled the phone from her ear and looked towards it bewildered.

"What? What do you mean? What did I do to you, Rollie? I have never, nor would I ever do anything to intentionally hurt you and you know that. So how could I betray you?"

The phone went silent. Jenna adjusted her breathing.

"I don't understand you. You say one thing but mean another. I can never work out where I stand, or what it is you want from me, Rollie. I've always had your back. I've been here for you through thick or thin, good or bad, I've always been there. How can you do this to me?

Is this how you really treat people you say you love?" Jenna asked, in a quivering voice.

"Listen, Jenna, I can't do this right now," he said, as he cleared his throat. "I'll call you later."

Jenna knew to try and keep Rollie on the line would be useless. If Rollie didn't want to talk, then he wouldn't talk, and there would be not one single thing she could do to make him.

"Okay, Rollie, I'll talk to you later then. Stay well, take care and be safe," she said, defeated.

"I will. You too. Talk to you later."

"Bye, Rollie," she whispered down the dead phone line.

Jenna took hold of Hannah's hand, led her up the stairs and went inside the house. She placed her mobile phone on the kitchen nook and stared directly at Holly.

"What did he say?" she asked.

"Nothing! He pretty much said nothing. He blamed me," she answered. "I can't believe he wouldn't stay on the phone long enough to give me the answers I wanted. I've waited endlessly for this day to come. The day to have my opportunity to get my answers and have my say. I wish he would've had this conversation with me once and for all. I guess once again, I'm the fool. I had hoped and prayed we could've worked past this mess and get things back on track. But Rollie doesn't work that way. If things get too hard, or too close to his heart he shuts it down."

"I'm sorry, Mum," Holly said, reaching out to grab her hand.

"It's not your fault, Holly. I just don't know how to handle this situation with him anymore," she answered, tears forming in her eyes. "I can't stand the thought of him being out of my life, but I don't understand his absurd behaviour. The games he plays are way out of my league."

"Do you want me to ring, Laura?" Holly asked. "She'll know what to do."

"No, it's okay. I'll ring her Holly. Maybe she can make some sense of this because I sure as hell can't."

The minute Laura answered the phone, Jenna broke down like a baby. "Oh my God, Laura. You're never going to believe who just rang me," she babbled. "And when I finally answered he wouldn't tell me anything. He blamed me for everything that happened."

"Slow down, honey," Laura interrupted, "Tell me what he said?"

"He told me I betrayed him and that I fucked him up. He also went on about how Doug was meant to be his mate."

"So there you have it, my love. It's right there in a nutshell. He just told you that he fell for you. He told you that you turned him into an asshole because he fell in love with you and Doug is supposed to be his friend."

"STOP SAYING THAT!" Jenna screamed, "That's not what he said."

"I'm sorry my darling, but that's exactly what he said." Laura stated, in a caring tone.

"I. I can't listen to this. He isn't like that. He knows I'm not like that. Laura, please help me," she pleaded, "I can't do this anymore. I think I'm losing my mind. I don't know what to do. I love him so much and miss him every single day, but I can't go on like this. I want this pain to stop!"

"Alright honey, take a deep breath and try to settle down. I know this is hard for you because you are who you are. You're a lady who believes in honesty and loyalty. But you need to understand not everyone thinks like you. Remember you told me about the time he asked you should he marry Candice or not?"

"Yes. I remember. What does that have to do with anything?"

"I think he was trying to tell you then. I think had you of said no don't marry her and be with me, he would have."

"Jesus fucking Christ, Laura stop it! I can have this same convo with Doug, I don't need it from you too."

"Okay, well let's try this then. Do you remember what I told you before about people like Rollie, Jenna? Do you remember me telling you that acceptance was the key to understanding his lifestyle and his behaviour?"

"Yeah, I remember, but I still don't really understand what you were talking about," Jenna replied.

"You don't have to understand it, you just have to accept it. Men in Rollie's position are expected to act in a certain way. He and all other bikies have an image to uphold and protect. You see my darling," Laura continued. "Rollie can't show any sign of weakness. He can never act in a way that could make him appear soft. In his life choice, he must deny himself some of the things he may want most, in order to function and be respected within his own world. And in this case, the thing he has to forsake is you. Could you imagine what his brothers would say if he made a move on his best mates wife? Regardless of what normal people think, bikies can't do that stuff. He would be frowned upon and could even get kicked out of his club. Nope, I'm sorry, honey. There was simply nothing else he could do. I guess he will just continue on down his lonely path and have to learn to live without you."

"But, I don't want him to be lonely. I want him in my life forever." Jenna cried.

"I know you do honey. I know you do. But what you don't know, or perhaps you just can't see is that for Rollie, you are like kryptonite is to Superman. You buckle him and bring him to his knees. You make him want to risk his reputation. And in his eyes, once he has done that, he has nothing. So for him. He can't win."

"How? By loving him?"

"Yep, that's exactly how. He's a really smart man, Jenna. He's not stupid. He will always do what needs to be done. No matter who he hurts, even if it kills him to do so."

"Yeah, like me."

"Yep, like you. You've got to understand, Jenna, from what I can see, this whole experience was never about hurting you. It was all about loving you."

"Well if that were true, why didn't he just say so? Why couldn't he tell me? She asked, puzzled at the concept. "I'm sorry Laura, I love you dearly, but nothing you or anyone else can say will ever convince me of that."

"What if Rollie told you himself?"

Jenna sat on the couch and continued to listen without answering Laura's question. She had no idea what she would do if Rollie ever did confess such a love to her. She decided she wouldn't add that to the list of her confused feelings as she had way too many already.

"My suggestion to you my love, is that you take all the good that Rollie taught you and you run with it. Forget the bad, but embrace the good. He taught you so much, Jen. Use it to your advantage and continue to rebuild your life. One day all of this will make sense to you."

By the end of the conversation, Jenna began to feel the anger she had stored up towards Rollie melt away like water from a melting glacier. Laura was right. Rollie had taught her a lot about life and a lot about herself. She understood her naïve nature had been sharpened and her eyes were opened much wider than ever before. She accepted that not everything Rollie had been done to hurt her, but had been done instead, to protect himself. Jenna could not be sure what effect she'd had on Rollie, but one thing was for certain; she was hurting him as much as he was hurting her. Maybe it would be best to apply some distance. She certainly had no intention of causing him any further heartache, havoc, or grief.

In the weeks that followed, Rollie and Jenna had a few uncomfortable phone conversations, both attempting, with an amount of passion, to forge forward past the damage that had been done. At one stage, she even told him not to worry about trying to explain the situation anymore because she felt she understood his actions. Rollie happily accepted that offer without hesitation. But in the back of her mind, an unwavering desire to hear the words come from his own mouth, gnawed away at her almost daily, until finally she thought she may be able to make it happen. Jenna had told Rollie she needed some of the herbal medication they had been helping the professor trial for her mother's husband. Rollie agreed to get it for her and promised to bring it over to her himself. Jenna panicked. This would be the first time she would come face to face with him since the whole situation had unfolded.

He called her early the following Saturday morning to arrange a time to drop the medication off. Jenna went about her business trying not to think about him coming over. When she heard a car pull into the driveway she nervously swallowed and unlocked the front security door.

She cautiously greeted Rollie and walked away from him.

"Hey, Rollie," she said with her back to him.

"Hey, Jenna, how you doing? Have you been alright?" he asked, "Where are Doug and the girls."

"Yeah, I'm okay. They're not here. They've gone birthday gift shopping."

"Ah, that's right, it's your birthday on Wednesday hey?"

"Yeah, it is. Don't remind me," she laughed, trying to break the astronomical awkwardness between them. Never before had she felt such tension. She thought to herself she would need a chainsaw to cut through its thickness. A knife certainly wouldn't do the job. Rollie continued to make small talk and gave Jenna instructions on how the medication should be used. Jenna stood there pretending to listen. She knew more about that medication than he did. She saw an opportunity to get an answer, so she took it.

"Rollie, are you ever going to be able to tell me what happened between us?" she asked. "I've tried to let it go, but I need to hear it from you," she added.

Rollie looked at her and hesitated.

"Yes, I will Jenna. I will tell you. I promise you that. But, not now. I can't do it now." he said, shoving the medication into her hands whilst backing out the door.

"Please, don't go. Please, stay and talk to me. I need to know what happened."

"I told you I'd tell you. I'm just not doing it now."

Jenna burst into tears.

"I will never give you another chance to hurt me, Rollie. If you can't spend five minutes with me now and tell me, I will never give you another opportunity," she cried, as he escaped out the front door and headed for the stairs.

"I gotta go Jenna. You just settle down. I'll speak to you later. I promise" he said, fumbling around in his pocket for the keys as he reached the bottom of the steps. He looked up at Jenna's pain etched face and jumped into the driver's seat of the Mercedes-Benz that he had promised to buy her when they worked together. Jenna crouched down on the front veranda with her head in her hands and sobbed as she listened to the car speed away. She clutched her chest truly fearing her heart would break in two. She had never believed Rollie could hurt

158

her this way or in any other way, especially not to her face. Now she understood she was very, very wrong. The only words she could mumble to herself were, "Never again, my friend."

Jennifer Brockie

Chapter Eight

In the Aftermath

As close as she was to Rollie, the idea of romance or passion between them had not existed in Jenna's mind. Yet the anguish she saw in his eyes the day he drove away and the woe she detected in his voice every time they spoke since, forced her to question their closeness. The two of them were cautious around each other, in spite of their proximity. They had their own lives, separate beliefs and both married to another, yet the yearning to be close proved powerful. What touched her the most, were the greetings they shared with one another. The smell of his aftershave mingled with his sweat as he wrapped his huge arms around her tiny waist and smelled the top of her hair. He made her feel welcome, wanted, or needed, a sense of belonging perhaps. After an absence, she was always one of the first people he saw. Maybe it was to reassure her of his safety, or maybe he needed to be reassured she was still there. Whatever it was, the desire for closeness was unquestionable. They had become a part of each other's lives; they had become a part of each other.

The true madness of it all began in midwinter, just after her birthday in May. The threat of snow came every night, but just like Rollie, it never came. Her thoughts and emotions were wound tight, caught up in the chilly whirlwind of winter. She was unable to lose her wakefulness for the fear of being visited by yet another dream or nightmare. Instead, she took herself on long sorrowful walks until well beyond the witching hour. She would quietly dress and sneak outside, then make her way down to the creek. She'd veer off the footpath, deliberately delving into long, wet coarse grass, as though it would lead her to another place, in another time. But it never did. It always led her to the same place; home. A place she no longer wanted to be.

Three weeks after the reconnection with Rollie, Doug moved their family to a new home in a leafy suburb several hours away from their old house. A place away from her memories and away from her past with Rollie. Doug craved the distance between her and Rollie. He begged for forgiveness and the right at being given yet another chance. Jenna loved her new five bedroom house with her in-ground swimming pool, complete with a cascading waterfall. The caramel brick house was pretty, almost perfect in fact.

The first few weeks flew by in a breeze with all the unpacking and decorating that needed to be done. Doug was impressed by Jenna's motivation to paint every wall, door and windowsill. He praised her efforts every afternoon when he arrived home from work. Jenna usually just smiled and nodded, not ever really listening to much of what he said. She didn't hear much in those days. She could hear the sprinkle of rain on her roof. She could hear the chirp of the magpies in the morning. She could hear the roar of a Harley Davidson motorcycle as it roared away in the distance, but she could not, or would not hear the sound of people's voices. She would watch their lips move and the animation of their body language, but she didn't listen to the words they were speaking. She no longer wanted to be influenced by others thoughts or feelings. The only time she did listen, and actually hear what was being said was when she spoke to her children, or when Rollie called her. One afternoon as Jenna tapped away at her keyboard, on one of those rare moments she had not been thinking of Rollie, her phone rang, and to her surprise, it was him.

"Hey, Jenna. How you doing?"

"Hey, Rollie. I'm okay. How about you?"

"Yeah you know, you know."

"No, I don't know, that's why I'm asking," she said, giggling like a teenage girl.

"I'm okay," he answered, laughing back at her. "So, what's happening?"

"Not much actually. I was actually just sitting here sitting wondering if people could die of boredom."

"What do you mean? Die of boredom? I thought you would've been flat out now Doug got you a new house?"

"No, I'm already finished doing all that. You know me, keep going till it's done. I've already painted everything that doesn't move and I've changed the furniture that many times people aren't sure if they're visiting the right house."

"Sounds like you," he said. "Hey, I've been thinking. No, it didn't hurt, smart ass," he added before she could interject. "Do you want to come back to work with me?"

"Ummmm, what?"

"I said, do you want to come back on board and help me get rid of these paintings? Candice is already back to her normal fucking shit. You know, as useless as a tits on a bull."

"Seriously? So she's still doing the same old thing?"

"Yep."

"You can't really say you expected much more from her, can you? What made you think buying her a bigger and better house would make her change, Rollie? She is what she is."

"Yeah, a lazy cunt! She still does nothing. Dirty fucking washing everywhere. I don't even have a clean or ironed shirt."

"I don't know what to say, Rollie. I don't think she can change. She's a spoiled brat. And in her eyes, you married her, you deal with it. You might have to wash and iron them yourself."

Jenna listened as Rollie explained his logic with buying the new house and his hopes that handing Candice more responsibility would force her to grow up. But she couldn't grow up.

She didn't want to grow up. Candice insisted on living her life on the edge, taking risks with everything and everyone at every corner. She thrived on living in a world full of drama and rumours. As soon as Rollie mentioned the word rumour, Jenna remembered the call she had received from Brad the plumber last week.

"Talking about rumours, Rollie. You know my mate, Brad? The plumber guy?"

"Yeah."

"Well, I got a call from him last week telling me that there is a rumour going around that you and I had an affair."

"What the fuck?" he yelled. "Who said that?"

"You know that little blonde that works in the café around the corner from your old work building? Her! She told Brad that Mike, your leading hand, is telling everyone that we had a steamy affair in your office and he walked in on it."

"What the fuck! I'm so sorry, Jenna. Fuck that weasely little cunt. I'll go front him. I'll fire up like a demon over that shit. You're not like that."

"Don't go causing any trouble, Rollie. I can't deal with anymore crap right now. Besides, I don't want you getting in any trouble. Just leave it. I just thought I'd better let you know that's what people are saying."

"Na, fuck him! He's not getting away with saying shit like that. I'll deal with it. Leave it with me. Now listen, back to the offer I made you. Do you want to come back to work with me or not?"

"I. I don't know Rollie. I really don't. Doug will hit the roof if I do."

"What the fuck? So, it's back to that then is it? That didn't take long, huh?"

"What? What didn't take long?"

"It's only been a couple of months, for fuck sake, Jenna and already you're letting him tell you what to do. For fuck sake! Didn't I teach you anything?" he asked, angrily.

"Rollie, I, I can't afford to piss him off right now. I've got nowhere else to go now you took my job off me."

"Well, now I'm giving it back. So now what's your excuse?"

"Look, I want to come back. I do. I loved my job, you know that. But Doug is really trying right now. He's trying to make things work. So much so, he's not drinking and he's controlling his temper. He even brought me a whole heap of Van Gogh and Monet repo's so I could start a small sideline business of my own. Something Holly can help me with. Something I can control and run. Something that no one can take off me.

"Ah, Good for good old, Dougy then huh? How fucking generous of him."

"Rollie, please don't be angry with me. I'm not trying to piss you off. I just don't know what to do, and I can't stand people yelling at me."

"I'm not yelling at you, Jenna. I'm just a bit fucked off that you're already back to exactly what you were before this all happened. I thought I'd taught you something. I thought I taught you to stand on your own two feet and not to take orders from anyone. Listen, the job is there if you want it."

Jenna sat silently and listened. Rollie was right, she could feel herself slipping backwards. Back into the girl that did as she was told, when she was told and how she was told. Jenna began to realise she had reverted back to being the same doormat she'd always been. "You know what Rollie? I will take the job. I can sell yours and my paintings together. Maybe we can salvage what we started and make some money, just like we were supposed to."

But, the job never happened. Jenna, hesitant to upset Doug, and Rollie hesitant to chase her, she never returned to work with him. And that, possibly became the catalyst for everything else that followed.

Once Jenna's paintings arrived from China, Holly and her set about getting their own little business up and going. As they went through the paintings, sorting them out for inventory, she came across a particular piece, a sensational oil painting by Vincent Van Gogh called, "Effects of Autumn". The same piece caught the sight of Holly. Almost in perfect synchronization, they both commented on how the piece resembled Rollie. As Jenna gazed deep into the painting she began to believe that the picture represented Rollie perfectly. His presence in her life had caused the same chaotic havoc as the harsh autumn had caused in the picture. Standing there nestled in the sea of colour, finely weaved with green, gold, red and brown stood a tree. It was the tallest tree. It looked tired as it had become leafless and withered, caused by the raging winds and natural rejuvenation process provided by Mother Nature. But yet, the tree stood tall and proud, the same way in which Rollie stood. As Jenna stood there immersed in thought, she realised that he'd had the same effect he had on her life. He entered her world, whirled around like a tornado, ripping things out by the roots and then left, leaving behind him a mass of destruction. But just like the tree in the painting, there Rollie stood, tall and proud. She stared at that painting long and hard before something struck her like a bolt of lightning. She got it! She finally realised what was happening in her life. All this time she had believed she was saving Rollie, loving him, nurturing him, yet at the exact same time he believed he was doing the same things to save her. She finally understood she needed to let that tall tree stand on its own and weather its own storm. She accepted she would have to do the same because for them to be together would make the devastation in that painting look like a walk in a well-maintained park by comparison.

After the realisation of what was occurring settled in, Jenna knew she had to let Rollie go. It was no longer a want, it was now a necessity. In order for her to reclaim her life and to build some kind of future, she needed to find a way to finalise their friendship in her mind. He had become a part of her, so removing him would be comparable to removing a limb. In the end, she decided causing a problem so they would have another disagreement would only fuel his fire, so instead she decided to end it in a loving and giving way.

She finally settled on giving to Rollie the same picture that had provoked her thought and inspiration. She quietly hoped he would look into the picture and somehow be struck by the same recognition. She arranged to have the painting framed in an antique frame to match the theme. When the gallery called to say it was ready she gathered it up with a bottle of red wine and delivered them to the clubhouse. Jenna timed it perfectly, knowing full well Rollie would not be there. She had no desire to see him, no desire to reignite her longing to be with him, so instead, she left it with the members who were present at the time. Jenna knew his brothers would be sure that he received it. She handed it over, hugged them and left. As she sat in the carpark she typed Rollie a message explaining that she had left him a gift, but that she could not see him or speak to him anymore. He tried to call her phone over and over. She just sat there and stared at the screen as her salty tears poured down her face.

The long drive home through the concrete jungle weighed heavy on her heart. Not only was she leaving Rollie behind, but also every other friend she had ever made through his acquaintance. These were his people. They owed him their loyalty, they owed her nothing. Jenna knew that what she was doing would once again alienate her from the real world, yet it was something she knew she had to do. She had to do it for Rollie. She had to do it for herself. She simply could not be near him, around him, or even think of him. Jenna accepted that Rollie and she were two different people from two separate worlds. Although their passion for certain things in life was identical, their worlds, forced by the hands of others, drifted so far apart, she now believed that not even their love, that had erupted between them, could close the great divide. Not without causing too many others far too much pain. Instead, she sucked up their pain like a thirsty vampire until it all but crippled her. But as the days turned to night and the lonely hours set in, she would sit under the stars and think of nothing other than Rollie. She thought of the anguish their friendship caused them both and recalled the pain it caused others. She missed his presence and the joy he brought her. She reminisced about the conversations, the friendship, the love and the caring they bestowed on each other and she missed him every single day. Her only hope was that eventually the sorrow would leave her, evaporate like water on hot cement. She could only wish that one day, Rollie would become nothing more than a distant memory. A fond memory with any luck. Little did she know, the decision she made that day, would only be the start of something even more explosive.

As the weeks slipped away so did Jenna's health. Her cheeks began to sink into her face, her rings slipped from her fingers, and her clothes hung off her shrinking body. Her resistance to speak to people, or to listen to them grew by the day. Instead, she immersed herself so far inside her work she created a space in which she didn't need to engage with others. She began writing day after day, letter after letter, word after word, then sentence after sentence, and paragraph after paragraph, until eventually she had written an entire book about her relationship with the beloved Rollie. She hoped the release of the words she kept well hidden in her heart would have the same effect as a valve on a pressure cooker. But nothing she did would relieve the pain, not even Rollie's acceptance of every word she wrote. She knew she could never release a book about bikie's without his approval so she lowered her guard against him, called him and asked if it would be okay. Rollie agreed and later confessed to Doug that he felt if anyone deserved to do what they wanted in their life, it was Jenna. He wanted her to make money. He wanted her to be happy. The only conditions were that she protect the identity of the club and that he read every word before it went to print. Naturally, Jenna agreed and handed over chapter after chapter. Even in hindsight, there was no way of telling just how much trouble that act would cause for each of them.

Due to their hesitation to see one another, Doug became the courier, delivering each chapter to Rollie as it was written. Doug would sit with him while he read them and then return them back to her. Each time Doug would return with a chapter, Jenna would notice there were no corrections marked out in the white space.

"Doug? Is he reading these chapters, or are you guys just stuffing around when you take them over?"

"Na. he's reading them alright because whatever's in them is affecting him. He pours himself a drink, lights up a cigarette and sits quietly on his own and reads them."

"So, he's happy with how they are? He doesn't want any corrections?"

"Not as far as I know. He must be alright with them, but I can't say he's happy with them. He certainly doesn't look too happy by the time he's finished reading them. He always looks pretty fucked up actually. I know he'd give me a kick to the head if he heard me say that, but he does. It looks like he's had his heart ripped out through his nose with an anchor. He's even asked me if I've read them. When I say no, he says well you should. I just tell him I don't read."

"He's probably right, Doug, you should read them," is all she said. Jenna pictured Rollie's suffering face and began to cry. She didn't know how to help him or how to ease his pain. She couldn't even do that for herself.

To Jenna's knowledge, Rollie had told Candice about the book, but he never allowed her to read the chapters as they arrived. She was angry over it, but all appeared well until one afternoon when she did find one. For some reason, Rollie had insisted on keeping one of the chapters with him in the house. Knowing Candice never did any housework, he slipped the manuscript under his mattress knowing she would never lift it, so therefore never find it. Candice must have been on one of her snooping expeditions and came across it. Before too long all hell broke loose.

"Don't you ever contact my husband ever again you home wrecking fucking slut!" she screamed down the line. "I found your stupid fucking book and I burnt the cunt of a thing. Just fuck off. Stay away from my husband."

"What's your problem, Candice?" Jenna asked, trying to remain calm.

"I found your fucking book. It's fucking stupid. Rollie wants you to fuck off. He hates you! He thinks you're not right in the head. Now fuck off you stalker!"

"Candice, I can't write the book without his approval, so if he wants me to not write it, he can tell me himself. Now lose my number. I am sick of you and your selfish attitude. Don't call me again. Got it?"

"No, fuck you! Don't tell me what to do you fucking old slutty cunt. If I tell you something you listen! I'll ring you whenever I want. He is not helping you with your stupid book, your stupid family or your stupid fucking life. Now fuck off and die!"

"See ya, Candice. Remember what I said, don't call me ever again," she said, hanging up the phone.

Jenna seethed with anger. She wondered how much longer Rollie would allow Candice to do this to her. After all, this mess was as much his as it was hers. Probably even more so; he had created it.

A few hours after the call from Candice, Jenna received a text message from Rollie. It simply read: "I'm sorry about that Jenna. I've left her. I'll be at the clubhouse if you want or need me."

Jenna panicked. Had she caused this? She momentarily ignored the message and thought about Candice. Jenna knew she had done everything she could have possibly done to help that girl and her marriage. Despite knowing it was all wrong. She knew Rollie was unhappy, but he'd married her. They had to try everything possible before throwing in the towel. Jenna had warned Candice about the partying, she told her about her drugs and drinking and she explained to her on several occasions what Rollie really did want out of her and his life with her. Each time Jenna told her, she would come good for a week or two before quickly slipping back into who and what she really was. Jenna now knew Candice was nothing more than a self-centred, uncaring, narcissist and that she was powerless to help her. Her thoughts quickly jumped to Rollie. Was he okay? Should she be there for him? What should she do? She knew to run to him and comfort him would only reinforce his decision to desert his marriage. She knew she couldn't take on any part of this decision, no matter how much she wanted to. She understood he had to make this choice himself, without any influence from her. Later that evening Doug went to the clubhouse to check on Rollie.

He stayed with him for several hours drinking and talking. At around two in the morning Doug arrived home, fuelled with alcohol and accusations.

"What the fuck is going on with you two?" he screamed in Jenna's sleeping face.

"Oh my God, Doug, not this again?" she answered, rolling away from him in her bed.

"Yep. This again. You're gonna tell me what the fuck is going on with you two," he yelled louder.

"Nothing is going on. Nothing has ever gone on. And if you haven't noticed, he doesn't even talk to me that much now."

Doug pushed her over onto her back, straddled her body, snatched hold of both her hands and held them tightly above her head while digging his nails deep into her flesh with all his might. "Stop fucking lying to me!"

"I'm not lying to you. Nothing is going on. Nothing ever has," she whimpered, trying to break free of his hold.

"You're a fucking liar. If nothing was going on he wouldn't be more worried about you than his fucked up wife."

"Ah, so here we go again. Again with the wah wah wah about how Rollie loves me more than he loves you and more than he loves her shit. I don't know why Rollie does anything that he does, Doug. It's pretty obvious he doesn't love me more than you because he devastated me for your sake. Why weren't you man enough to ask him these questions while you were there with him, rather than manhandling a woman less than half your size, Doug? I'm sick of this shit! I can't do it anymore. Both you and Candice are off your tits. Fuck you and fuck her!" Doug jammed his face hard into hers, pushing her nose to breaking point.

"When I find out what happened between you two, I will kill you cunt, believe that! Was he better than me? Does he have a huge cock? What's it like being a bikie mole?"

The questions and accusations continued until the break of day. Jenna just lay there, too frightened to move or to speak. Instead, she listened to everything that she was and everything she had done. All of which were foreign to her. But as the sun appeared from on the horizon, Doug's anger subsided. He lay on the bed and dozed off to sleep. Jenna slipped outside quietly and wept. Now her world truly was upside down. The man she cared about more than any other at that moment was alone and grief stricken. She could do nothing to try help save him. She couldn't do anything to stop Doug from doing this to her. She couldn't leave him and she certainly didn't want to stay. All she could think about is why Rollie wasn't doing anything to stop all this from happening. Did he truly want to destroy her? Because if that was his plan, he was more than half way there.

Although Jenna grew quiet in those early days the continual abuse drove her further down the tunnel of silence. Holly now seventeen and Hannah twelve, were the only people she communicated with and even then it was only when absolutely necessary. She still tended all their needs, but she did so silently. If anybody other than the children put their hands upon her she would shudder and walk away. If anyone spoke to her she smiled and nodded, never really hearing a word they said. Her resentment for everybody she knew grew day after day. She began to blame them. All of them. If it hadn't of been for them, none of this would have ever happened. If her sense of responsibility and commitment didn't rule her life she could have been free. Just the way Rollie had told her she should be. He had warned her, he told her regularly how badly these people were treating her.

"You're not their fucking doormat, Jenna," he would say. "Stop letting them own you!" But they did own her. Doug reminded her daily that she was his wife, not Rollie's, therefore he owned her. Doug's self-inflicted illness owned her. Ever since the day he was diagnosed with severe cirrhosis of the liver, he told her, "I have nothing to lose now, if you dare to leave me, I will hunt you down and I will gut you like a fish." And, Jenna believed him. But it wasn't only him, it was her children who owned her. Her friends owned her and above all her moral compass owned her. She tried endlessly to shake the thought of Rollie off every single day. Her thoughts screamed at her to get out. Her mind had become a prison and no matter how hard she tried, there simply was no escape. Her only happy thoughts were of Rollie and the work they had once done together. Visions of his pain etched face ruled her world. She wondered if she would ever be able to forgive him, or herself for the mess both their lives were now in. Jenna's descent into madness had begun, or at least that's what she thought.

One afternoon as Jenna enjoyed the warmth of the sun by the pool, Holly came and sat down beside her.

"You know I love you, don't you, Mum?"

Yes. I know you love me, Holly and I love you too."

"Do you love me enough to see a doctor?" she asked.

"A doctor? Why would I need a doctor?"

"Because you do. This crap with Rollie has gone on too long. I think it's making you sick."

Jenna looked at Holly, stood up and walked away.

"Don't walk away from me when I'm talking to you, Mum," she said, following Jenna to the opposite side of the pool. "I'm only saying this because I care.

I'm worried about you. "All this stuff with Rollie has been going on for years. Both of you are as stubborn as each other.

175

Neither one of you will fix it, but neither one of you can let it go."

Jenna turned her head and refused to listen. Holly took hold of her hands and squeezed them tight. "I want you to listen to me, Mum. I'm serious! You both keep cutting each other off then run straight back to each other. I think it's pretty obvious that you love each other very much. You are always so sad because you miss him so much. This is hurting us, me and Hannah, but it's killing you, Ma. You need to sort this out with him. Screw Dad. He doesn't own you and he certainly doesn't deserve you. Just go! Me and Hannah will come with you. "It's either that or you really do need to see a doctor."

"You have no idea what you're talking about, Holly. Just leave me alone," she said.

Eventually, the choice would be taken out of Jenna's hands. Holly went behind her back and booked an appointment with the family G.P. Since the doctor had known the family for over fifteen years she helped Holly book Jenna an appointment with a leading psychologist.

On the morning of her first appointment, Doug guided Jenna into the outer office of the psychologist's office and waited for her to take a seat. He told the receptionist her name and handed over the Medicare card before checking on her one more time as he left the office. Jenna sat and looked around the room, wondering how in the hell these control freaks had managed to pull off this one. The next thing she knew, a lady, perhaps in her early forties, dressed in caramel slacks and an orange button-up shirt, called her name from one of the practice rooms. Jenna just stared at her.

"Hi, Jenna. My name is Carmen. Come in and take a seat."

Jenna followed slowly behind and sat down on the comfy blue couch.

She has lived the life of a stranger for far too long. There are layers of secrecy within her. She knows the Jenna she would have to show today, would not be the same as the Jenna who writes her own stories, or who attends her children, or the Jenna who once loved to cook. She knows today is about revealing her most inner secrets. The secrets of her travels up the rickety railway tracks and the clickety-clack of what she heard on that journey.

"So it looks to me like your family are really worried about, Jenna. Do you mind if I call you Jenna?"

Jenna said nothing.

"In the notes I have here from your doctor it says you have stopped communicating with your family and your friends. It says you barely eat anything and that your health is becoming adversely affected by your behaviour. Is that correct?" she paused. "Is there anything you want to tell me about that?"

Jenna cleared her throat and sipped on her bottle of cold water. "No. not really."

"So, you can talk, you just choose not to. Is that correct?"

"I can talk just fine. I just have nothing to say."

"So you never have anything to say? To anybody?"

"My family are exaggerating. I talk if I need to. I don't see the point in talking anymore."

"What do you mean?"

"I mean why talk if nobody listens?"

"Well, I'm listening, Jenna. Will you talk to me?"

Jenna fidgeted on the couch. "What do you want to know?"

"It's not about what I want to know. This appointment is about what you want to tell me. This is about helping you get back on your feet and back to your normal life."

"Oh, I see. So they want me to go back to my normal life, huh? No real surprise there actually."

"You'll need to be more specific with me. I don't know what you mean. I have no idea about what's been happening. You'll need to tell me."

"Not to be rude, but I'm not telling you jack shit if this is about giving them what they want. That's how I landed in this mess...... giving them what they want. Especially, Doug." Jenna said, growing agitated.

"No. you've got that all wrong. It doesn't matter who made the appointment, this is about you. These appointments are made to help you feel better. How about we start at the beginning."

"Okay, how about we start with you telling me if I am stark raving mad? I swear to God I think I'm losing my mind."

"Firstly, you are not mad. People who are mad, don't know they're crazy. They think they're normal. So stop worrying about that. Secondly, how about you tell me what caused you to shut down and maybe then I can tell you what I think."

"What caused me to shut down huh? Well, let's see. What part do you want to know? The part about how my so called loving husband is controlling me through his terminal illness, which in actual fact he caused himself?

Or would you prefer to hear about the betrayal of my boss, who was also supposed to be my best friend?"

"What do you mean your husband is controlling you through his terminal illness?

"Well, he was told over ten years ago to stop drinking. He didn't listen and now he has cirrhosis of the liver. He has left treatment for so long they can't fix it now, not unless he has a transplant. I love and hate him all at the same time. He is so abusive to me. Its got to the stage where I can't stand the sight of him. But my conscience won't allow me to desert someone who is dying."

"I'm afraid with his disease, Jenna, you can't do anything. You're not God and you're not a doctor. He created a problem for himself and that is something he will have to deal with. You cannot stay with someone because they are ill. If they are mistreating you, or you are unhappy, you need to leave regardless. Now, with your boss, or best friend, what happened there?" Carmen asked.

"Well he asked me a question one day, a question that I have to admit I did not understand, so I answered it the best way I knew how. Apparently, it wasn't the answer that he wanted to hear and he ditched me, taking my job, my health, my happiness and my only chance of freedom with him."

"I'm a little confused. What do you mean?"

"You're confused. Do you want to try being me? Nothing about Rollie's questions are ever what they seem."

"Why is that?"

"Are you positive everything I say to you is confidential?"

"Yes. I give you my word on that. The only thing I have to report to the police is if I think you might murder someone, or harm yourself. You are quite safe here, Jenna. Nothing you tell me will ever leave this office."

"Oh okay. It's all good. I just can't put him out there like that."

"Like what?"

"Rollie isn't like other people. He can't say what he wants, when he wants, especially not over a phone."

"He can't?"

"Nope. He can't. You see, Rollie is a bikie and the police tap his phone." Jenna half giggled, as she watched Carmen grow uncomfortable in her seat.

"Oh, I see," she said. "So what did he mean when he asked you the question?"

"I don't know exactly. His question seemed quite direct to me at first. He asked me what I wanted from him. I thought he meant in the work capacity, but everyone else thinks he was trying to ask me something else. My darling husband," she slurred with sarcasm, "seems to think Rollie is in love with me. As a matter of fact, heaps of people think he's in love with me. But I think they're all just crazy. The whole lot of them are jealous of how close he and I are. Oh, ooops, sorry, I meant, we were."

"What do you mean were?"

"Well, we don't talk too much anymore. It's too hard. His wife and my husband both think we had an affair."

"Did you? Did you have an affair?"

"Oh hell no! I don't roll that way. I'm ruled by my conscience. I could never have an affair, my guilt would kill me."

"Did you want to have an affair? Did you want to be with this man?"

"I just told you, I don't do affairs. If I were to be with any man, he would have to be single and so would I."

"You didn't answer my question, Jenna. Did you want to be with this man?"

"To be completely honest with you, I never ever thought about him that way until all this mess started."

As the two-hour session began to wind down, Jenna once again asked Carmen did she think she was mad.

"Jenna, you are far from mad. You, as a child and then again as a woman have gone through so much in your short life. How you have managed to stay afloat and not shut down way before this is a miracle."

"But, what about this obsession with Rollie? Why do I think about him constantly? Why do I pine away for him? Is it me who did this to him?"

"No, Jenna, you didn't do this to him. He did this to himself. He did this to you both. From everything you have told me about all your conversations, with all the text messages and with every action this man has done, you did not cause this. This problem has been caused through Rollie's own inability to speak. I know you struggle to hear these words Jenna, but from what I've heard here today, this man is in love with you. You are the key to his world. You need to speak to him and work this out one way or another."

Jenna continued her sessions with Carmen for the following two months. Not only did she need constant reassurance of her sanity, but she also needed someone to talk to. Jenna felt comfortable to speak to someone who could not repeat or manipulate any of her words, or judge her on her feelings. By the end of the sessions, Jenna and Carmen became quite good friends and still on occasion meet up for coffee.

Although no longer mute, Jenna remained fairly quiet around people. Her words instead became thoughts and she often lived entirely in her own head. But before too long she began to socialize once more, but on a very limited basis. She selected her friends carefully and mainly only attended family functions, parties and meetings on a purely have to basis. Then in the following February, something happened to make her smile once again. After all the heartache brought about by Rollie and the realisation that she would have to stay and take care of Doug now he was dying, a little miracle happened. Baby Bethany, Jenna's second precious granddaughter had entered this world. Harrison and his wife had given birth to their first child. The baby was delightful. She really was a bouncing bundle of pure joy. As Jenna cradled her in her arms and stared into the face of pure innocence, her heart once again began to beat at a normal pace. She found herself smiling every time she thought of the baby. Baby Bethany was proof the world truly could provide miracles and here she was; a wonderful reason to live a wonderful life.

Chapter Nine

It Is What It Is!

"It is what it is," was always one of Rollie's favourite expressions. He'd used it often and in many different contexts, but usually in a situation where he didn't want to explain or give an answer to a question. Those words would become a mantra for Jenna because she still had no answers to any of her questions. She found great strength in those words, the same way she had once found strength in him. They were his words so they had to mean something and eventually, they did mean something. Not only to him, but to her also. Their bizarre and twisted relationship, the one which had no name, or no meaning was exactly that! Once Jenna accepted that she slowly began to move forward.

The bumpy road to recovery was arduous, full of highs and lows, and fraught with ups and downs. In the years that followed, Jenna struggled to hold her deteriorating life together the best she could. Her efforts were made much more difficult each and every time she laid eyes on Rollie. To make things worse, she saw him everywhere she went. At times she even believed they had to possess some kind of magnetic pull between them, because if she was there, so was he. She ran into him in shopping malls, hotels, acquaintances houses, driving on the roads and even at places of business. One afternoon, as she dropped Holly to work, she almost walked smack bam straight into him as she was leaving the store he was entering.

At another time, she saw him in the distance in a mall but had to travel in the same direction to exit the centre. God bless his soul, he ducked into a handbag store to avoid her any inconvenience. You can imagine the looks he would have received from the workers, as an almost seven-foot tall guy, built like a body builder, who also happened to be a bikie, hid in amongst the latest Louis Vuitton's and Versace bags and wallets. Jenna anxiously grinned and quickly made her way past the store and into her vehicle, before making a speedy getaway. Life that way became almost bearable, but it couldn't stay that way forever. Although Rollie tried to make the separation easier on Jenna, the people they both knew and loved, didn't. It didn't take too long before they started complaining, wondering why she insisted on having nothing to do with them. One afternoon as Jenna stopped by her local shopping mall, she ran into one of the high ranking member's wives, Sarah.

"Well, looky here," she said from behind. "If it's not little Miss Jenna. Where've you been girl?" she asked, wrapping her arms around Jenna's neck.

"Oh my God, Sarah. It's so good to see you. How've you been?" she asked, hugging her back.

"I've been good, babe. What about you? Where've ya been stranger?"

"I've been around, hun. I've just been crazy busy. What have you guys been up to? How's Joe? How's the rest of the boys and girls?"

"They're all great babe. Why don't ya come up and see for yourself? Everyone will be up there tonight."

"Oh hun, I would so love to come but I can't come up there anymore."

"What the fuck? Why not?"

"Because I can't. You heard I had a huge run in with Candice, I suppose?"

Sarah laughed so loudly the other shoppers turned and looked at her. "Ha ha, yep. I sure did and so did everybody else."

"Oh no. So is everyone pissed at me?"

"Oh hell no! Everyone is stoked. And what's even better, me and her had a huge run in just after you two did and now she ain't allowed up there at all anymore. Rollie told her himself that she wasn't welcome. We told him he might have to put up with her bitch ass attitude since he decided to get back with her, but we told him we don't have to. Everyone hates her. I tell ya what, ya wouldn't know the place now that trouble making bitch is gone."

"Really?"

"Yep, really. Come up tonight, babe and catch up with everyone." "I can't, Sarah, I really can't. I don't want to run into Rollie."

"Why not? I'm sure he'd love to see you."

Needless to say, Jenna didn't go to the clubhouse that night, but she did begin to associate with her old friends once again. Not too much at first, but as time went on she began going back to the bike and tattoo shows, some parties and private dinner invitations. Each time, she cautiously asked who would be attending. She eventually managed to avoid Rollie almost entirely. Although there were times in which she couldn't.

The one thing Jenna refused not to do for Rollie was to have his back. If something happened which involved him and she heard about it she always made sure she told him. One of these occasions occurred not too long before the club's up and coming annual run. Although she herself, still had no desire to see Rollie, she arranged with him to meet one of her foster daughters so she could pass on a message. It was arranged that Rollie would collect Emily from her house at seven that night. At around six thirty that evening, Jenna received a call from Emily.

"Hey, Mumski, I won't be able to meet with Rollie for you tonight because I don't have a sitter for Lucy."

"What do you mean you have no sitter. I thought Ang was watching her for you?"

"Yeah she was, but she got caught up in work. So I can't go unless you want to come watch her for me."

"Leave it with me, Em. I'll hunt around and see if I can get someone to watch her."

"Why can't you just do it?"

"Because Emily, as I've told you a trillion times before, I don't want to see Rollie."

"Stop being such a sook. Just stay inside, he won't even see you."

"Wait. I'll ring around and call you back."

Jenna didn't completely trust Emily. She couldn't be sure she was not setting her up. Emily would've done almost anything to get her and Rollie together. There wasn't much she wouldn't try to get the job done. And, she had been spending a fair bit of time with him lately, while he was helping her to buy a new car. Jenna called everyone she trusted to see if they were available to watch baby Lucy. Once she couldn't find a suitable sitter she called Emily back.

"Alright look, I've rung everyone I know and no one can watch her tonight. I'll come over with the Holly and Hannah, BUT, you meet him out the front of your house."

Emily laughed, "You're such a sooky la la. Alright, I'll meet him outside."

"Stop being a smart ass, Em. I mean it. At a quarter to seven you're going outside to wait for him. I don't want to see him."

At ten past seven Jenna heard the car pull up outside, Emily got inside and the car pulled away. After they left, her nerves settled a little and she spent the time playing with Lucy and tidying Emily's house. Around an hour later the car pulled into the driveway. It sat there idling. No one got out and the car did not move. Jenna snuck to the front screen door and unlocked it. She went back to the lounge room and continued to play with the baby. Lucy squealed in delight as Hannah tickled her chubby little belly. Holly got down on all fours and pretended to be a dinosaur. The noise was deafening as the girls all played together. After a few minutes, Jenna began to wonder why Emily hadn't come back inside the house. A concerned frown formed on her face as she continued to wonder. Just then, she decided to go peek out Emily's window. Maybe they still had things to discuss she thought. As she straightened up and turned around, she almost lost her footing. Standing right behind her, where she'd been playing with Lucy, was Rollie. Jenna nearly walked straight into him. She gulped hard and opened and shut her eyes. This could not be happening she thought. What the hell was he doing here?

"Hey, Jenna, how've you been?" he said, holding his arms open to her.

Jenna opened her eyes wide, unable to mutter a word. She just stood there.

"Are you alright?" he asked, moving in closer to her.

"Oh fuck," she mumbled quietly as she automatically fell into his arms. "Hey, Rollie," she whispered as she held onto him tightly. He looked and smelt so good to her. They held each other for the longest time. Once he finally let her go, she stood back and observed the shock on his face over Holly and Hannah's growth. He had not laid eyes on Hannah in a few years.

"Wow, Hannah! Look at you," he said, holding his arms out to her. "The last time I saw you, you were a little girl. Now look at you, you're a young lady. And a very pretty young lady at that," he added.

Hannah rushed to Rollie and hugged him tight. "Hey, Rollie. I've missed you. Where've you been?"

Holly still reeling over the paintings greeted him a little less lovingly, but she hugged him just the same and told him how much she missed him.

After being reacquainted with the girls, Rollie asked Jenna to come outside to talk. She hesitated. She really had no desire to get too close to him ever again. Their former closeness and then their sudden separation had almost killed her once already, she might not be so lucky the next time around. After a little more persuasion, she agreed to talk on the front porch.

"Gees you've lost some weight, Jen," he said.

"Yeah, it's called being so stressed out, Rollie," she answered coyly.

"So how've you been? How's Doug?"

"I've been alright Rollie, but Doug, not so good." She didn't dare mention the violence or abuse for fear that he would have a go at her. She still had no tolerance for anyone raising their voice or being nasty to her. "His illness is getting worse. His liver is now causing other complications in his body."

"Fuck! That's not good. Is there anything they can do?"

"Nope. Well, they can, but he won't let them. Listen, I'd actually rather not talk about Doug. What's been happening in your world?"

"Not much really. Same old same old," he said. "Oh, that and I moved out from Candice again. I'm done with her for good. I'm living in the city with James now."

"Really? That's not good."

"Yeah, it is good actually. You going to the run tomorrow?" "Ummm, I'm not sure. I did think about it."

"Come on, come to it. You'll have a ball. Please, come? It's gonna be huge."

She looked into his pleading eyes and agreed. "Okay. I'll go."

Jenna tossed and turned all night long. The smell of Rollie's aftershave lingered on her skin and his words played on loop through her mind. The morning couldn't arrive quickly enough for her. She wanted to see him again. She wanted to be near him and to hear his voice. She didn't know exactly why, but she missed him ever so much. She knew she was heading down a dangerous path, but she promised herself it would be only for that one day, then she would stop herself again. Rollie must have felt the same way. At around eleven o'clock her mobile rang. It was Emily telling her Rollie wanted her to hurry up and come up there. He asked her to call in the shops and get his cigarettes for him. Jenna giggled, commenting that not much had changed.

When she arrived at the clubhouse there were cars, bikes and people everywhere. She wondered how she would find him in that crowd. She went inside, hugging her friends as she entered. She found Emily down the back harassing one of the members.

"I've got his smokes, Em. Where is he?"

Emily looked around and started yelling. "There he is Mumski, he's standing over there." She said, pointing to the middle of the room. Then, just as if time and sound stood still, he turned to look directly at Jenna. His face lit up like a lantern and a smile spilt out across his lips. He raised his huge arm and motioned for her to come to him. She fought her way through the crowd and stood beside him, trying to hand him his cigarettes. He brushed by the smokes dropping instead to hug her. He squeezed her tightly and welcomed her. "I'm so glad you're here, Jen," he said before standing back up tall.

"I'm glad to be here, Rollie," she said smiling back.

The rest of the day and then into the night becomes rather perplexing for Jenna. For some reason, Rollie didn't go on the ride, preferring instead to stay back at the clubhouse. She wondered why he had so desperately wanted her to come if he wasn't even riding. Then the after party became even more confusing. The first half of the night was like every other party in the clubhouse; great conversation, good booze, extraordinary entertainment and the company of many cherished friends. Rollie periodically came over to Jenna on the leather sofa and spoke to her, but being the gracious host he usually was, he had to mingle with all the other guests also. Jenna knew that and it hadn't bothered her in the slightest. But as the night grew on, Doug became aggravated and annoyed at Jenna, accusing her of ignoring him and treating him like shit. Jenna looked at Emily wondering what she had done wrong. After all, she hadn't really moved off the couch and she only spoke to people who came and spoke to her. As Doug's aggression grew, Jenna's nerves once again began to play havoc with her mind. She knew exactly what was in store for her when she got home. Hours and hours of torment and abuse, so once she watched him start to yell and carry on, she knew she had to leave before he got himself escorted out of there. The clubhouse was no place for that kind of absurd behaviour. Jenna insisted Emily stay and enjoy the rest of the night. She asked Rollie to keep a watchful eye on her. He agreed to do it but got a little upset that she was leaving.

"Are you really going now? It's only early," he complained.

"I know, Rollie, but I've really got to go," she said, as one of the young guys come rushing over spurting off at the mouth about Doug's behaviour.

Rollie looked at Jenna questioningly. "Are you right to go home, Jen?"

"Yes, Rollie. I'll be fine," she said, glaring at the young guy.

"If he lays one hand on you, Mumski, you call me and I'll come kill that cunt," she yelled. "I hate that prick."

"Emily, stop it! It's all good. Now I've got to go."

Rollie leaned down wrapped his arms around her and reminded her he was there if she needed him. He kissed her gently on the cheek and said, "Goodnight."

The remainder of the night became a nightmare for Jenna as she endured Doug's endless abuse. In between his bouts of anger she would sneakily call Emily's phone and check on her.

She felt bad leaving Emily there on her own considering she was supposed to be her guest.

Each time she called her, she reminded her to be on her best behaviour because Rollie was watching her. Behaving for Emily had always been a challenge. She liked sex, drugs and men way too much for Jenna's liking, but she was a grown woman now at almost twenty-three. Twenty-three with the intelligence of a two-year-old on a generous day would be the result that came from the decision of Jenna to leave Emily at that party. Emily somehow managed to convince Rollie that Doug might come and harm her throughout the night if she went back to her own place. Rollie in his infinite wisdom decided to let her stay with him at his place in the city.

Now if you listen to his version, he was doing it for Jenna, he was doing exactly what she'd asked him to do; protect Emily. But if you listen to Emily's story the ending goes quite a lot different. This is a part of the story that Jenna can never tell because she was not there and still to this day does not know what actually happened. The only thing she knows for sure is how angry she was about Rollie taking Emily home with him under any circumstances. She was angry at Emily for instigating the whole idea and fronted her with it.

"What the hell, Emily? Why did you stay at Rollie's place?" she asked.

"Because I can," she said, sheepishly.

"What do you mean because you can? You shouldn't be staying at men's houses, Emily. It's totally inappropriate."

"Oh shut the fuck up would you," she said. "I'm glad I stayed there because now I have him in a position where he's gonna have to do what I want."

"What the fuck, Emily? What the fuck is that supposed to mean? What drugs are you on?"

"None yet, but I will be when Rollie gets them for me."

'Ah, so that's what all this is about? You think he's gonna get you drugs? Well, I'm telling you, you smart ass manipulative little fuck. If he gets you anything I'll be ringing Candice. She can sort you out," she said, as she slammed down the phone.

Emily then rang Rollie and tried to dob. Rollie then tried to ring Jenna, over and over again. Jenna would stare at the phone screen and curse. "Fuck you, Rollie. Fuck you and everything about you. It's one bullshit thing after another with you. Stop calling me," she screamed. Eventually, he did stop trying to ring her and eventually sent her a text message instead.

"Please answer your phone, Jenna." It said. Jenna ignored it.

Then the next one read: "I don't know what that bitch told you, but I didn't touch her." Jenna ignored it.

After several more unanswered texts, Rollie lost his patience and called Doug's phone.

"You tell Jenna to answer her fucking phone!" he yelled.

"Mate, you know her better than that. You know what she's like, you can't tell her nothing. If she don't want to answer you, she's not gonna. Why? What's going on?"

"I don't know exactly. All I can make out is that she thinks I fucked that skank, Emily."

Doug erupted in laughter, "I certainly hope you didn't mate, she's full of fucking herpes."

"I didn't fucking touch her. Can you tell Jenna that? Just do your best to get her to call me when she calms down."

Jenna never did call Rollie over that incident, instead she reverted back to the way things were before the party.

As the date of the big bike show began to close in, Jenna began to feel a little anxious. She hadn't felt that way in the longest time and began to wonder why. She had already promised Sarah and the new member Michael that she would be there. They'd made her promise, and the one thing she wouldn't do is break one of those. As the afternoon commenced the butterflies began to settle. The record breaking crowds gave her a sense of peace. Even if Rollie did turn up, she would have little to no chance of running into him anyway. The show was a wonderful event. Bikes and stalls everywhere, people smiling, chatting and walking around in the warmth of the sun. It really was an amazing day, but as the afternoon came to a close, Jenna and the girls made their way back to the club tent. She and Michael stood off to the side, overlooking the water as they chatted about the party a few weeks before. Then as though someone clear ran a knife through her, she had the urge to turn around and run. Her legs were stuck, they wouldn't even move an inch. The anxiety she had suffered all that time ago, took over her. Her heart began to race and her breathing became short and shallow. She looked at Michael who kept chatting as though nothing were wrong. She held her gut and spun around in a rush. Staring straight at her, as he spoke to Doug, was Rollie. Standing beside him was another guy and a rough looking woman, with her breasts half hanging out of her super low cut top. She seemed to be all over Rollie. Jenna just glared.

"I. I've got to go, Michael."

"What's wrong bub? You look like ya seen a ghost," he said, taking hold of her elbow.

"I'm fine, buddy, seriously. I just need to go."

"Alrighty, well give us a hug and I'll see ya next week then, hey? Don't forget to ring me on Monday."

"I won't," she said leaning in to hug him.

She made her way back under the tent, grabbed her handbag and hugged Sarah goodbye. She told Holly and Hannah to go tell Doug she was leaving. When they returned, Jenna hugged each of the members and told them she would see them soon. As she got to where Rollie was sitting she realised she could not leave without saying goodbye to him. That would have been a massive sign of disrespect and the other members would have thought it extremely rude. Jenna adjusted her top, took a deep breath and tried desperately not to make eye contact with him.

"I'm going now, bye Rollie,' she said, her voice quivering.

Rollie looked at her with the same familiar anguish in his eyes. "You going already?"

"Yep."

"Okay then, bye, Jenna. Take care hey."

Jenna stormed away without looking back, knowing she had hurt him. She knew it must have ripped his heart out for her to hug every single person under that tent besides him. But she didn't care. She remembered the incident with Emily at the clubhouse and now this. She hoped her actions had hurt him. She wanted to hurt him. For the first time ever, she truly wished she could have stabbed him right through the heart. She wanted him to feel her pain. He had hurt her so deeply for so many years and yet for him, life just went on. He obviously hadn't lost any sleep over the incidents because here he was with another woman; another woman who was also not his wife. Obviously she had been wrong about him. It wasn't his moral commitment to his wife and to Doug that had stopped him from declaring this supposed undying love her.

For the very first time, she was forced to accept that everyone had been totally deluded about his feelings for her. He hadn't cared about her at all. He perhaps just wanted to have some entertainment on the side. But whatever it was, she should have known better than to expect anything better than behaviour like this from a bikie.

In spite of his misgivings, he was never far from her thoughts and it didn't take long for her to notice his absence. She no longer ran into him at random places, the calls between the two of them had ceased and the majority of people that she mixed with stopped talking about him in front of her. If she ever hinted at where he was, people would just fob off her questions. She began to wonder what was going on. Had she really hurt him so badly that he now chose to avoid her completely? Then one night as she spoke to one of her friends on the phone, she blurted out a question.

"Tash, have you heard anything about Rollie?"

"I thought the subject of him with you was closed?" she said.

"Well, it is, usually. It's just that no one has mentioned one word about him for months. I might not want to see him, but I do need to know that he's okay."

"I don't know if I'm allowed to say anything. Leave it with me and I'll speak to Mark tonight."

Over the next few nights, the fretful sleeps attacked Jenna like a disease. All the rumours she'd heard about Rollie slipping into drug addiction began playing out like scenes from movies. She had never taken those rumours as anything other than just that; rumours. Rollie hated drugs as much as she did, so she knew it was merely the rumour mill running at full steam. That is, right up until one particular night, she dreamt she had walked the streets of the city looking for him. A vagrant appeared from nowhere and approached her. In a thick drunken slur, he asked her if she was looking for Rollie. Jenna stood there, shivering, just staring at the homeless man. He pointed his long bony finger in the direction of a dilapidated building with a sign above the door, which read, "No-one loves you? We do!" Jenna walked disorientated towards the building. She placed her hand on the putrid metal handle and pushed. The door wouldn't open. She pushed it again. Still nothing. She dropped to her knees and began to weep. She raised her head as three apparitions appeared. "Don't quit now, you're almost there," they said in unison. They all pushed the door together and it flung opened. Jenna turned to thank them but they were gone. She climbed the wooden stairs, searching floor after floor until she found him. Rollie roamed around a clinic full of lost souls. His head hung low as he wandered around aimlessly in a dark green surgical gown which hung from his skeletal frame. His once sparkling eyes had sunk into his head, his lips had turned grey and he looked at her as though she were a stranger. When she spoke to him, he looked right through her. Not an ounce of recognition registered in his face. Jenna bolted upright in bed almost choking on her tears. She dried her face, settled her breathing and called Tasha at two twenty-eight in the morning.

"I'm so sorry Tash, but have you heard anything?" she blurted out.

"Jen, it's after two in the morning. Can't this wait till the sun comes up?" she mumbled.

"No. no, it can't. I can't do this anymore. I can't handle the nightmares. I can't handle not knowing if he's okay. Tell me what you know. If you love me, you'll tell me."

"Alright," she said, "Let me get out of bed so I don't wake Mark up."

The next few minutes dragged on like hours. When Tasha finally came back to the phone, Jenna wished she hadn't rung her.

"He's gone, Jen."

"What do you mean he's gone?" she asked as her emotions threatened to choke her. "Is he dead?"

"No," she laughed, "He's not dead. He's left the country. He doesn't live here anymore." "What? What? Are you fucking nuts? Of course, he lives here."

"Nope. He doesn't. He's gone to live in Asia."

"Asia? Why would he go to Asia? Seriously, stop fucking around Tash. Where is he?"

"Jenna, listen to me. He is gone!"

Only his death could have shocked her more than that statement from Tasha. Rollie, who had always shared his dreams with her, had never mentioned anything about travelling to Asia, let alone living there.

The very next morning, Jenna begged Doug to ask around and find out what was going on. After their usual argument about her letting Rollie go, he eventually agreed. As it turned out, Rollie was due back in the country for a visit in two weeks' time. In two weeks' time, it would be his birthday. Jenna knew exactly what to do. She went and brought a bottle of his favourite aftershave and tied it off with a bow. She arranged for Doug to take it to him on the night of his arrival back in the country. But when the night arrived, Doug insisted she go with him to the clubhouse while he spoke to Rollie. When they arrived, he refused to take the gift inside.

"I aint giving him shit. Come in and give it to him yourself if you want him to have it," he said.

"I'm not going in, Doug. I can't. Can't you just do this for me?"

"Nope! Fuck you. Wait here then."

Doug went inside the clubhouse emerging about thirty minutes later. Walking out behind him was Rollie. Jenna's heart skipped a beat. He approached the car and looked inside.

"Hey, Jenna, how's things?"

Jenna jumped out of the car and wrapped her arms around his neck. "Don't you hey Jenna me! Where the fuck have you been? What the hell is going on? What's this shit about you living in Asia? Rollie what the actual fuck?" she rambled, not allowing him to answer.

"It's okay, Jenna. I'll be living part time there and part time here. It's something I've got to do."

"But, but, how will I know you're okay? How can I see you?"

"Well, you don't want to see me anyway. So why now? I'll give you my number for over there. That way if you want me you can call me."

"Don't you ever do anything like this ever again, Rollie! You could've been dead for all I knew. Don't you ever scare me like that again, EVER!"

Rollie flew in and out of the country on a semi-regular basis from that time on. With the distance now between them, his strength and resistance against Jenna grew, but so did her need for him. Things were beginning to make sense to her now. All the things Carmen, the psychologist, had told her, the things everybody else had told her and the things she had been blocking were finally sinking in. Rollie really had loved her, and she, in return had hurt him beyond belief. The only remaining confusion she had was why he had never confessed his true feelings for her, to her. She had never expected him to be a knight in shining armour or to ride in on his white stallion and save her, but she had expected more of a gallant behaviour from a man with his status. She knew he was a man of honour, but what about the honour her owed her? Did that mean nothing? Did he truly not care what she suffered because of him? As always she rationalized it to herself. Maybe he had not been able to grasp the concept that she was a lady? A lady who was strictly guided by her moral compass and as such, she demanded to be treated that way. It was not in her nature to pursue a man. Maybe Rollie had never received that message? Maybe he would never would?

As the pages on the calendar began to turn, and without a single word from Rollie, Jenna once again began to doubt her rationale. She wondered why she had bothered to listen to others, especially because she had already learnt that people only ever said what they wanted you to know, or what they thought someone wanted to hear. All she knew for certain was that she could not return to her place of silence. Instead, she widened her social network and began mingling a lot more often with her friends. One Thursday evening, Charlotte, one of her best friends called her.

"Hey, lovely, what's happening?" she asked. "Are you going to the Fearsome Devils party on Saturday night?"

"I'm not sure. Are you?"

"Yeah, I'm thinking about it. Max asked me to go."

"Everyone is talking about. You should go, it'll be a great night." Jenna said.

"Make a deal with you. I'll go if you go."

"Okay, deal. I'll find out if Tash, Michelle and Nelly are going, and if they are, I'm in too. It's not like I have to worry about running into Rollie."

"Yeah, well that's true. It's a bit far to travel for a party," she laughed. "I can't wait. This is gonna be awesome," she yelled with excitement.

Jenna and Charlotte went shopping together to buy new outfits and shoes for the party. Charlotte brought a little black dress with a netted tutu attached at the waist and a pair of silver strappy sandals. Jenna brought a new pair of tight fitting jeans, a black top with a low scooped back and finished it off with a pair of eight-inch heels. She loved to wear heels to the clubhouse. They made her feel tall, nowhere near as tall as the men, but taller than a child to say the least.

As the morning of the party arrived, Jenna struggled to wake. Her body felt as though it were weighted down like a ship in the harbor. She lay in her bed wondering why she felt this way. She had no fever, no cough, no sick feeling, and nothing else to complain about. She decided it had to be a case of the, "Oh, I don't want to do this today's" so she forced herself up and ploughed on forward with her day. At nine fifteen that night, Charlotte arrived to collect her for the party. The same feeling swamped her, but she knew she couldn't let the girls down.

They had all prepared for this party for days in advance, so on she went. As the girls entered the bustling clubhouse, Jenna was stopped by Sarah who wanted to have a chat. Her friend circle moved on without her, made their way to the bar and got themselves some drinks. Once she wound up her conversation with Sarah, she made her way over to the bar to get her own drink, then joined her friends sitting on the leather couch. The party was a hit. So many happy people everywhere, having such a good time. It didn't take long for her mood to change and she began to thoroughly enjoy the evening.

"Next round is on me," she said, making her way over to the bar. As she stood there chatting and laughing with the bartender, she could feel a presence behind her. She spun around quickly and said.

"Can you help me carry these, please, Nel?" her mouthed dropped open. "Oh ooops. I. I'm sorry, Rollie. I thought you were one of the girls," she said.

Rollie laughed at her. "It's all good. How've you been, Jenna?"

"I'm good," she mumbled. "But…. What are you doing here?" she asked, staring at him blankly.

"Oh well, sorry about that. Last I knew this was my clubhouse. I can leave if you like?" he asked, teasingly.

"No, no. It's me who's sorry. I didn't mean it like that. I didn't expect to see you here," she said, breaking out into a laugh. "When did you get home? How long will you be here?"

He pulled her in hugging her tightly while he smelt the scent of her hair. "It's so good to see you, Jen."

As she held him tight enjoying his embrace, she noticed out of the corner of her eye that the girls she had come with were getting loud and obnoxious. She stood up straight and watched them closely as Rollie began to answer her questions. The girls' behaviour continued to escalate. As they were her guests, she knew they were her responsibility. So without a second thought and to protect her reputation, she marched towards them leaving Rollie standing there with a stunned look upon his face.

"Charlotte, get your bloody legs out from behind Michelle's head, you've got a dress on. And, Michelle, pull your frigging top up. They've already paid for entertainment thanks," she yelled, as she approached the group of intoxicated women. The girls laughed and continued to entertain themselves.

Jenna looked across to the bar as she realised what she'd done. She looked around for Rollie, but he was gone. She felt so guilty for cutting him off mid-sentence. All she could do was sit and wait for him to reappear. But when he did reemerge, he looked angry. Jenna hesitated, not wanting to approach him while he was mad. He looked at her, screwed up his face, shook his head and yelled at the top of his voice.

"I'm leaving. I'm going to the strip club. Who's coming?"

Several of his brothers cheered as they left the clubhouse together.

Well, so much for apologizing and trying to make it up to him, she thought. Maybe she had put too much importance on herself? Maybe he hadn't really wanted to see her anyway? Either way, Rollie once again left the country a few days later without uttering so much as a single goodbye to her. Jenna had no choice other than to accept it for exactly what it was and that's how she learnt to use his saying, "It is what it is," to her advantage.

Jennifer Brockie

Chapter Ten

It's written in the stars: The Tarot Reading

Around a week after Rollie left the country, a phone call came through that made Jenna feel a little better.

"Hello there, lovely. It's me, Stan. What are you up to today?"

"Stan? Rollie's cousin, Stan?"

"The one and only."

"Oh, hey, Stan. How are you going?"

"I'm fine and dandy. So, what's happening? Are you going to be home today?"

"I certainly am. Why? What's up?"

"I thought me and Collette might come and see your lovely self."

"That'll be great," Jenna said, giggling. "What time were you thinking?"

"How about now?"

"Yep. Sounds great to me."

"Put the jug on, we're on our way."

Jenna disconnected the call with a smile on her face. She decided to make a batch of scones, one of Stan's favourite treats. Even though she had only met him a few times before, she really liked him. He felt familiar to her. Self-confidence and pride oozed from him. On their very first face to face meeting, Stan told Jenna so much about his and Rollie's childhood that she felt like she had known them both their entire lives. Stan explained the family connection and who was who within the family. He also relived Rollie's mother's death and the impact it had on all of them, especially the impact it had on Rollie. From all accounts, of Stan's version of events, their entire family were exceptionally tight-knit. The two boys as teenagers had been inseparable and were as troublesome as each other. Stan idolized Rollie, but Rollie's lifestyle was not appropriate for what Stan had in mind for his own future with his wife and children. Jenna thought back to the day that Stan had told her it was okay to love Rollie, but to be careful she didn't get hurt. He had told her to always remember to love him from a distance, but not to ever put herself in a place where Rollie could have to tread on her. "Remember this, Jenna: he is a bikie above and beyond everything else that he is." Jenna had screwed up her face and laughed when Stan told her that. She rationalized that statement to herself believing that Stan simply had no idea of what the lifestyle entailed, or how much Rollie had grown as a person. Little did she know, but in time she would find out, Stan's recommendation would be exactly what she needed to do in order for her to live her life.

Just as she pulled the scones out of the oven her phone rang again.

"Sorry, Jenna, but something came up with Josh at school. Can you possibly come down here and we'll meet for lunch instead?" Stan asked.

"Of course. Is Josh okay?"

"Yeah, he's fine, just a bit of boy mischief. Do you want to meet at Kev's Diner? He has the best chicken."

"Okay. No problem. Give me an hour and a half and I'll see you then."

Jenna rolled her eyes and giggled. He is so much more like Rollie than even he could imagine, she thought, as she changed into a dress and heels, fixed her face with light day make-up and sprayed herself with her favourite perfume.

When she arrived down the coast, she found a perfect parking space right around the corner from where she was meant to be. When she got out of the car, she realised she had parked directly in front of a spiritual healing store. Not usually drawn to things like that, she found herself intrigued by what was inside the windows covered with the heavy black velvet curtains. She knew she had somewhere else she had to be, so she walked on by and went to check in the diner for Stan and Collette. Since they hadn't arrived yet, she decided to go back and take a look inside the quaint little store. As she opened the heavy glass entrance door, a thick scent of incense wafted to her nose. Surrounding the store were waist high, glass cabinets filled with the most beautiful crystals, rocks, and stunning jewellery made from both silver and gold and finished off with lovely crystals. She was immediately drawn to a pink quartz bracelet with a tag attached to it which read: Wear pink quartz every day and all forms of love will flow straight to you. Jenna picked it up and rolled the beads between her fingers. Sounds of the ocean filled the air via the music being played in the back room of the building. A water fountain flowed in sync with the music from its position on the counter. Jenna became startled as a woman emerged from behind a purple curtain and greeted her.

"Welcome, my friend," she said, with a Russian accent.

Jenna gave her the once over, checking out the gypsy ensemble this woman had put together. A long red velvet skirt, an off the shoulder white peasant shirt, black ankle boots, a thick silver chain belly belt that jangled when she walked, a matching red bandana tied around her long black locks and massive silver hoop earrings to set it off. She couldn't help but think how stereotypical the outfit was.

"Are you here for a reading?" the woman asked.

"Oh no. I was just looking, thank you," Jenna answered.

"I think you should have a reading," she said, "There is something you need to hear."

"I couldn't have a reading even if I wanted to, I have a lunch engagement and I'm already late, but thank you anyway."

"You will be back. I'll wait here until you return," she said.

Jenna tipped over a stand of wellbeing cards as she hastily backed away towards the door. She apologized and left.

Over lunch, Jenna told Stan about her encounter with the strange lady. He laughed at her and told her not to waste her money.

"They're all a scam," Collette said. "I had a clairvoyant party once and the so called psychic got every single persons info wrong," she laughed.

"I'm not really into it too much either now. I haven't been since I studied necromancy and divination in uni. It kind of scares me," she said. "Give me your hand," Stan said, reaching out to take Jenna's hand in his. "I'll give you a reading for free. I can see travel. I can see money. I can see love and I can see," he paused. "You will still go see that fraud the minute you leave here," he added, laughing.

"I'm not going to see her, Stan. So shut up!" Jenna answered, laughing back at him.

Stan was right about one thing though, the chicken at Kev's diner was amazing. Jenna ordered chicken fettuccini and salad. When the plate came out, overflowing with beer battered chips, fresh garden salad and her chicken, she mentioned how convenient it would have been if Rollie were here. He could finish the food on her plate relieving her of the embarrassment of all the food she always left behind. After sharing a bottle of sparkling white wine and good quality conversation, Jenna decided she really better make a dash for home before the dark grey clouds above decided to open up. Jenna hugged them both and headed off around the corner.

As she made her way back to her car, she couldn't help but notice the gypsy woman standing in the doorway of the spiritual healing store. She tried not to make eye contact with her. She opened the door to her car and threw her handbag on the front seat. She watched as the gypsy woman went back inside the store and shut the door. Jenna sat in the driver's seat, placed the keys in the ignition then looked once more towards the store.

"Ummm, excuse me, how much would a reading be if I decided to have one?" Jenna asked, as she leaned in through the store door.

"It's $70.00 for half an hour, but, I think it's something you should have. Understand?" the woman said.

Jenna went all the way through the door, before following the gypsy woman to a table in a darkened room at the back of the store.

She took a seat in a large wooden chair with claws for arms. The table was covered in purple velvet with tiny silver suns and moons all over the top. A mood lamp threw off soft colours around the room. She nervously placed her hands in lap and began to wonder why she had even entered. The gypsy shuffled a deck of beautiful tarot cards. She closed her eyes and began to say some kind of chant in her native tongue. Then her eyes shot open staring directly at Jenna. "Divide the deck into three stacks," she said, placing the cards in front of her. "Is there anything you want to ask the cards?"

"Ummm, no. I don't even know why I'm here really."

"You are here because you need to be here. Understand? Are you sure you don't have any questions about anything or anyone you would like to know about?"

"No. just tell me what you see," Jenna said, becoming more doubtful and apprehensive with each minute that passed.

"There is someone you want to ask about isn't there?" the gypsy said, leaning in closer to her. "You want to know where he is, don't you."

"No. really, I don't. Who? I just thought it would be fun to see what you could see, and if any of what you tell me is true."

"Ah a sceptic," she said, "We shall see. You won't be a sceptic for long, Jen. Understand?"

"Ummm, how did you know my name?" Jenna asked, her heart skipping a beat.

"Mirela knows all. I know you worry about your children. There is no need to worry for your children, they will be alright. Understand? They may have some struggles in their lives, but they will work it out. I know you worry about money. There is no need to worry about money. You will be wealthy beyond your dreams if you stop sabotaging yourself and your destiny. Understand?"

"Do you mean I should finish writing the book?"

"Write all the books. No, you don't worry. The books will write themselves. Understand?" she said, in her predominantly Russian tongue. "Jenna you don't need to worry about him. He will be okay."

"Who? Doug?"

"He will be okay too. Don't worry about his sickness. He will be alright. But the one I talk of is the one who is separated from you by water. Lots and lots of water. It's not just the water that separates you either," Mirela said, studying the tarot card she held in both hands, "It's something more. It's a shadow, a dark vengeful shadow that controls and threatens to destroy you both. Understand?"

Jenna shuffled in her chair as her hands became cold and clammy. "What shadow? Who are we talking about? You're starting to frighten me. Maybe I should just go," she added rising from her seat.

"No! You sit!" the gypsy yelled. "You need to hear this. You sit."

She sat back down.

"The one you seek is in danger. He is in danger of himself. He is somewhere else, separated by oceans of water. He made this choice to set you free. You are a naïve girl, Jenna. You can sometimes be selfish. Understand? You worry for your hurt, but you don't think of this man's hurt. He gave you time, but you did not listen. He gave you love, but you resisted. You hurt this man with more pain than any other pain he has ever felt before. You made him suffer for your ignorance. He thought you understood his intentions and that you rejected him. Understand?"

"Oh my God, are you talking about, Rollie?"

"Yes. The man you almost destroyed. I don't understand his position of power. He might be army? He might be big business man? I can't see what he is, but he is very, very powerful man. Very, very dangerous man. A man many men fear. Understand?" she asked, slipping between her English and native tongue.

Jenna stared straight through the gypsy. There was no way in hell she was going to explain to a stranger that Rollie was a bikie. So instead she sat.

"You are about to receive monies. Monies from a man, not your father but like your father. Before he passes over the claws of an evil manipulator will rip the heart and soul out of your family. She will lead the weaker one behind her. They will steal most of yours and your only true sister's inheritance. You can't stop such evil. Not evil like what's in her, she was born that way. She was born from filth and lies. That evil will suffer when it least expects it. Everything that meant anything will be snatched away from her when she least expects it. You will never forgive either of the evil half-sister's their sins. And, you shouldn't, they can never be trusted. They will always only ever think of their own. Understand?" Jenna gulped hard in disbelief. How could this stranger know any of this information? What she had just described about the two daughters of her mother, were exactly correct. Jenna had no need to heed her warning though because as far as she was concerned she only had one sister left. The only other one she had, had passed away many years before. And, the two the gypsy woman spoke of were neither her blood nor her kin. They meant absolutely nothing to her.

"The man from over the water will always be in your life, Jenna, even if you don't want him to be. He will always watch out for you and he will always help you. He will help you with a new business venture sometime in the very near future. You will have many times you will try and cut him off, but I will tell you, it will never happen. He is a part of you, the same as you are a part of him. He was sent to you by something bigger than all of us. He was sent to find you. He has done that now. He will always be with you. If not in body, than in spirit. Ponyat'? The shadow, the selfish, childlike girl he once married is the one for you to watch out for. She will unleash a world of trouble for you. She will try to destroy you with the evil she has inside. She will lie, cheat and plead her nevinnost', or how you say, her innocence, as she recruits whoever she can to destroy you. Understand? She knows you stole her husband's heart, so she now she curses you. She blames you for him falling out of love with her. She knows that it is only you he will change for. It is only you he would deystvitel'no, sorry, truly share himself with. Understand? Be careful, Jenna, she is bad, bad character. She hates you. Understand? She does what she needs to get what she wants. And one of those things is to destroy you. But it will not happen unless you let it. Ponyat', sorry, understand?"

Jenna looked at the clock. The reading had gone on for way over an hour.

"Ummm excuse me, Mirela, its way past the time."

"No. You stay. You don't pay extra. You need to hear this. Many years will pass before this man will understand this bond you share with him. You both sometimes see this bond as a curse. But, it is not a curse. Curses come in the shape of evil. This bond you two have is not evil. The bond you share with this man is made of something stronger, much stronger. It is made of the most pure emotion known to man.....love!" she exclaimed. "He will force himself to suffer over and over again until eventually he will learn, hc is no more a match for this challenge than you are. The destiny for both of you ends

213

together. Together you would be rulers; a king and his queen. Understand?"

Jenna sprung out of the chair, pulled her handbag up onto the table and rifled through her purse. She pulled the seventy dollars out, placed it in the gypsy woman's hand and ran out of the store.

As she pulled her car away from the gutter the heavens opened up and pelted down on the windscreen. The rain had always been a welcomed visitor to her; it masked the storm she had brewing inside. She needed it today to mask the horror of what she'd just heard. She wished she had of listened to Stan, she wished she had just left directly for home straight after lunch. The things the gypsy woman had said to her mulled around in her mind, especially the things about the shadow. Jenna thought of her friendship with Candice and wondered how it had become so bitter. She recalled the phone call she received from Candice the night she found the letter she had sent to Rollie. Jenna tried to explain to Candice that the letter was not in any way a love letter, but instead a letter expressing her disappointment in how things had ended and letting him know how important he was to her and her family. Candice would have none of that. Instead, she cursed and screeched like a banshee, making threats and ordering Jenna to never contact her husband ever again. Jenna asked Candice why the relationship she shared with Rollie was any more a love affair than the relationship she shared with Ivan, considering it was those two who people suspected were actually having an affair.

Jenna told Candice for the millionth time over that she had never had an affair and had no intention of starting to have one now. She could not understand how such a beautiful well-mannered young woman had turned into such a conniving, manipulative, foul mouthed person. Her thoughts quickly became untangled as a blue Ford sedan swerved into her lane forcing her to slam on her brakes, sending her car into a spin up the edge of the highway. As she pulled her car to a stop the guy from the blue Ford sedan rushed over and opened her door.

"I'm so sorry. I didn't see you there. Are you okay?" he asked.

"Yes, I'm fine thanks. It was just as much my fault. I wasn't watching."

"No, it was all my fault. Like I said, I'm really sorry. Look at you, you're shaking like a leaf. Do you want me to call someone?"

"No. I'll be fine. I'll just sit here a sec and I'll be right."

"Well, I'll stay with you until you calm down."

By the time the other driver walked away, Jenna had completely settled down and had forgotten most of what she had been thinking. She drove the rest of the way home thinking about how there really were some decent people left in the world.

The following Thursday afternoon, Stan called Jenna and invited her and Doug out to dinner. After some resistance and vaguely explaining how she now had very little to do with Doug, she decided she would go anyway. They finally agreed on a local steak house. On their arrival, Stan insisted Jenna tell him everything the psychic had told her.

"What makes you think I saw the psychic, Stan?"

"Because you did. I know you did. Come on tell me what she said. Jenna erupted with laughter. "Okay, I did see her. She told me to beware of a nosy guy who lives on the coast. A guy who'll want to know everything the psychic told me." Stan playfully dug his elbow into her ribs. "Come on. Tell us. What did she say? Did she look like a witch?"

"Na, she looked like an old fashioned gypsy actually. She was really freaky. I had to really listen to what she was saying. I think she was Russian or Bulgarian or something," she said, as the waitress approached the table.

"Hi guys, are you ready to order yet or do you need a few more minutes?" she asked.

"I know what I'm having," Stan said. "I'll have the creamy garlic prawns for my entrée, then I'll have the rib eye fillet, stuffed baked potato and salad thanks. What did you want, my love?" he asked Collette.

The waitress took the other orders then scuttled away like a busy little beetle.

"So, come on, out with it. Stop being such a holdout, Jenna."

"My God you're persistent, Stan!"

"I know. That's why you'll tell me. That way I'll finally shut up," he laughed. "Well, I guess that's true. You know, she was pretty good actually. If you ever want to see a psychic, Collette, she would be the one to see. She even knew my name without me even telling her."

"Really?" Collette asked, "Was your wallet open or something? Did she see your licence maybe?"

"Nope. I had nothing out of my bag at the time. It was really freaky."

"Yeah, you already said that," Stan said. "Now come on, out with it."

"Wow! Hold your horses. I'm getting to it. She told me just about everything that has been happening in my life. She told me that all my children would be fine. She said they would grow up and be happy healthy people."

"I could've told you that for free," Stan said, "You've got great kids. Of course, they're going to be okay. What else did she say?"

"I'm getting to it Stanley, so stop talking and let me tell you," she giggled. "She also knew all about my stepfather and that he was going to die. She told me to beware of two of my sisters. She told me that they were going to steal all his cash while he's still alive so there would be nothing much left in his will. And, I can tell you, I'm pretty sure she was spot on with that one because we think they're already doing that now."

"Fuck! Really? What can you do to stop them?"

"Absolutely nothing. They have power of attorney over his estate. Do you want to know the rest of the reading or are you happy now?"

'No. I want to know the rest. What else did she say?"

"She knew all about my writing and my books. She told me not to stress over them as they would be really successful. She told me I would be quite comfortable financially and that I would have a great life."

"What? So that's it? Nothing about me?" Stan asked.

"Why would she mention you, Stan?" she asked, laughing.

"Because I'm special. Na, I'm just kidding. Did she say anything about Rollie?"

Jenna wriggled in her seat. "No. Why would she say anything about Rollie?"

"Oh, I don't know. I just thought she might've mentioned him. Oh well, happy days then," he said, as he began to eat his dinner.

Jenna thought about what she had just done and began to feel guilty. She knew she had just lied to Stan about the reading. She justified her little white lie by thinking she hadn't actually lied, she had just left out a major part of it. There was no way she could share with Stan, let alone anyone else, what the gypsy had told her about Rollie. She felt weird about all that the old woman had said to her. She still needed time to think about what everything had meant. Besides, she still had no idea what to make of that part of the reading. How does one make sense out of constantly being told that the person she had always viewed as her best friend really was in love with her? Jenna had reviewed her feelings for Rollie over and over again for the last few years. But no matter what conclusion she came up with, something always shot her theory down in flames. Besides, on top of the confusion with Rollie, Jenna's ego was still reeling from the sting delivered to her by the old gypsy woman. How dare she call her selfish? The one thing she had never viewed herself as being was selfish. In actual fact, she was the exact opposite and she made sure of that. She shared and cared with everyone she knew and loved. How dare that woman have the audacity to say she hadn't cared about how all this drama had affected him? Of course she cared, but she was powerless to change it.

She sat and wondered how anyone, including the old woman, could even think she would ever deliberately hurt Rollie, especially considering he had never confessed to her exactly how he actually felt about her. He had told her a million times over that he had loved her but never once had he said he was in love with her.

Over the next few months, Jenna spent a lot of time with Stan and his wife Collette. She truly enjoyed his company. She felt an affectionate familiarity towards him. His presence somehow made the distance between her and Rollie seem a little less. He shared her opinion of Candice and understood Rollie and his eccentric ways. Not many people could actually do that. Some of the stories Stan shared with Jenna left her wondering if they were speaking of the same person at times. She sometimes wondered if he had Rollie confused with someone else. Her favourite stories about their adventures were the ones he shared that left her in stitches of laughter. Her all-time favourite was the one of Rollie being exceptionally drunk and hitting on a gangster's daughter. That story left her speechless. This was not a side to Rollie she had ever seen before and it made her wonder which side of him was fake. The one he had portrayed to her, or the one he portrayed to others. Needless to say, regardless of which side of his personality was his true side and which one was his fake side, there was one side to him she never had to doubt, the side that made him help her if she needed him.

Jennifer Brockie

Chapter Eleven

Fiascos

Despite the best efforts of two of Jenna's half-sisters to avoid it, three months after her stepfather passed away, she received a small amount of inheritance from what should have been a multi-million dollar estate. But, it would not come before a final act of vengeance.

Blinded by his alcoholism and resentment against all authority, her stepfather, heavily influenced by the two sisters, embarked on a mission to wreak havoc before his final curtain fell. Not unusual behaviour from such twisted souls, they together, set about unravelling the single remaining thread of family fabric; the baby of the family, Raven. Relying on Raven's fragile nature, the two sisters began to manipulate her thoughts and ideas regarding their father and tried to rationalize the charges brought against him for interfering with a minor. Only, they hadn't counted on the fact that Raven had first-hand knowledge of his behaviour and had witnessed his sickness with her own eyes. Jenna had disowned him the minute the charges were laid and refused to have any further connection with the man. Raven had followed suit. However, the promise to be left with a great deal of wealth saw the remaining two sisters defend and oblige their father, creating excuse after excuse for his pedophilic actions. Their bizarre exploits resulted in the four girls entering into a bitter battle resulting in restraining orders and an irreparable split within the family. Jenna and Raven went one way, the other two another.

As his death drew nigh and his mental state deteriorated further, Jenna's stepfather requested for her to come and see him. His desire to clear his conscience became an obsession and he relentlessly pursued the issue. Jenna vehemently refused the request resulting in her being disinherited. Raven stuck by Jenna's decision and also declined the request. The other two sisters, twisted with anger, then attempted to have Raven cut out of the will also, but with Raven being his natural daughter, he refused to do so. With resentment building in their hearts, the two sisters went about exerting their authority as the power of attorneys over his estate. Once they realised they could do absolutely nothing to change Jenna or Raven's minds, they began to sell off his assets and filtered the majority of the money out of the estate. By the time the will was read, the estate left Raven with a minimal amount of inheritance. Needless to say, the minute the money hit her account, she went directly to the bank and deposited exactly half of it into Jenna's account.

After the money cleared in her account and much deep consideration, Jenna decided she would like to open a swanky jazz bar in the inner city. A really hip and happening jazz bar which she wanted to name, The Blue Wasp Bar. She had been obsessed with Jazz music, particularly post-hop by John Coltrane and Miles Davis and Soul jazz by Jimmy McGriff, since her trip to New Orleans. She felt the atmosphere would be perfect for the Brisbane people who wanted to enjoy something a little different. Her intention was to make the place a theme inspired one. One in which the decor and the dress code fit in with the era. Her friend Charlotte was to be her partner and to share in all the costs and responsibilities. They had already lined up a few talented musicians waiting to take their place in the spotlight.

Jenna and Charlotte understood it would take more than cash, or class to set up a place like this. To be successful, they needed the backing from someone in the know. They needed someone who had connections within the industry. Jenna spoke to Rollie about it during one of his visits.

"You can't just open a place like that, Jenna. You'd make yourself a target for anyone to extort money from you. Especially with two women running it," he said.

"I know. That's why I'm asking you to help me."

"You know I'd do anything for you, but, I don't live here now. How do you want me to manage things from over there?"

"Can't you come back?

"You know I can't do that."

"Well, I don't know. I don't know what to do. Now Doug doesn't work and it doesn't look too good with his health, all the responsibility has been placed on me. I'm the one who has to make the money to keep this roof over mine and the girls head. You know how it works with writing. If you don't write, you don't get paid. And, I haven't been in the right frame to write for a while now, thanks to someone always upsetting me. If I lose this place, Rollie, I have nowhere else to go." "I know. Look, leave it with me and I'll see what I can do. I'll see if I can pull a few people together, we'll all go have lunch and talk about it properly before I fly out."

Jenna wrapped her arms around him and squeezed him tight. "Thank you, Rollie. You really are the best."

A few days later, Jenna received a call from Ivan.

"Hey, Jen, it's Ivan. How's things?"

"Ummm good thanks. How about you?"

"Yeah, I'm all good. Just calling to let you know that Rollie flew out this morning and asked me to give you a call and arrange a lunch so we can talk a little more about your business."

"Pardon?" she said, "What do you mean? When did he go? Where did he go? And will he be back for the meeting?"

"No. He had business he had to attend to so he asked me to do this for him. You know I'm a brother now, right?"

"Ummm, no. I didn't even know you were trying out to be a Fearsome Devil. Congratulations," she said. "Ivan, can I call you back? I have something I've got to do first, then I'll call you straight back."

"Yep, no worries. I'll wait for your call."

Jenna ended the call and dialled Rollie's number. The call went straight to voicemail. He must be still on the plane she thought. She waited an hour and tried again receiving the same result. By this time, her anger was brewing wildly. She couldn't understand why he had done this to her again. Why was it that every time he came home to Australia, he left without seeing her before he left? It was becoming a pattern she thought. She wondered why it was so hard for him to at least pick up his phone and say goodbye. She wondered why he bothered to be friends with her at all. He obviously didn't mind upsetting her. She decided to send him a private message through Facebook.

The message read: "What the hell, Rollie? What have you done this time? If you didn't want to help me all you had to do was say so. Why do you always do this? Why on God's earth would you set me up with Ivan of all people? Are you trying to set me up to fail? Have you forgotten he's Candice's best friend? I'm sure my business will do great with him at the helm. Do you want me to lose what little money I have? And while we're at it, why would you leave the country again without saying goodbye? You know what? Screw you! I've had it with you. Just forget I even asked. Just forget I ever existed. I really do hate you this time. You knew I needed you, but just like always, something else was more important. Don't call me or message me. I'm not doing this anymore. Have a great life OLD FRIEND!"

Jenna thought about all the things the psychic gypsy had told her the day of the reading, and how that reading, plus the opinions of others, had taught her to accept Rollie and his strange ways. But what was the point in being tolerant of his bizarre behaviour at the cost of her constantly being hurt and disappointed by the things he did? So much for the gypsy saying he would always help her. She began to think the only person Rollie wanted to help was himself. She also thought about everybody insisting on his undying love for her. She shuddered, shook her head and laughed sarcastically. How could he possibly love her? No man in their right mind would treat a woman the way Rollie treated her. If they did, the woman certainly would not return that love for very long. She decided to accept the fact that Rollie was exactly what he said he was; a selfish, self-centred man.

Later that night Rollie tried to call Jenna's phone. She looked at the caller- id, threw it on the couch and screwed up her face in disgust. By now, her disappointment towards him had grown to astronomical depths and she truly feared what she would say to him if she answered that call. She didn't trust herself not to say something which she couldn't take back. Instead she ignored the call, poured herself a wine and went to sit by the pool. She looked up into the black velvet of night and watched as beautiful sparkles of light shot across the skies. She wondered why life had to be so cruel. She wondered just how long the hurt from his constant betrayal would continue to rule her life. She just wanted to forget. She wanted to forget she ever met him, that she ever knew him, or that she ever loved him. It was becoming distinctively clear that he would always be nothing more than a disappointment to her. He could never keep his word to her, and she began to wonder if he even ever truly tried to. As the blanket of night began to slip down around her shoulders she decided she would try and sleep off the mood before making a final decision on the whole situation in the morning. As it stood now, she wanted him to stay away from her and let her move on with her life.

Strangely enough, when she did go to bed, she fell instantly into a deep sleep. As the hands on the clock ticked by, Jenna's mind took her to a distant place. She saw herself lying in a huge hand carved, four-poster king size bed. Her body, partially covered by a white satin sheet with red rose petals scattered all over the top. To her right, on a nightstand was a tall crystal vase filled with long-stemmed red roses, two half-empty champagne flutes and streams of soft sunlight filtered in through white organza curtains. Her long blonde hair fanned out across the pillow and a smile broke out across her face. The luxurious sheets caressed her naked body. The scent of familiar aftershave wafted to her nose as she lied there feeling thoroughly content and happy. The next thing she knew, a strong tattooed arm wrapped around her middle, pulling her closer to him. He began to smell her hair while kissing the back of her neck. Jenna turned over to return the embrace........ She bolted upright in her bed and gasped for breath. For the first time ever, she had dreamed of her and Rollie together in a way not familiar to her. Unstoppable tears poured from her eyes as the loneliness took hold of her.

No matter how hard she tried to deny it, she missed Rollie in so many ways, even though, she never imagined it would be in this way. She laid there and wondered where this dream had come from. She truly had no idea what to do now. There truly was no escape from Rollie, not even in the privacy of her dreams.

When she arose the next morning, although she felt drained, she also somehow felt strong and determined. Somewhere in between her dream and the break of day, she decided no matter how hard it would be, or what emotional carnage it would cause, she decided once again to try to forget about Rollie. She really had no choice; he didn't know how to be a part of her life and she was through trying to educate him. As part of her morning routine, Jenna had to check her social media pages and email. When she opened her Facebook page she found a message from Rollie. She contemplated deleting it without reading it but then decided against it. His message read: "Once again, I'm sorry, Jenna. What happened was completely unavoidable. I had to leave the country straight away and didn't have time to let you know. No, I haven't forgotten who Ivan is, but he will do as I ask, not what Candice wants. You have to trust me. I know what I'm doing." She stared at the computer screen in disbelief. "Funny that," she said out aloud. "How was it that he found time to call Ivan if he hadn't had time to call me? What is it with this guy? Does he really think I'm that stupid?" Jenna closed the message and ignored it.

Rollie called her later that day and kept right on calling until she reluctantly answered her phone. "For fuck sake, Jenna, can you stop breaking my balls over shit?" he said sternly. "I said I was sorry and I am. What happened over here was important and I had to leave straight away. The only reason I asked Ivan to call you is because he was with me at the time I got the call.

I understand your worries about him, but you don't really think he's stupid enough to cross me, do you? Besides, I told him he can't do one single thing without my approval. So stop stressing. It's still all systems go. I told you I'd help you and I am. You just have to trust me."

Over the next few weeks, Jenna and Charlotte had an absolute ball spending most of their time with Ivan and two other members of the Fearsome Devils. They searched each day for the perfect property to make the bar a huge success. They lunched, they laughed, they shared many different things, but Jenna still refused to let her guard down when it came to Ivan. In the back of her mind, she always remembered that he was Candice's best friend. His loyalty was to her, and not to Jenna. Despite what Rollie might say or think, Jenna knew better when it came to those two and their antics. She had seen firsthand the lies and deceit they hand-fed him.

On one of these afternoons, after a busy morning of building hunting, Jenna excused herself and went to freshen up in the hotel bathroom. When she emerged, Ivan was waiting around the corner for her. He gently took hold of her arm and pulled her towards him.

"Jenna, we really need to clear the air between us. I need to know why you don't trust me?" he asked.

"Oh come on Ivan, let's not do this. Let's not pretend we both don't know where your loyalty lies," she answered, as she went to walk away.

He tightened his grip on her arm. "Don't walk away from me," he said. "Please. I need you to listen to me. Look, it's no secret that Candice is one of my best mates. No-one is trying to tell you any different, but what I'm doing here, with you, is for Rollie."

"You need to understand my loyalty is to him before anybody else, even before Candice. He's my brother. I don't expect you to trust me like you trust him, but I'm as good as it gets at the moment. Besides, we've always gotten on pretty good haven't we?"

"I guess so. But, it's not so much that I don't like you, it's more the fact that I don't trust you. Have you got any idea how much grief Candice has caused for me over the years? Better question, do you even care? Could you even imagine the amount of lies she has told Rollie about me, to get me out of his life? Do you have any idea what she'd do to this business if she could get herself involved in it? Sorry buddy, but it's not a chance I'm prepared to take. I've only got one shot at this and I've got to get it right."

"Believe it or not, I do know, Jenna and I do care. But it's hard for me too you know. I got put in a real hard spot with this one, because I can't let Rollie down and that puts Candice off side. She's that fucked off with me for helping you, she's barely even talking to me. But like I told her, it's too fucking bad. Rollie's my brother and he wants to help you, so that's exactly what I'm going to do. And, I'll do a good job at it," he stepped in closer and took her hand. "You know why she hates you, don't you, Jen?" he asked.

"To be honest, Ivan, no, not really, I don't. I've tried to be friends with her. I've tried to help her and all she does is put me down. The only thing I know for sure is that she hates me having anything to do with Rollie. Even though it's him that keeps the friendship between him and me going."

"You're right. She does hate you. Being honest, she hates you with a passion. And she does hate you having anything to do with Rollie and she always will.

But do you want to know why she's like that?"

"I suppose you can tell me if you want, not that it will make any difference to me now, Ivan. After everything she has done to me, and all the rumours she's spread about me, I hate her just as much as she hates me."

"I understand that, but I'm going to tell you anyway. Candice hates you the way she does because she knows how much Rollie loves and cares for you."

"And? Why is that such a problem?"

"Jenna, you don't seem to understand. Rollie doesn't just love you like a friend like you think he does. The man is in love with you. Everyone, other than you can see that. It's a jealousy thing. Candice thinks if you were gone, Rollie would love her again. She doesn't realise how much damage she has actually done between him and her. She really thinks it's all your fault. She has told me several times if you'd just die, her life would be happy again. Her hatred for you is so strong if she could've had you chopped up into little pieces and thrown into a river she would have had it done by now."

Jenna gulped down hard. Oh my God, she thought, now his brothers were saying he was in love with her too. Jenna didn't know what to say to that statement so she brushed straight over it, choosing to instead focus on what he'd said regarding Candice's desire for her to die.

"Don't you think I already know that, Ivan? I know if she ever meets anyone willing to do it for her she will. She even told me that herself. But I don't live my life that way. I refuse to be bullied or live my life in fear. If she can get it done, well kudo's to her. I just hope she doesn't have anyone she values too much though. The one thing I have that she doesn't have, nor will she ever, is I have many people who love me and would do anything for me. So if she's that stupid, I wouldn't want to be her and to suffer the consequences that will come her way. And, just to add to that, I hope she realises, if anything ever does happen to me of a violent nature, she is the first suspect on their list. You see, I'm not like her and I have very few enemies."

"No, Jen, you're taking me the wrong way. I'm not trying to tell you to be scared of her. She wouldn't dare do anything to harm you. She knows only too well what would happen if she did. All I'm trying to say is, don't worry about her. She is my mate and I do love her, but I won't do anything to jeopardize this deal for you and Rollie, and neither will she. I'm only trying to assure you that I have your back and to explain why she's like she is."

"Oh okay. Well, provided she never finds out about anything that we are doing together, I guess I can deal with that. Besides, I don't have to go through you anyway, I can go through, the other member, Paul. I really do like him. He's really cool."

"Yeah, I noticed you two get on pretty well. Is that why you ring him instead of me?"

"Yes. I trust him. I like him a lot and besides, he hates Candice too," she said, smiling. "He's a smart cookie, unlike you. No disrespect meant, Ivan."

"None taken. I respect how you and Candice feel about each other. Alright cool. We have that sorted then. You go through Paul and only tell me what you need to if that makes you feel better. I'll let Rollie know that's what's going to happen."

"Okay, deal," she said, as he pulled her in and hugged her tight.

Jenna felt much better with the new arrangement. She knew she could trust Paul. Even though she hadn't known him long, he made her feel secure. They truly enjoyed each other's company and before too long they confided in each other on a regular basis. Paul's efforts to make her trust him astounded even her at times. Once, he even warned her about Rollie's predetermined visit. Paul understood her desire to keep as much physical distance between Rollie and herself as possible. He understood that every time Rollie left the country, Jenna's heart would break a little more. He knew if she didn't have to see him she wouldn't. Her respect and admiration for Paul only grew fonder. Jenna knew, if anyone found out he'd told her that information about Rollie's arrival, he would be in real trouble. She never spoke a word about it to anyone and neither did he.

Things began to change for Jenna ever so quickly once it become common knowledge that her and Charlotte were about to open their jazz club. Strange things began to happen that neither of the girls could have expected. People began to approach them and asked them if they could be somehow of any assistance. At first the girls thought the offers were genuinely nice gestures, but it quickly became apparent there was nothing nice about the offers at all. People that really should have known better, the same people Rollie trusted, began to ask if they could perhaps take over the leadership role since Rollie was out of the country. They suggested that he couldn't do a very good job at protecting the girls or their assets from such a distance. Jenna thanked them for their kind offers but flatly refused to cut Rollie out of the deal. Her resistance left her open to a world of abuse. The more they attacked him or criticized him, the more she defended and protected him. Instead, she went to Paul and told him what was happening.

"I really don't know what to do, Paul. These people who are meant to be close to Rollie are telling me, to get rid of him and forget about him. They keep asking me why I can't see he's just using me and that we'd be better off without his help. One of them even told me that once we get it all set up he will come back and take the whole club off us and give it to Candice. They're saying they'll take better care of us than he would and they'll take a much smaller cut, leaving me and Charlotte with the majority of the money. I'm scared, Paul. I really don't trust them. But, when we say no thank you, they get shitty. One of them threatened to burn the place down before we even get the doors open if we don't reconsider. I really don't know what to do."

"What the fuck? Who said all this? We gotta tell Rollie about this, Jenna. No-one and I do mean no-one, should be saying shit like that to you. They shouldn't be asking you anything at all. When Rollie finds out about this, shit is really gonna hit the fan."

"You know I can't tell you who, Paul. I'm too scared. And there's something else that scares me about telling him. What if Rollie thinks this is all my fault. He did say to only deal with you guys so he might think we went to them. But, we didn't approach any of them, they came to us. I don't want him to get angry at me. I can't stand it when he yells at me."

Paul rubbed the top of her head and smiled. "Don't be scared, babe. He won't get fucked off with you, it's them who's gonna have the problem. You got to stop worrying so much about him yelling at you. He yells at all of us," he said, laughing.

"No. Please, Paul, let's not tell him. I'll just tell him I've changed my mind and I'm not doing it now. Please don't tell him any of this shit happened. He already thinks he doesn't have many people here who care about him anymore."

Paul agreed to keep her secret on the condition she told him if anything else like that happened ever again.

Jenna sent Rollie a private message via Facebook simply saying: "Thank you for all the help you guys have already given us, but we've changed our minds. Sorry to waste your time, Rollie."

Rollie replied by saying: "I'm sorry it didn't work out without me being there, Jenna." She felt so guilty not telling him the truth of what happened, but she certainly didn't want to tell him the things that had occurred. With the dream of the nightclub down the drain, Jenna needed to come up with a new plan to make her money into something that could sustain her and her children's lifestyle. Her real dream was to one day own her own publishing house, but she had nowhere near enough money to buy one of those. So instead, she scoured the newspaper classifieds to see what was available. Mostly there were ads for coffee shop franchises and she had no interest in owning one of those. She figured something would come up, she just didn't know what and she didn't know when. Then one day, simply out of the blue, she received a Facebook message from a guy claiming to be a good friend of Rollie's. His name was Richard Robertson.

In the beginning, Richard told Jenna that he had lost contact with Rollie over the years and pleaded with her to reconnect them. Rollie had been hesitant and wisely resistant at first. He asked Jenna what Richard was like these days as he had not seen or heard from him in so many years. She told him he seemed genuine enough and was desperate to touch base with him.

After a little while, Rollie allowed her to give Richard his phone number. But not before warning her not to enter into any kind of business deal with Richard. He had become suspicious at Richards offer to give her a third ownership piece in his up and coming multi-million dollar business for free. Rollie once again warned her that nothing comes for nothing in this world and to always remember that. He had insisted that if Richard was prepared to give her that share for free, that it would be fraught with strings attached and could be laced with danger. Jenna had been reluctant to listen at the time, desperate to find a new interest. However, it wouldn't take long for her to wish she had of heeded his advice.

When Jenna first met Richard he seemed like a nice enough man. Polite, well-mannered and with good intentions. He had been attempting to start up a new bike and car show which was to travel around Australia from state to state, presenting stunt shows like no other show had ever offered before. Jenna liked the idea believing it could be a huge success. She explained to Richard that in order to run such a show it was imperative that he and his team follow simple instructions and be careful not to step on other people's toes. In Brisbane, in the time before bike clubs were illegal, many different clubs would hold many different events throughout the year. Some held tattoo shows, some held bike swap meets and others celebrated their annual runs. These events were usually scheduled in a way to ensure they didn't clash with dates from any other clubs. Despite Richard Robertson thinking he was a bikie, he didn't seem to possess the knowledge of how these things were supposed to work. In his infinite wisdom he decided he would run his show when and how he liked, regardless of what anybody else had planned. Jenna tried to explain to him that it just couldn't happen that way and that he'd run into trouble if he showed no respect for other peoples schedules.

Over the following few months, Jenna became somewhat of a consultant for Richard's company, in the hopes of keeping him out of trouble. Everything started off reasonably well until Richard's true character began to appear. Richard struggled with any kind of criticism whether it was in his best interest or not. Jenna grew restless and doubtful towards him and his intentions. Never in her entire life had she met anyone with the problems Richard Robertson displayed. His resistance to follow simple rules and protocol astounded her. No matter how many times she explained to him that the men from the biker community are men of their word, he would give his word to someone and then think nothing of it and break it in a heartbeat, never once thinking of the consequences of doing so. People were becoming frustrated and annoyed at his ethics. Jenna was asked several times to explain to him how things had to work. In the end, no matter how well the community knew and trusted her, they simply ran out of patience with his ignorance. Before too long he had made several enemies within the community. Jenna simply had no other choice than to walk away.

After walking away from the collapsing company, it quickly became apparent, there had been an ulterior motive of Richard contacting her in the first place. It had become abundantly clear it was to in fact to destroy her relationship with Rollie. Unbeknownst to Jenna, Candice and Richard had remained firm friends over the years and had hatched a plan to remove Jenna out of Rollie's life once and for all. From the moment, she decided to end her friendship with Richard, the blanket of secrecy was removed.

Jenna's relationship with Rollie descended deep into the pits of hell, as lie after lie would be laid at his feet like some kind of sacrificial offering. Rollie seemed to lap up each lie like a cat to a milk dish. No matter what Jenna would say in her own defence, he preferred instead, to listen to the lies of a madman and his manipulative ex-wife. Being no match for the two creatures from the underworld and fed up with declaring her innocence she eventually decided to give up on her friendship with Rollie for good. She had finally had enough. She realised that the twenty years of loyalty and friendship between them had really meant nothing at all to him. As far as she was concerned, he should have known that every word those two released from their drug afflicted lips were nothing more than lies. She decided that if he chose to believe them over her, then so be it. She would forge forward with her life without him. Despite the sadness, a wave of relief washed over her as she realised the reign of Rollie had finally come to an end.

In the meantime, the girls who had worked for Richard's company, as promotional models, had begged Jenna to open a company and take them with her when she left. The young girls, all aged between eighteen and twenty-three loved their jobs but had no work to do now the company had been closed. They explained to Jenna that Richard had never paid them one red cent for the months of work they'd already completed promoting the show. After a great deal of thought, Jenna decided she would do it. She felt she would be able to help the girls while gathering information for a new book about the life of bikini models. It really should have been a win-win for the girls and for Jenna, but none of them could have ever imagined the hostility and grief they would receive from Richard Robertson.

Once Jenna legitimised the business, work began to flow freely to the company. All the girls finally had paid work they could go to and Jenna began her documentation for her new book. Needless to say, Richard was not at all happy and went about trying to cause trouble wherever he possibly could. His first port of call was to try and damage the company name to other bike clubs within Brisbane. But unbeknownst to him, Jenna had been well known in the community for many years and had many people to vouch for her professionalism. The next thing he tried was running around to the venues at which the girls worked and told the proprietors that Jenna herself was a bikie. To most people, that statement would be completely dismissed instantly, knowing that females could never become a member of such a club. Others on the other hand, would need more reassurance. On one such occasion, one of the Fearsome Devils members had to go and have lunch with one of the hoteliers and explain that although Jenna had been around the club for several years, she was not in fact any kind of member. The manager from the pub had told him that Richard had expressed that the club was going to make the pub a target for drug dealing and encourage the girls to engage in sexual conduct. The member insisted this was nothing more than a pathetic lie. He assured the manager that one of the pre-requisites for getting a job within her company was that the girls understood there would be absolutely no sexual conduct at all. As a matter of fact, any girl who got caught acting inappropriately would be instantly dismissed. It wouldn't take very long until word spread from pub to pub to steer clear of Richard Robertson and his lies.

Eventually, the only thing left for Richard and Candice to do, was to try and cause Jenna problems with the Fearsome Devil's club itself. That would be a mistake neither one of them would forget. Being the absolute genius' they are, they started a vicious rumour involving the club. That attempt backfired badly. Richard ended up fleeing the state while Candice plummeted further into her underworld lifestyle and continued to live for free off Rollie and his good intentions in his house.

As the fiasco with Candice and Richard came to an end, Doug implored Jenna to give their relationship one last try.

"Come with me to Vietnam, babe," he asked. "You need to get out of here. All the shit those two have caused you never know when some fuckwit will turn on you again. We can start a brand new life. In a brand new country."

"I can't, Doug. I can't just pack up my life and move across the world. What about my kids?"

"They can come with us. We'll pay for them to move over there too."

"What about your health? Do they even have doctors over there?"

"Of course they have doctors there, Jenna," he laughed, as he spoke. "Besides, it's only a couple of hours by plane. I can come back for my appointments."

Jenna stared into nothingness saying not a single word.

"Well? Will you come?" he asked, interrupting her thoughts.

"I….I can't, Doug. I'm sorry, but I really can't."

'Why? Why can't you, Jenna? Give me one good reason."

She clasped her hands together and began to squeeze them firmly.

"You can't can you? You can't give me one good fucking reason can you?" he yelled. "You're going to sit here and wait for that fuckwit, Rollie to come back aren't you?"

"Doug, stop being stupid. We don't even talk anymore. Besides, he has shown me what he really is."

"And, what's that, Jenna?"

"He's an asshole. He is a using, manipulative asshole, Doug," she raised her voice. "Is that what you wanted to hear? Well, there you go you heard it. You heard it from me. I hate his stinking guts. I've got it through my thick head. He is no friend of mine."

"Yeah, whatever! I've heard it all before. You'll hate his guts till he makes up some fucked up excuse and then you'll forgive him like you always do. Well, you know what? I don't give a fuck any more. I'm going anyway. You know how to contact me for when the next lot of shit starts. But you remember something, babe," he said, taking her face into his hands and squeezing her cheeks. "If I find out you're having anything to do with him, I'll be back."

"I'm not going to have anything to do with him, Doug. I don't know how many times I've got to tell you the same thing."

"You better not," he said, squeezing harder. "Because if you ever end up with him, I will kill you. That's a promise!" he yelled, flinging her face from his hands.

So now with Rollie out of her life for good, and Doug finally giving her the space to breathe, Jenna embarked on reclaiming her own life. This time, she could do it her way. After all she had been through, she wanted to make her own mark on society.

She re-enrolled in university to finish her bachelor's degree and concentrated on writing a bestselling novel. One night just as she sat down to finally relax after a huge day of study, she switched on the nightly news. She set her sights on the television and low and behold, there was a picture of Rollie in the right-hand corner of the screen. Jenna dropped her glass of ice water, sending it shattering across the floor. She blinked her eyes wildly and turned the volume up. This can't be right she thought. What the hell is going on? The accusations of the news reader forced vomit to her throat. She picked up her phone and shook. She had no desire to talk to Rollie ever again. But now, with what she had just seen on the news, she knew she had to tell him. The thought of calling him sickened her. She knew she owed him nothing. The battle in her mind raged on before finally, the remembrance of her loyalty to him forced her hand. She dialled his number, then just as quickly hung up. There was no way she could handle listening to his voice. Instead, she typed him out a text message.

The message read: "Hello, Rollie, it's me, Jenna. I just thought you might be interested to know, that you are, as we speak, featuring on the nightly news. They are very serious allegations. I'd suggest you check it out." She did not add one smiley face, a single kiss, or even a goodbye. She felt she had done her job. She had warned him, he could take it from there. The next minute he messaged her back.

His message read: "Can you call me?"

She answered: "No."

His next message: "Please, call me, Jenna? I need to know what has been said."

Jenna looked at her phone and shook her head. Nope, she thought.

He can ring Candice or even Richard if he liked, but she sure as hell was not ringing him. She put her mobile down and picked up her landline phone and called Nellie.

"Oh my God, Nel, did you just see who was on the news?" she asked.

"I did, I did. I was just trying to call you. You know you're going to have to tell him. That's pretty serious stuff."

"I already did. The minute I saw it I knew I had to tell him. I just sent a text. I don't want to talk to him. Mind you, he asked me to call him. I said no."

"Jenna, don't be so mean," Nellie said.

"It's not being mean, Nel. I can't talk to him after what he did to me with Candice and Richard. I'm never going back down that path again."

"I hear you girl. I can't say I really blame you though. That was the single most stupid decision he ever made."

Just then Jenna's mobile began to ring, she walked over to it, picked it up and said, "Oh no, Nel. That's him. What do I do?" "Answer it, Jen."

"No. I can't," she said, with a quivering voice.

"You should. You'll hate yourself if you don't." Nellie said.

"Hang on then, I'll call you back."

Jenna answered her phone reluctantly and listened to what he had to say.

"Jenna, don't you dare hang up until you hear me out….. please. Tell me what they said on the news."

"Why don't you ring your lovely ex-wife? Or, better yet, why don't you ring Richard Robertson? I'm sure they'll tell you the truth," she said sarcastically.

"I don't want to hear it from them, I want to hear it from you. You know what, fuck what the news said. Tell me if you believed what the newsreader said?" he asked.

"Of course I don't believe it, Rollie, it's about drugs and murder. I know you're not like that."

"Thank fuck for that," he said, "So how've you been?"

"Are you serious, Rollie? Are you seriously asking me how I am? What the actual fuck? You don't care how I am. You could give a flying fuck about me," she said, anger rising in her voice. "I haven't heard from you in months and you ask how I am. How about asking how I was when all that shit went down with your junkie mates, Candice and Richard? You chose to ignore my messages then. You know what, Rollie, screw this shit I'm going."

"Don't you fucking dare hang up, fuck you, Jenna," he yelled.

Jenna froze, not used to him raising his voice to her.

"You listen to me," he said, "if you had of bothered to call, not message me, when all that shit went down, none of this would've even happened. How many times have I told you before about listening to people's shit and letting them put words in my mouth?"

Jenna began to cry. She said nothing.

"Haven't I told you a million times before if someone says something to you about something I've supposedly said to call me and ask me if I even said it?"

"Yes," she whispered.

'Well, why didn't you do that? Why did you let it get to this without even saying one word to me?" he asked softly. "You know how much shit people talk, Jen. You've always known. I don't get why you let it get to you. I keep telling you to ignore the drug fucked cunts. Especially with that fucking Richard. I told you directly that I hate that cunt. I also told you why I can't get rid of Candice."

"I know you did. It just hurt me really bad with all the nasty things they were saying and all the trouble they got me in. I'm not like you, Rollie. I take everything to heart."

"Yeah, I know you do."

They spoke for the next twenty minutes discussing all the rumours and lies people were spreading about them both. Some they laughed over and some made them angry, but before too long, it was as though they had never stopped speaking at all.

It wouldn't take long for Jenna to once again miss Rollie the way she always had. It wouldn't take her long to begin thinking about what it was she truly wanted from him. Then she realised the answer was simple; she wanted him to come home. She knew he couldn't do that because of his commitments, but she could not for the life of her understand why he couldn't email her, or call her once a week, to at least tell her how his life was going. She understood the more he spoke to her, the more he missed her because she felt the exact same way. But the yearning to have him in her life in some regular capacity was overwhelming. Now, with the anti-association laws and VLAD laws in place in Brisbane, things were only going to get worse. Her dreams of him one day returning to Australia to live were dwindling.

No matter how hard she tried to shake it off, her mind constantly thought of the anguish Rollie and her bikie friends had in store for them. She just couldn't understand the government, or the way their new laws were supposed to work. Was Rollie not an ordinary man, just like every other man? Did he not have the same feelings, goals and nightmares as all other men? Why had they needed to make such an unjust law?

Regardless of what the police or government think, bikies are exactly the same as they are. They bleed the same colour, they shed the same tears, experience the same love and battle the same hate. The only real difference with these men compared to any other is the fact they belong to a brotherhood. In reality, shouldn't that be their choice to make? In such a multi-cultural country, which is supposed to be free, how could a group of men and women, who make up the government, make these choices for others? Her thoughts began to scare her. Would they soon be able to choose a sole religion for the entire country to follow? In all her life, she had never thought the level of discrimination with these men could ever have truly happened. But it did. And when it did, many people got hurt deeply by it. These were the thoughts and many more like it that began to roll through her mind day after day. She knew that not all bikies were innocent, nor had she ever proclaimed that to be so. But, she had always said, don't judge a man by what he wears upon his back, judge him by his actions. If someone breaks the law, whether it be a bikie or a priest, prosecute the man, not the entity. In this supposed modern day world we live in, aren't we meant to have a choice about the way we live our lives? Slowly she began to understand the depth of all those suffering thanks to these crazy new laws.

Jennifer Brockie

Chapter Twelve

Resistance

One lazy Sunday afternoon, as Jenna was in her kitchen baking a Chantilly sponge for the guests she had coming for dinner, her phone began to ring.

"Hey, it's me," the caller said, "I'm just calling to give you the heads up. You know, that bitch has finally won."

"Which bitch?" Jenna asked, "And, what exactly did she win?"

"The biggest bitch of all, Candice. She finally got Rollie to sell his house."

"What? What did you just say?" Jenna asked.

"Yep, she finally got him to sell it. From what my source told me, she sold it for a lot less than what it was worth too."

"Oh my God! You can't be serious?" Jenna cried, "That can't be right. It can't be true," she paused, "If it is the truth, well, that's it then. It's all over. She has now literally cost him everything he ever worked for."

"It is true, Jenna. I drove past just to check it out for myself and there it was, a huge sold sign plastered across the front of an auction sign, right out the front of his house."

"Oh my God. I really don't know what to say. I feel so bad for him. I can't believe he would let her do this."

"Me either. He always told me he'd be back to live in it eventually. Maybe he had to sell it? Or maybe it was his way of fucking her off and detaching himself from the fucking thing?"

"He always told me the same thing. You know this means he won't be coming home?" she added, "But you know what? You're wrong and so is he if you're thinking he'll be able to get rid of her that easy. There's no getting rid of her. She's worse than an incurable disease. She'll go her own way until the cash he's given her runs out, but as soon as she spends it, she'll be straight back on to him for more. It's how she is. It's her way. And, in all honesty, it's his way too. He can't seem to cut her off no matter what she does to him or to anyone else. She'll leech off him until the day he dies. Even then, you can be guaranteed he'll leave her everything he has left in his will."

"Na, I think you're wrong there. He's not that stupid."

"Hey, I didn't say that. I've never once said or even implied, he was stupid. It's that exact behaviour that makes him, him. Everyone thinks he is an ass and most of the time he is. But, he isn't really like that. He is… well, not when it comes to me," Jenna laughed, "but to everyone else, a person of his word. He told Candice he would take care of her, and so he has. I only hope now, now that he has literally lost everything he has ever worked for, that he realises his time of providing for her is over. He left her emotionally years ago, now he needs to understand she's not his responsibility anymore. He needs to concentrate on rebuilding himself. He needs to build a brand new life for himself and let her do what she should have done years ago; move on and look after herself. Let her find some new sap to draw her existence from. Maybe now, he'll concern himself with what he wants and needs rather than what she wants. I hope with all my heart he can finally do it. I wish him all the luck in the world."

"Yeah, me too. Let's hope he can."

In the wee hours of the following morning, Jenna awoke from a fitful sleep. She bolted upright in her bed covered in a cold sweat. She swung her legs over the edge of the bed, dropped her face into her palms and began to sob. The realisation that Rollie was never coming back hit her like a tsunami. Visions of his cheeky smile flashed before her eyes. Memories of all the crazy things he had ever said or done flooded her thoughts. She rose from her bed and paced the house. She tried everything she could think of to stop her mind from racing. Maybe it had been Rollie's idea to sell the house? Maybe he wanted it gone? Maybe he never wanted to come back? Maybe he needed the money? No, that can't be right she thought. He would have told her. Actually, why hadn't he told her? Was it a secret? Was he ashamed? She poured herself a tall glass of water and went to sit by the pool. As the water cascaded down the waterfall, she began to remember something Rollie had told her in the very early days of their friendship. "Nothing is forever, Jenna and everything can be bought and sold." Jenna giggled to herself as she remembered telling told him there was no price for love, loyalty, honesty or friendship. She told him no matter what, she could never be brought or sold. Rollie had answered her quite simply, "No, I don't think you can." As the early morning summer sun began to peak out from the edge of the horizon, she headed back to bed to rest her weary head. She knew no matter what she did or what she said, nothing could undo what had already been done. Maybe Rollie was right? Maybe nothing is forever?

Her downtrodden mood hung over her like a cold wet blanket for the next few days. She thought constantly of everything Rollie had lost since she'd known him. From cars to businesses, friends to family and now finally his home. How much more could one man stand to lose? Their common goal had always been to gain wealth for a future, not to squander it away. Realising nothing she could do would shake off the niggling feeling that he needed her, she eventually made the decision to travel overseas to visit him. She knew she couldn't change anything, but she knew her compassion towards his situation would make him feel slightly better. She typed out a straight forward five-word message and sent it to his phone.

"Can I come see you?"

Within a few short minutes he replied.

"Why not?" Were the only two words he typed back.

She knew she had been right. He did need her. Just like in the old days, when Rollie really needed reassurance, it was Jenna who could give it to him. Butterflies danced in her stomach as she thought about the millions of things she had to say to him. So many things she could never tell him over the phone. Maybe this would finally be their chance to get their issues sorted once and for all?

She knew she would be greeted with great resistance from her friends regarding her decision. Breaking the news to them would be the hard part. She fully expected them to start their hate campaign against Rollie all over again. They had all grown weary of waiting for him to come and fix the damage he had caused and constantly encouraged Jenna to move on without him. They wanted her to be happy. They no longer cared if Rollie was happy or not. She chuckled as she thought about their suspicions of him killing her. "If you go over there and don't give him what he wants, he'll take you out to a field and have you shot, you know, Jenna," was her favourite.

Jenna grinned at the thought, knowing full well that Rollie could never harm her, no matter how much he may want to, or how close she drove him to that kind of madness. What her friends didn't understand, or rather, didn't want to understand, was for Rollie to hurt her, would be like him harming himself; because no matter who he was with, or what he was doing, he would always love her unconditionally.

After the initial text that Jenna had sent, and Rollie had answered, he quickly reverted back to his usual ways of ignorance. She sent him three more texts asking where to go and what to do, but each message was greeted with silence. She even contemplated cancelling her trip until the morning she had a major run-in with Charlotte. Charlotte had berated Jenna to the point of tears.

"When are you going to get it through your pretty little head, Jenna? He's a fucking manipulator. That's why he doesn't answer you. He wants to control you. He doesn't want to let you go so you can move on with your life. He can't be here, or have you with him, so he's not happy, therefore, he wants you to be unhappy too. Fuck him off and forget about him altogether. Let him deal with his own shit. Please, don't go over there."

Jenna thought about everything Charlotte had said. Maybe she was right? Maybe she shouldn't go? But then again, Charlotte had not heard the disappointment in his voice a few months earlier when he had asked her once again to come to him. Jenna had ended that phone call, drowning in a pool of emotion. When Rollie had asked her to come, Jenna made up every excuse known to man. If the truth were told, her resistance to see Rollie was all about self-preservation. She knew to go and see him, knowing full well that eventually she would have to return to Australia and he would have to remain where he was would be too much pain for her to bare. It was hard enough for her to hear his voice on the phone, let alone see or touch him in person. She was scared. Scared of him, and even more scared of herself. She knew, as did he, that if she went, she wouldn't want to return home. But, all that had changed now, Rollie had literally lost everything and she knew he'd need the shoulder of someone he knew truly loved and cared for him. So regardless of what Charlotte, or anyone else for that matter, had to say, or how hard it would be for her to leave, Jenna was going to be there for him. The following afternoon, Jenna decided she would call Rollie instead of texting him. Her hands trembled as she dialled his number.

"Hey, you," he said, answering his phone immediately.

"Hey Rollie, how are you?"

"Not bad. Yourself?"

His deep voice seemed vague and distant.

"I'm all good, Rollie?" she answered, her voice quivering as she spoke. "Can I ask you something?"

"Yes, of course, you can. You know you can ask me anything. What is it?"

"Well, I got a strange call a couple of days ago from one of our friends. Did you sell your house?" she asked, hesitantly.

"Yep! It's gone. I sold the fucking thing."

"Oh my God! So it is true?"

"Yep, one huge head fuck off my plate."

"I am so sorry, Rollie. I can't believe you have now officially lost every single thing you ever worked for here in Australia."

"How do you think I feel, Jenna?" he asked, his voice rising. "Don't you think I know?"

"I. I don't know what to say, Rollie. I really don't."

"You can't say anything. It's gone!"

"You sound so angry," Jenna said, softly.

"I am angry, Jenna. I'm not angry with you. I'm just angry. I' m angry at Candice. I'm angry at everything."

"It'll be okay, Rollie. You can always start again."

"Fuck that and fuck her. I shouldn't have to."

"I know, but it'll be alright. It's not your fault, you thought you were doing the right thing by letting her live there."

"It is my fucking fault. I married the fucking thing. Everyone warned me, but I didn't listen. But, at least now she is out of my life for good, thank fuck!"

She spoke to Rollie for a few minutes longer trying to soothe his battered ego. The hurt she heard in his voice weakened her. She could not believe that Candice would go this far. She couldn't understand how any woman could strip a man of everything he ever owned and still hold her head up high.

"Anyway Rollie, that's why I really wanted to come and see you," Jenna said, as she wound down the conversation.

"Yeah, that would be good. I could do with seeing your face. Let me know the minute you're here," Rollie answered.

"Will do. I can't wait to see you. I have so much to tell you. I miss you so much. I miss the old days when you were….."

"Jenna," Rollie interrupted, "I've got to go. I've got business I have to attend to. Ring me when you land and I'll take it from there. Don't stress, I'll make sure you catch up with us."

Ending the call, she stared at the phone. Us? What the hell did he mean by that? Over the next few days, the words

Rollie had said on that call played on loop through her mind. Confusion once again consumed her. She could not work out what the 'us' was meant to mean. Had he meant the club? Had he meant someone else? What the hell had he meant? No matter what he had meant, Jenna now had to think. She needed to make a decision on whether or not to go and see him. She had poured half of her lifetime into this twisted relationship she'd shared with him and she was prepared to be there for him no matter what he had done to her, but yet, he still didn't seem to understand. She had no intention of travelling halfway around the world to see 'us'. This was not meant to be a catch up and party visit. She had planned to see Rollie; and Rollie alone.

Not usually confrontational by nature, Jenna had put a lot of thought into this trip and decided to use it to the best of her advantage. Her intentions had been to soothe Rollie over the loss of his house and reassure him that he could start over, the same way as he'd done so many times before. However, once she had done that, she had planned to ask him for the answers to the questions he had promised to tell her for so many years. She needed to know, she needed to hear it from him. She had heard everybody else's version of the events, now she wanted to hear his. He had promised her he would tell her anything she wanted to know if only she would fly over to see him.

After all these years, she now had the courage to do so. But, his statement had bothered her. Would she get an opportunity to get those answers if she was to spend time with "us"? She began to wonder if he ever had any intention of telling her at all. It quickly became apparent that he'd either forgotten about the answers or simply had no intention of giving them to her. Once again, she felt betrayed by his ignorance and his hesitation. She knew if she went over there and he disappointed her again, her contempt for him and his lack of caring about her needs would change her view of him forever. She decided it was better if she simply cancelled her trip.

Over the next few weeks Jenna attempted to throw herself back into her work, constantly staying busy, with the intention of forgetting about Rollie altogether. If a thought of him dared enter her mind, she would simply reminded herself of his arrogance and lack of compassion. She managed to control her thoughts magnificently while she was awake, but as she slept, her subconscious would not provide her with such relief. Each night, just as she would drift off to sleep, she would be startled awake by his face. Sometimes he was smiling and other times he would be sad. The visions of him haunted and tormented her. She knew she could not live a normal life with such emotional turmoil guiding her thoughts and visions. She remembered how sick she had once become due to her own silence. She knew she deserved better than that and she was determined to find it. Jenna finally understood she had to put an end to this once and for all. It was time for her to move on; without, Rollie. After all, she now had the power to do so. He had already taught her everything she needed to know on how to be tough and resilient.

One afternoon soon after, she lifted her gaze from the computer screen and watched the plump droplets of rain plummet to the earth. As the summer, storm brewed overhead and echoed the rhythm of her heart, her phone began to ring. Rollie's number flashed up on the screen. She picked up the phone and looked at it blankly. Tears sprung to her eyes.

"I can't, Rollie. I really can't answer you. I have to let you go. I have to move on with my life," she whispered to herself.

The phone finally rang out as she placed it back down on her desk. It rang again and again and each time it was him. She picked up the phone and switched it off.

Gentle tears dripped down her face as she looked out of her office window and watched the storm gather strength outside. She walked out into it and stood there, vacantly embracing the drops from heaven as they fell upon her shoulders. Her heart ached and doubt washed over her like a tidal wave. A clap of thunder whipped through the sky as a bolt of lightning struck the ground in the distance. Within that moment, she knew she had made the right decision. She knew couldn't take that call, or any other call Rollie might make after that. She desperately wanted to answer him. She yearned for the solace his words could give her. But, she finally understood, that no matter how many times she answered him, he would not answer her. Not the answers to the questions that consumed her thoughts. She stood there with her hair plastered to her cheeks, placed her hands over her heart and fell to her knees. All of a sudden, a bolt of rationality hit her. She lifted her head up high as if the lightning had struck her and an electric wave of blissful acceptance soared through her veins. In that moment, she realised she no longer needed the answers. She had never needed them. Jenna had finally found her peace in knowing that she had always had them. The answers had been in her heart right from the beginning.

END

A Closing Word From Jenna

In reality, I knew there was no blame in a situation like ours. What happened between Rollie and I was a twist of fate that neither one of us could have predicted or controlled. The day Rollie first knocked on my door, he had no idea what he was about to set in motion, and neither did I. Yet that first knock and that persistence to make me love him turned our entire lives upside down. Both of us distorted and manipulated by what was the "right thing" to do. It changed us both in a way that neither one of us could have ever imagined. However, the changes he brought about within me, will be with me forever. Rollie had succeeded in doing something no-one else had ever been able to do before.

I, Jenna, the abused, had become Jenna the free, thanks to the strength Rollie had instilled in me. With his ignorance and sometimes cruel lessons over those years, Rollie knew, unlike me, that I would eventually find the strength within myself to overcome any obstacle thrown in my way. Whilst I questioned his motives and doubted our friendship, he never did. He knew in order for me to conquer my demons that he would have to take a watchful back seat and let me fight those battles alone. Let me assure you, some of those lessons were extremely bitter pills to swallow. At times I got so caught up in my hate for the man for not helping me, I believed I would never be able to forgive him for his lack of action. Yet, I did forgive him and in the end, it taught me to love him even more.

Thanks to the things he did, or lack thereof rather, I now possess the courage and the confidence to move forward with my life without fear of judgement. I no longer require the acceptance by certain members of my dysfunctional family. I now comprehend the true meaning behind the word friend and in doing so, choose them wisely. I no longer agonize over what Doug or Candice, or anyone else believes about the situation between Rollie and me. I no longer listen to the opinions of others regarding Rollie, as I can see clearly the results of the decisions he made by removing himself from temptations way. Thanks to his guidance, I no longer crave the approval of my beloved publishing world or the notion of being ostracized by them, for my choice of subject. My subjects may not fit into their publishing lists and may indeed be controversial, but I am a natural born writer with different tales to tell. So, controversial or not, I shall tell them to all who will listen. And above and beyond everything else, I no longer allow myself to be judged by anyone and that, truly is the meaning of freedom. After all these years, I can finally be me!

As for Rollie and his path, well, he still has some distance to cover. Although he taught me to be me, he still wrestles with his desires as his commitments to his lifestyle takes priority in his life. He is an honourable man and as such, he will always conduct himself in that manner. Unfortunately for him, his loyalty will continually come at a price. Whilst his greatest love on earth will always be his club, it comes at the cost of forsaking the true possibilities of real love awaiting him out there. That is something I struggle to accept, as I know it's one of the few things he is yet to experience. My heart goes out to him in more ways than he could even imagine; for at the end of the day, it is I who knows the true price he has paid for his lifetime of dedication.

Notes in Closing

Finally helping Jenna to close the chapters on this book, I found myself shocked and somewhat embarrassed by some of my prior thoughts I'd previously had on bikies. Through Jenna and Rollie's story, I learnt that the myths surrounding some of these men were quite troublesome and incorrect.

Right up until the story was close to completion, I have to admit, I had my doubts about Rollie's commitment to her. I felt his treatment of Jenna was cruel and unusual from time to time, especially because he had persistently claimed to love and care about her. It was not before I began to see the struggles that Rollie himself faced alone because of his love for her that I began to understand him.

Rollie had inadvertently backed himself to a moral corner and refused to release the pressure for the sake of his own emotions. Rollie's intention had been to make Jenna see through the veil of deception placed before her by the media and to make her love him as his friend. But being a human being, Rollie found himself in a situation where he had fallen for Jenna. He found himself in a constant battle between what he wanted and what was morally right. After all, Jenna was a married woman and to top that off, she was married to one of his best friends. Not only that, he too was married and to make matters worse, it was against the rules of the club to pursue another man's wife.

In "The Bikie Effect" we witness a complication that occurs on a regular basis in everyday life. Many people, not just bikies, have found themselves in the exact same situation that Rollie found himself in. The difference here is how the situation was dealt with. One of the biggest myths I've heard when it comes to bikies, is the one where in which the biker will take whatever he wants, whenever he wants, whether it's a woman or a possession, Rollie proved that to be nothing more than a false accusation.

Throughout this book, Rollie has actually revealed quite a few fallacies that plague these men and their chosen lifestyle. His actions have made me question the rumours that are often spread about bikies. If he would force himself and the person he loved the most through such heartache for the sake of morality, could bikies really be as bad as people have made them out to be? The proof of Rollie's real nature is evident by the fact that if she would allow him, he would remain in Jenna's life today.

What this book has actually succeeded in doing for me, is to educate me on the fact that bikies ARE real life human beings. I will never again judge a man by the way he dresses. Whether he wears a designer suit or he wears a patch on his back. I for one will judge ONLY on an individual basis from this time forward.

Notes in Closing

Jennifer Brockie